Kate Triumph

A Novel by

Shari Arnold

ISBN 13: 978-1502596871

To my dad, Richard Arnold, who always
believed I should be a writer.

One

The Jigsaw Club is filled to capacity and yet they still let me in. A bouncer named Sid checks my ID and then tells me he likes my boots, even though he isn't looking at them. Inside the club there's enough light to find the bathrooms. But not the exits.

I take a spot near the back where the wall is sticky and smells like beer. I don't know much about beer, my mom drinks wine. She says it relaxes her, and I'm okay with that. We both know she needs to relax.

"Be careful, Kate," she called out right before I left the house. "Be home by midnight. And — be careful."

If I know anything it's how to be careful. Normally this wouldn't be my scene but I like the band. Their first two CDs could be considered the soundtrack to my life — that is, my life of solitary confinement.

The stage lights zigzag across the crowd and I spot a few kids from school. One or two make eye contact but that's all they do. Their eyes slide on past me without a hint of recognition. They've had a few years to perfect this maneuver. I'm the only one not fooled. They sway back and forth to the music, their faces occasionally lit when they respond to a text. Or pretend to. Normal looks good on them. I fight back that familiar twinge of jealousy I always experience in their presence. I tug the sleeves of my black shirt down over my hands and tuck them into my armpits. It's about a thousand degrees in this club, but I feel cold.

The band stops playing halfway through the next song. I figure there's some kind of technical difficulty, but then a guy from just off stage grabs the mic and tells us all to head toward the exits. *Quickly,* he emphasizes. But no one moves. We all must be thinking the same thing: *If this is for real shouldn't the house lights come back on?*

1

The musicians drop their instruments and run from the stage — that is, everyone but the bass player. He pauses only long enough to unplug his guitar and take it with him. From stage left the smoke appears. It clouds the stage lights, diluting their colors into murky renditions of blue, orange and red. It swirls about the ceiling as if it's looking for someone. And that's when I notice the flames.

Fire!

Everyone starts moving at the same time, but there's nowhere to go. They slam into each other like bowling pins, some are knocked over while others tip sideways and then stabilize. I'm frozen until the smoke reaches me. It moves in through my nose and tickles the back of my throat. I push off from the wall only to get knocked to the ground. My hands splash into something wet on the floor and then slide around as I try to climb up onto my knees. Something slams into the top of my head and I slip sideways, nearly face-planting to the ground. My head is pounding, the pain so intense I begin to choke. I breathe in, slow and then fast, trying my best to fight off the possibility of blacking out. I only need to rest for a moment. Just one moment should help.

"Kate! Get up!" Someone tugs at my arm and then all at once I'm on my feet. A blurry figure grabs my hand and pulls me toward him. And because I'm barely able to stand I allow it to happen.

"Stay close," he yells and then drags me behind him. My rescuer uses his body like a bulldozer, plowing through the shapes and shadows around us. When he knocks a young girl to her knees he pauses only long enough to help her to her feet before we're on the move again. The stage lights skimming through the crowd bounce off his hair tinting it an electric blue and then a clownlike orange. I've yet to catch a glimpse of his face.

We crash out the side entrance and the cool night air feels like a gift I will never return. One deep breath after another fills my lungs and my knees begin to shake. I'm coughing, he's coughing — I feel like I might collapse.

"You should go," he says. His voice is scratchy. He still hasn't released my hand.

The alleyway is dimly lit, but I can make out a strong jawline and dark hooded eyes. There's something familiar about him. My stomach clenches and I wonder if I know him from school. No, that can't be right. No one from school would risk their life to save mine.

"Thank you," I say and he nods. The words barely make it past my raw throat. When I don't look away he takes a step back into the shadows.

I open my mouth to say something more but then stop when I feel a warm drip of moisture trickle down the side of my face. I want to believe it's rain, *please let it be rain*, but when I look up at the sky all I see are stars. I turn my face away and hope he hasn't noticed. Maybe the darkness will keep my secret this time.

No such luck.

His grip on my hand tightens, as if he's sensed I'm about to run. "You're hurt." His other hand reaches out to me but I jerk away. I'm looking at the ground, my long hair covering my face, when he says, "Don't let them see you." He releases my hand one finger at a time and then steps further back into the shadows.

"What's your name?" I ask. I have to know.

He hesitates for a split second and then says, "Jonah."

"How'd you—"

"Go, Kate. Now!"

I stare into the shadows one last time, and then I run. I run past the choking wall of teenagers lying on the sidewalk outside the club. I run past the fire trucks and security guards. I run until the blood spilling from the jagged wound in my skull begins to cloud my vision. And even then I don't slow down until the blood finally stops and the pounding in my head ceases to nothing. I reach up and let my hand move along my scalp until I'm convinced. My hair is matted with dried blood but my skin is once again smooth.

There's a Chinese food restaurant across the street from me that advertises all you can eat wontons, and the flashing neon sign above the door tells me they never close. I slip through the front door with my head down and hurry toward the restroom. I stick my head under the sink and scrub at my hair until the water changes from rust colored back to clear.

The bathroom mirror is dirty, just like the toilet, sink and floor, but right now I can't think of a better place to be. My face is paler than normal, which emphasizes the streaks of dirt and blood across my cheeks. I wet down a paper towel and do my best to clean it all away, but the rough texture of the towel only turns my cheeks a raw looking pink. My eyes widen in the mirror when someone starts pounding on the wall.

"Restroom for customer only," an angry Chinese woman says once I open the door.

I shrug my shoulders and duck behind my long wet hair. I have no reason to hide from her — not now — but I do it anyway.

"Two egg rolls to go," I tell her, handing her a five dollar bill.

She doesn't smile. Her suspicious eyes pin me to the wall while she rings out the line of customers back at the cash register. When she hands me my small bag of egg rolls she mumbles something about a woman's shelter a few blocks away, and then she pushes me out the door.

I eat my egg rolls on the bus. My shirt is slightly wet and my hair is dripping, but I'm clean. No one would guess I was injured tonight. Not even my mother.

"I take it you didn't like the band?" she asks when I walk through the door. She glances up and smiles over the neatly folded piles of laundry distributed evenly along the back of the couch.

I shrug and say, "Not so great live," and head toward my bedroom.

I know to keep my lies simple and my explanations short. Unnecessary rambling is a sure sign of guilt. Thankfully my mother doesn't come too close otherwise she'd smell smoke, blood and egg rolls.

"Are you packed, Kate?" Her voice carries down the hallway. "We need to leave a little earlier tomorrow than we'd planned, so you should pack tonight. I have a stop to make before our flight."

"I'm almost packed. I'll be ready by morning."

"Kate?" she calls after me and I stop directly in front of my bedroom door.

I slide my finger along my shiny door handle, anticipating her next words. The handle is smooth to the touch. And pink. I picked it out when I was five years old and it has survived seven different houses, seven different bedrooms and seven different towns. Just like me.

"Yes?" I say when she hesitates.

"You can still change your mind."

"I won't," I tell her.

"It's just that—" she continues but I cut her off.

"I'm going. It's important to me." My hand grips the door handle and I open my door. Just inside my doorway I wait for the argument. The same three words that preempt every disagreement my mother and I have.

It's. Not. Safe.

But this time the words are different.

"Alright, Kate. Alright," she says, followed by a sigh.

I slide my suitcase out of my closet and the noise stirs the small cat lounging on my bed.

"You've been in that exact spot all day, Lefty," I say.

But he doesn't care to acknowledge that comment. Instead he crawls into the top portion of the open suitcase, as if to say *you're not leaving without me.*

Lefty is all white except for one gray spot right above his chin. I love that spot. I call it his soul patch, like he should be reading obscure poetry in a café somewhere downtown. But he doesn't like it much. He does his best to remove it every time he takes a bath.

He came to us when I was eight. He showed up one night at dinnertime and after a few minutes of howling I opened the door and he walked right in. My mother was hesitant at first, until she realized he was the one friend that would always keep my secrets.

Besides, how can you turn away a three-legged cat?

I go through the motions of packing but all I can see is Jonah. If only I could shine a flashlight into the memory of his face just to see the color of his eyes. He seemed so familiar to me, as if I knew him. Or I'd seen him somewhere before. I think back through all the schools I've been to, Boston, Chicago or possibly here in San Diego. There have been so many schools, so many kids. But no Jonah. Perhaps I've seen him around my mother's boutique? But that doesn't seem likely either.

There's a soft knocking on my bedroom door and then my mother calls out, "Goodnight, Kate." She doesn't open the door. No goodnight kiss or bedtime story for me. Now that I'm seventeen we're past that. But there are times I wish she'd tuck me in, tell me everything's going to be alright, like she did when I was younger. And I could pretend to believe her, for just one night. Like I did when I was younger.

My mother and I live like roommates, best friends who exist for each other alone. Or "codependent," I believe they call it. She says there's no one she'd rather spend time with, but I know that can't be true because as much as I love her there are days when I'd kill for someone else to talk to.

Someone who doesn't *have* to love me. They just do.

"Goodnight, Mom," I call out now, but it's too late. She's already moved on down the hall.

I grab my iPhone and crank my favorite playlist. I fill my suitcase with running shoes and running clothes — everything I need for tomorrow's track meet — and, oh yeah, one pair of pajamas. Outside my window the night is settling in as one by one lights are turned off and sleep is the uniform goal in the beachside community. And down the hall my mother joins them.

I love it when the house is quiet, my favorite time of night. I dance around my bedroom where I know no one is watching me. That is, no one other than a three-legged cat. Here I can pretend the rest of the world doesn't exist.

For the moment I'm not a freak.

I'm just Kate.

Two

Seattle

Most runners don't eat the day of a race. But I eat everything. Grapefruit followed by a side of pancakes and waffles is my early morning tradition while my mom sips her coffee out of habit not thirst. She's overly nervous this morning. I know this because for the last half hour she's been avoiding my eyes.

"It's so beautiful here," I say, staring out over the Puget Sound. "Maybe we should stay a day or two longer."

"No." Her coffee cup connects with the table, sending a splash of warm liquid out and over the side of the cup. "I can't, Kate." I watch her dab at her hand with a napkin. She should probably run it under cold water or something and I open my mouth to suggest just that, but she cuts me off with, "We have to leave tomorrow."

When her cell phone rings she sends me a smile that resembles an apology. "This is Olivia," she chirps into the phone. Her hands flutter around the room, straightening everything until even the TV is shifted a little to the right. "Of course. I'll have to hurry, but I should be there in thirty minutes."

"Kate," she calls from the bathroom. "Can I drop you at the stadium a little early? My appointment has been changed."

I stand up and watch as my napkin falls from my lap and onto the floor. Before I can bend over to retrieve it my mom swoops by, leaving in her wake a trail of musky perfume. She moves on toward the doorway and I notice my napkin has magically made it back onto the table.

"That's fine," I say. "You'll be back in time—"

"Of course, Kate. It's only a short meeting with the buyers. I'll be back in time to see you race."

I nod my head but she doesn't notice. She's throwing clothes into her suitcase while she simultaneously makes the bed.

My mom is a jewelry designer. Actually she's more than that. She's an artist. She turns metal into expensive gifts cheating husbands buy their wives or their mistresses. And occasionally she makes something for me.

But she's also known for obsessively cleaning when something is troubling her.

In the bathroom mirror I watch her spin around the room like a whirlwind. Nothing in the small hotel room is safe from her relentless hands. When she begins to straighten the coffee filters I slide my palms down the sides of my running shorts.

"Mom. I'll be fine."

She glances up and her hands pause. We look so much alike I could be staring at myself twenty-five years into the future. Her auburn hair is just past her shoulders, like mine. Her body tall and thin, like mine. She blinks her green eyes and that's where the similarities end. My eyes are blue.

"Two races," I say. "It's only two races and then we go home."

Her shoulders rise as her chest welcomes a much-needed breath. She grips her hands together in front of her as if she's holding them prisoner and says, "Yes. And then we go home."

. . .

Husky Stadium is crowded. The University of Washington's purple flags flap loudly like applause as I stride up the stadium steps. High school students draped in their school colors are swarming the stadium in droves. Their eyes search out familiar faces and occasionally I hear my name called but not once do I acknowledge it. It's always some other Kate, some other girl's face that lights with recognition and smiles or waves in response.

I put my earbuds in so I don't hear them, those other Kates and their friends. I turn the volume to loudest and jog in place.

And then I see her, one of my many ghosts. Her blonde hair is pulled back in a ponytail. She's smiling at someone I don't know. Their conversation is animated and fun, whatever they tell each other is so hilarious they throw their heads back or double over with laughter. You can't fake that kind of happy. She catches me watching her when she turns to grab her backpack off the ground.

It's not her, I tell myself. *It's never her.*

And just like that I'm seven years old again.

"Don't look down, Kate," she'd said that day in her yard. "You'll chicken out if you look down."

"I'm not scared!" I yelled back. I had no reason to be.

The tree wasn't that tall, and its branches had always held us before. My mother explained it again and again when I asked why, WHY? and why some more.

Perhaps it was the storm the night before that had weakened the tree. Or perhaps it was simply more evidence that life isn't fair.

But Alice's mother needed more explanation than that. She needed to know why her daughter spent three weeks in a coma due to severe head trauma while I — the girl who cushioned her daughter's fall by hitting the cement first — didn't even need a check-up.

"It's just one of those things," my mother explained first to the doctor and then over and over again to every person who asked. "A freak accident," she called it.

But all I heard was "freak." The word got caught up inside my head, bouncing back and forth like a tennis ball, until I thought I might go crazy.

When Alice did wake up she wasn't the same. She had to learn how to talk, walk and eat again. And during rehabilitation she discovered her only friend had unexpectedly moved away.

"Kate?"

The voice is so close I jump. My eyes focus back on my surroundings and I notice the girl I thought I knew has moved on toward the lockers. I don't have to look again to see it isn't Alice. Alice was smaller, darker. And from what I've heard she gets around now with a cane.

"Kate?" the voice says again. "Kate Triumph?"

"Yes?" I turn and find a dark-haired girl about my age smiling at me.

"I thought it might be you. I'm such a fan," she reaches out and touches my arm.

"What do you want?" I say.

This sets her back a bit. Her smile slips in the corners, but she soldiers on. "Seriously, everyone on my team worships you. My coach, Coach Thom over there," she points toward the stadium at a tall, bald man who, when he notices we're staring at him, waves a clipboard in the air. "He'd really like to meet you. He's been talking about you all year. He keeps a chart with all of your winning times up on the wall of our gym so we know what to aim for."

"I'm sorry," I interrupt. "Is there something you need?" This isn't the first time I've been approached by someone at a track meet. But I'm not looking to make friends today. No point. Friends are complications. And complications are something I've got enough of already.

The girl shifts her feet and forces her smile back in place with an enviable effort. "I just wanted to introduce myself. I'm Lyla." She holds out her hand and I take it reluctantly.

"And this is my friend, Todd."

Suddenly there's a guy at her side. I didn't even notice him. He must have been standing just behind me.

"Hi, Kate," Todd's voice is deep. Like he's swallowed something heavy. His eyes move down my body and get stuck somewhere between my waist and shoulders.

I should tell him my eyes haven't been at the height since I was seven, but I honestly don't care.

"It's nice to meet you," I say, "but I really need to check in with my coach." I try to move away when Lyla reaches out and grips my arm. Her fingernails dig into my skin.

I glance down at her hand, more than slightly annoyed, but she doesn't release me.

"I understand, Kate. But can you, *please*, promise to come say hi to my teammates? It would *really* mean a lot to them." Her eyes are pleading, her voice is pleading. I wonder if Lyla ever hears the word, no. I look at Todd to find the answer but he's moved over to a large group of boys standing near the fence.

"Sure, okay," I say. But it's a lie.

"Great!" Lyla jumps up and down, her ponytail swooshing around her pretty face. "Come to building C. That's where we're set up." Her smile is wide and perfect, like she practices it in the mirror every day. She gives me one last finger wave before she trots over to Todd.

"She said yes!" I hear her tell him.

Todd throws his arm around her waist, rubbing his hand up and down her side. His eyes, however, stay on me.

"I've alerted the officials about last week's track meet," Coach Elton announces once he's signed me in. "They're going to be watching out for you today." He glances up from his clipboard. "But I have you in the outside lane, just to be safe."

I grab a bottle of water from the cooler and once again try to convince myself that all athletes play dirty. Tripping the fast girl is part of being normal.

"Kate? You'll tell me if there's any trouble, won't you?" Coach is scribbling something on his clipboard but when I don't answer he looks up. "I can't have my star athlete injured. Especially not before we place in nationals."

We. It's such a misleading word, a word he always uses when he talks about us. We means me and you or me and him. But I'm a runner. I run alone. If I make nationals I make it as me. Not we.

"Sure, Coach," I say. You'll be the first to know."

I slip the cap back on my water bottle. The rest of my team is stretching while they discuss the fun that was had on the bus ride down. The bus ride my mom didn't even bother to ask if I'd like to be a part of.

She knows better.

A few girls notice me watching and start talking behind their hands. I look away but not before I hear my name, followed by a colorful word here and there. I know it isn't right to hate someone just because they're them and not you. But most of the time I do anyway.

"Do you feel ready, Kate?" Coach Elton asks. "Should we run through our workout one last time?" He sounds so eager I almost say yes, but I've already spent the last twenty minutes prancing around like his prized pony. "You sure?" he asks, when I stay silent. "We could talk instead, if you like. Is there anything that's bothering you?"

My only response is to walk away.

Coach doesn't care about me. To him I'm a sensation. An elusive number on a stopwatch.

Up until a few months ago he called me Four-minute Mile, not because that's what I run but because it's his dream for me. And it would've continued if Molly, the girl who runs hurdles, hadn't stepped up and said, "She's got a name, Coach."

Until that day I didn't realize Molly could speak.

I held onto my mask of indifference and vowed to thank her later, but the next time I saw her, she didn't see me. At least she pretended not to.

And that continued until I stopped looking.

When I joined the team a few years ago I used to smile down the line and try to make friends, but jealousy and envy were the only friends who would smile back.

My fellow teammates congratulate me on the field, and back at school they carve *bitch* in my locker.

But it doesn't matter. I don't run for them or coach or anyone. It's not about the records or awards. And it's definitely not about the trophies. They only collect dust in my mom's office.

I run to feel the power that is speed. It surges through my body and I feel free. No one can touch me when I'm running. Not even their words can reach me.

"There you are," a familiar voice says at my side.

I look up and find Lyla. She's got her smile in place, her pony tail still swishing.

"Thanks for doing this, Kate." She links her arm through mine and then Todd appears. His hand slides around my waist and suddenly I'm the meat in a Lyla and Todd sandwich.

"I really can't—" I begin, but Todd stops me.

"No worries, Kate. Just think of it as doing us a favor." His comment triggers laughter and when I glance behind us I find we're not alone. Todd and Lyla have gathered a posse of friends to tail us to Building C.

"Shit," I say under my breath.

Todd hears me and grins. His hand tightens around my waist.

When we turn a corner I find three more guys lounging along the wall. They straighten their position once they spy us.

I turn to flee.

"Not so fast, Triumph," Todd says. "Now see, that's what got you here in the first place." He lifts me at the waist and hoists me up over his shoulders. One minute I'm gearing up to scream, my hands and feet flailing out around me, and the next I'm being thrown through a door marked Janitor's closet. I kick and push at the locked door but it's no use. The door doesn't budge.

"Don't worry, Kate," Lyla says through the door. "He told us he'd let you out right after the race."

He? Who's he? I want to scream. But I stay silent. It's not like they'll answer me anyway.

"Go on ahead," Todd says. "I'll catch up in a minute."

His friends snicker at this as they move off down the hall, calling out lewd suggestions that thankfully I can't completely make out. But Lyla doesn't find it amusing. She threatens to tell Todd's girlfriend, a girl whose name sounds like Mekia or Mecca. I wonder if Mecca/Mekia already knows her boyfriend is a loser but chooses not to accept it like most girls at my school. I hear their footsteps move off down the hall. And then I'm alone. In a closet.

I search the wall until I find a light switch but it only reveals the other abandoned objects in the closet: a collection of cleaning supplies and a couple of brooms.

I may not know who initiated this little plan but I bet I can figure out the reason. A glance at my watch tells me I've got about five minutes before my first race begins.

I kick the door once then twice and then back up and kick it again, this time with a powerful battle cry that makes me sound like a ninja. But the battle cry doesn't work, and neither does the kick. The stubborn door doesn't budge.

"Hello? Is somebody in there?" A male voice calls out and I feel a stirring of hope.

"Yes! Can you open the door?"

The doorknob rattles but nothing more. I let out a deep sigh and rest my head against the cold wood.

"It's locked," the voice explains. "I can try and find the janitor—"

"Don't bother," I say.

"What did you say?"

"Just stand back."

"I'm sorry I didn't hear you, your voice is— "

"Get the hell out of the way!" I yell and kick the doorknob.

With a splintering crack the lock breaks free and I stumble out of the closet.

"What the—" a dark haired guy jumps back as I fly out of the closet. He's dressed casually, not like a runner. His gray-green eyes move from the broken door to me and then back again.

I glance away, cursing the heat rising in my cheeks. I hate that I'm in this situation, but mostly I hate that this guy — who just so happens to be ridiculously attractive — has witnessed it.

"The door sticks," I say with a shrug, and then take off toward the stadium before he can ask any questions.

Coach Elton is the first person I see when I reach the track.

"Triumph!" he yells, glaring at me. "Get on the line before you're disqualified!"

"Sure thing, Coach." My eyes sweep the crowd of athletes along the fence for Lyla or Todd, but I don't see either.

There are twelve girls already on their mark when the warning whistle blows for the 400-meter. Their nervous chatter and last minute stretches stop when I step on the line. One lap around the track. The sprint of death, as some like to call it. To win the race takes speed, and determination. But mostly speed.

My name is whispered followed by a curse or two. Apparently I'm not making any friends today. I feel their apprehension, their exclusion. Competition. It's always the same. But this isn't just any track meet. It's the nationals. If you're fast, you prove it today. But if you're me, you rein it in.

Lyla takes a step over the line. She wants me to notice her. When I look up she's smiling, but not at me. Todd and the bald coach are just behind me leaning up against the fence. Todd catches my eye and winks, while the bald coach reveals nothing.

Was this part of their plan? To get me all riled up before the race? Or to keep me from racing? Either way, I'm going to win.

I take a deep breath and pretend to tie my shoelace. I need to calm down. I need to think rationally and keep my head. At least that's what my mom would tell me if she were here. But she's not. She's somewhere in the crowd, watching from her seat. She doesn't know the things that go on at track meets. Nor will she ever know.

I take another deep breath and stare up at the sky. Thin patches of white clouds are attempting to hide the sun but I can still feel it against my skin. The air is crisp and the second whistle only seconds away.

A line of expensive name-brand shoes take their mark. My shoes aren't expensive, but they're my favorite. They're red with orange stripes and they clash with the forest-green tank top I'm forced to wear in support of my school colors.

The restless crowd feeds off the nervous energy of the athletes and their voices became a loud buzz in the background. The runners poised to compete twitch and shuffle restlessly like stallions at the gate.

I stay perfectly still. I know what I need to do: win the race and nothing more. But the thing is, that's not what I *want* to do. I want to fly.

The starter pistol fires and I hold myself back, allowing Lyla a brief glimpse at what it feels like to be at the front of the pack. We stay like this awhile. Whenever she slows, I slow. The look on her face when she continues to check my progress is clear as day. She thinks she's got me.

My coach is yelling at me, urging me further. Faster. The crowd is so loud, they're a crack of thunder on a sunny day. I stay with Lyla until we round the corner near the finish line.

And then I let go. Lyla's not smiling now. Her expressive face reflects her surprise when I sidle up next to her and hover at her side.

"Not today, Lyla," I tell her and her eyes flash at me.

"You're a bitch, Kate Triumph," she hisses between breaths.

"Yeah. So I've been told."

Her foot swings out like she's about to trip me just as my foot stretches slightly further than my usual stride. I avoid her leg and she goes down. Her cry of outrage kicks me into high gear.

Never before have I felt so free. I realize I'm moving too quickly but my legs are in control now. My legs and my heart, together they block out reason. All around me the crowd is collectively craning their necks — some even rising to their feet — to see the girl who can practically fly.

The other runners push with all their might, stretching the limits of their strength even though they know their fight is for second place.

I cross the finish line and turn around to observe my fellow racers. But my wait is longer than I expect. One by one they join me across the finish line, their faces a composite of shock and disbelief.

The moment it hits me my hands fly to my mouth.

What have I done?

The noise of the crowd surges to a deafening roar and from the corner of my eye I see the scoreboard is flashing two words. World record. World record, it blinks. I don't notice the number that precedes it. I don't care to know.

The judges are checking and rechecking their stopwatches and soon the rows of recruiters are clamoring out of their seats. I take a step back from the finish line. My hair paints the path of the light breeze circling the stadium.

"Freakin' fabulous," I mutter under my breath and sweep the crowd for my mom. Even from across the track her wide eyes reach mine. She isn't standing and cheering like everyone else.

She looks terrified.

Three

San Diego

"You ran too fast today, Kate," my mom says. These are the first words she's spoken to me since we got off the plane.

"Do I have to remind you it was a race?"

Her silence is my answer.

"Why, Kate?" she turns away from the road just long enough for the pain in her eyes to injure me permanently. "What happened? We've worked on your control so many times. What happened today was never supposed to happen." Her voice is bordering on hysterical, each word is a rock thrown in my direction. "I have multiple messages on my cell phone from reporters, not to mention the college recruiters who are practically offering me a second home just to train with you. They all want a piece of the seventeen-year-old girl who broke an eight-year world record. Any idea what I should tell them, Kate?" Her hands tighten on the steering wheel, each knuckle points toward the windshield like an arrow aimed at the sky. "How did they even get my number?"

"How about, no?" I offer quietly and then when she doesn't respond I say, "Steroids. Tell them I'm on steroids and that I just confessed to it and I would like to be disqualified from the race." It's not like I have a reputation to uphold.

For a brief moment she thinks about it, to her that would be a solution. Her eyes move over my face while she continues to hold something back.

"I won," I whisper. "And it felt pretty damn good."

My mother flinches, just like I want her to. "You always win," she sighs.

"Don't you want me to be happy?" I cry, even though we both know it's a childish thing to say.

20

"Of course I do, Kate, it's just—"

"It's the only thing I have." I don't mean to yell this, but the few times I've allowed the truth to slip out it always arrives loud.

"You have me," she whispers. "We have each other."

There's that word again. We. Is it wrong that I want a different version of we, someone more my age? Like when you have a best friend so close that you speak in "we." "We should totally get matching toe rings!" Or, "We think people with matching toe rings are creepy."

"Do you hear me, Kate? We'll always have each other," my mom says.

But we both know it's not enough. It will never be enough.

I sit back in my seat and close my eyes. There's a jar of air tightly sealed inside my chest. I'm not sure how much longer I can hold back from breathing. Truth be told, I don't know how much longer I can hold back from living. I slide the lid off a bit and allow some air out.

"I'm sorry, Mom." In the darkness I find her hand. It feels the same as it always does, soft to the touch but rough at the fingertips. "Next time I won't try so hard."

Her fingers tighten on mine. "Next time, Kate? Do you really think that's such a good idea? Especially after today."

Finally, the words she's been building up to say. That imaginary lid slams back on the jar.

"You want me to stop running." I drop her hand and pull my knees up to my chest.

"Just until this all boils over. I spoke with your coach—"

"You spoke with Coach?"

"He agreed it was our decision to make."

"You mean your decision!"

"You know it's for the best, Kate. It's not fair—"

And there it is. The word I hate more than anything. "Don't talk to me about fair! I have no life! You think that's fair? You're always worrying about *them*. About what *they'll* think or feel or do if they discover the truth about me. When will you start thinking about *me*?"

"Kate—"

"No. You know, just forget it. I know. There's nothing we can do. And if there were something, you'd do it. You'd do anything, give anything to make me different. But you can't." I lean my head against the window but even the cold glass can't cool me down.

"I'm trying, Kate. I saw someone today."

"I know. You met with a buyer," I say and start counting backwards. *10, 9, 8. Alice, Lyla, Todd.*

"No. Not a buyer. I saw a doctor. Someone who might help us."

"Help us what, Mom? Change my DNA. Make me less of a freak?" I'm half listening, half watching the Pacific Coast Highway rush by in the darkness. Even without looking I know I'd be able to see the white foam from the waves below crash up against the shore. It's soothing the way the waves are predictable. They move out, they move in, like a pattern.

But when I close my eyes I don't see the ocean, I see Lyla's smile, and the fear hidden behind it.

They're all the same.

I used to think it was hate. "They all hate me," I'd cry to my mom. She'd shake her head and say, "fear's only disguise is hate. They don't hate you. They could never hate you." Then she witnessed it for herself.

When I was much younger my mom and I never did playdates. She was always too busy building up her jewelry boutique to spend much time with other mommies or their kids. While she worked I worked, or pretended to. She sold precious metals and jewels while I sold drawings of princesses and castles. My mother made enough money to buy our first house while I made enough to occasionally buy us ice cream.

We were inseparable. Two auburn-haired, fair-skinned girls with only each other to count on. I didn't need friends or birthday parties. I had my mom. And then came kindergarten.

I knew it was a struggle for her to send me out into the world. I could tell she was fighting back tears. Her green eyes sparkled just like the emeralds I helped her clean after a new shipment.

But this was school, something I had to do on my own. One by one the other mommies walked away while my mother lingered, drawing out her departure. I figured she would miss me. I thought maybe she just didn't want to be alone. I didn't realize then just how different I was.

The call came halfway through the day. I remember my mom rushing into the classroom, her green eyes no longer sad, instead they were wide with worry. And fear.

"Where is she?" she shouted.

When I heard her voice I hid behind the bookshelf where my teacher had placed me, far away from the other kids. And far away from her.

I didn't want to go home. I liked school. We'd painted and colored all morning. Twice we'd ventured outside to get pushed on the swings. I'd even met a girl with black ringlets named Darcie. She'd smiled and held my hand while we stood in line at the drinking fountain.

"You're my new best friend," she whispered, and I smiled.

"Let's build a castle and we can both be princesses," I said, and she giggled.

Everything was perfect, just as my mom promised it would be.

Then after lunch one of the boys — Joey, "Joey Singer," he'd announced multiple times throughout the day — found the teacher's scissors and chased Darcie and me around the room, threatening to cut our first day of school dresses. He cornered Darcie behind the play kitchen and I felt it was my responsibility to come to her rescue, seeing as we were best friends and all.

I know he didn't mean to cut me. He was waving the scissors like a claw and when I reached for them he only tried to keep them from me.

He didn't mean to hurt me.

But the teacher was upset. She'd been distracted, as most teachers would be on the first day of school when four of her twenty-four students had not made it to the bathroom in time.

Darcie's scream sent her running.

Joey's scream and my hand made her stop.

There was blood all down the front of my new pink dress. It covered the pink polka-dot tulips that danced along my waist and across my shoulder. I remember looking down at myself and thinking, I won't be able to pretend it didn't happen this time.

By the time my mom arrived Darcie and Joey had already gone home. Their parents had also received calls at work. And the rest of the kids were sitting out in the sunshine listening to the teacher's assistant read an entire collection of Dr. Seuss books, while my teacher scrubbed blood out of the carpet.

Once my mom saw me she didn't ask any questions. She grabbed my hand and we left. That night she told me a story about how we were moving the boutique.

"Chicago is much prettier than Boston," she said.

"Does it have a river?" I asked.

"It does."

"Will I meet another girl like Darcie?" I asked.

"One day," she said. "But first we're going to try to learn our letters and numbers at home."

"Kate? Are you listening to me?" my mom asks me now. She reaches across the car and touches the side of my face. "Honey? Were you asleep?"

"Did you miss John?" I take her hand in mine and give it a slight squeeze before I place it back in her lap. "He wants to marry you. You know that, right?" It's not a secret the guy my mom pretends she isn't dating is in love with her.

"Honey, I'm trying to talk to you about something important here."

"Are you saying John isn't important?"

My mom rolls her eyes. "We'll see," she says, but again that we is her and me.

"I like him," I say. "He's nice and he loves you. What more can a girl ask for?"

"Kate."

"Seriously, Mom. Just because I don't have a life doesn't mean you can't."

"How about I turn around and get us two Chocolover shakes at Sully's?" my mom asks.

I close my eyes and allow the subject to be changed. "You always know how to distract me," I say.

"Kate? Is your seat belt on? This guy behind us is coming up way too fast." I feel her arm pin me back against my seat. The gesture is so familiar I almost smile. Was it possible to shield someone with simply a protective hold and a strong will? Perhaps it was purely instinctive. But when my mom gasps, I open my eyes. A loud crunch from behind jolts me forward and the breath is pushed from my lungs when my seat belt locks up. I look around, searching for answers but our car is spinning like the teacups ride at Disneyland.

And I want off.

I grip the dashboard but it isn't much to hold on to and I'm thrown into the side of my door.

What's happening?

Everything is moving too fast. And then it stops. I look up and follow the beam of our headlights to another car and the man behind the wheel. Trembling, I push my hair back off my face and stare into the eyes of the stranger. He stares back.

"Kate! Kate, are you alright?" My mom's voice. It's close. It's terrified. She's reaching for me. Touching my face, my hair. Trying to drag me back from the shock. But it's too late. I can feel my skin growing cold and damp and my heart is beating rapidly. Most of all I can feel the man's eyes watching me. He climbs out of his car and his face is clearly visible as he carefully lights a cigarette.

"I should call the police. I should check to see if anyone's hurt. Kate? Kate! Stay in the car. Do you hear me? Don't get out. It's too dangerous."

I don't answer. The stranger's mouth is moving. Is he talking to himself or me? I hear my mother open her door and then our car begins to fill with light.

"Don't they see us?" she spins around in her seat and stares out the back window.

"See us?" I ask blankly just as the man's stoic expression lifts into a smile.

The sound of screeching tires shatters his spell on me. And my mom fumbles for her seat belt. Closer and louder, the screeching becomes a roar. Once again I'm thrown forward with a crescendo of splintering metal and plastic. My fingers touch cold glass and then break straight through it.

Stop! Please stop! No more!

I hear myself screaming and then everything flips upside down. Instinctively I push against the descending roof and when the feeling of suffocation begins to overwhelm me, I close my eyes. A voice screaming at my side — *Mom!* — eventually fights through my panicked mind and I gasp in pain. Then finally our car comes to a stop.

I wrestle against my seat belt in a struggle to escape but the pain is like nothing I've ever experienced. It's everywhere. And it's too difficult to pinpoint. Is it my back, my head or my legs that feel like they're in pieces? When my breathing grows labored, I know it's my lungs. Blackness is beginning to fill in around me but I fight it off and reach across the car toward my mom.

Mom! I can't see you!

Did I say the words aloud? My mouth feels locked shut and there's a ringing in my head that is steadily becoming louder.

Where is she? I can't find her!

My left hand is flailing around the inside of the car until what I'm looking for finds me — my mom's hand.

I cling to it desperately and hear my mom call out to me — just once — before everything turns to absolute black.

Four

I am in hell.

If I could open my eyes I'm sure I'd find my skin is melting, sliding off the bone into a puddle at my feet. My feet. I can't move my feet. They feel heavy. Dead.

I'm dead.

I have to be. Except I'm on fire.

If I could only get my eyes to open.

"She's awake, Doctor," someone says. They sound far away and then close.

There's a woman standing over me. She's all in white, like an angel. She smiles at me and says, "Welcome back, Kate."

It's my mother. She touches my face and tells me everything is going to be alright. "You're safe here. The doctor wants you to know you're safe."

And then she's gone.

Or am I gone? No. My eyes are closed.

"I thought you said she was awake."

The voice sounds like John. My mother's John.

"John," I say, but it sounds more like a moan.

"Just rest, Kate," he says. "You're going to be alright."

I want to say, "I know," but my lips won't move. I want to see my mom again. I want to ask for her.

But all I do is sleep.

Five

The whispering wakes me. It drags me out of a place where everything is dark to a place where everything is dark. My room. It has to be my room. Just darker. And about a thousand degrees warmer than normal.

"Mom?" I call out. My voice sounds like I'm sick. Am I sick?

"How are you feeling?" a voice asks.

I open my eyes, but I don't recognize this person. She smiles at me and touches my hand.

"Would you like some water?"

"No. I mean, yes. Why can't I move my legs?" I lift my head and look for the object that is holding me down, making me feel heavy. And hot.

But it's just a blanket. My blanket. Purple flowers and grey clouds with Lefty nestled in between my feet.

"I can't move," I whisper. "My legs." I want the blanket off. Now. Only, as I think it, I can't seem to do anything about it. I manage to slide one of my arms out from under the blanket.

Where is the rest of me?

"I can't breathe," I say in between deep breaths. "I can't…"

"Just relax, Kate," the woman says. She holds me down when I try to sit up, but there's really no point, the only thing I can lift is my head. "Everything's going to be alright," she says.

I feel a prick in my left shoulder.

"What? What was that?" I say, and then the darkness creeps back. It fills in the corners of my vision until just her face is clear. She smiles one last time and I force my eyes wider, concentrating on her hair — dark and pulled off her face — then her mouth, which is thin and when she smiles she hides her teeth.

How did I ever think she looked like my mom?

My mom. Where is my mom? I want to close my eyes. It's so hard to keep them open. I'm searching my room, she has to be here somewhere, but the darkness is spreading. "Where is she?" I say. But I don't think the woman hears me. I barely do.

And then nothing.

"Hello, Kate."

My eyes are open but all I see is my ceiling. There's a light on in my room. A candle. It flickers and dances along the walls and smells like lavender. Just like my mom.

"Where is she?" I say. I remember this is a very important question. It's the only thing on my mind right now.

"How are you feeling?"

John. He's back.

I turn my head on my pillow and there he is. He's pulled my desk chair next to my bed. He's dressed in scrubs. I've never seen him dressed in scrubs. When he visits my mother he's always so formal. His shirts pressed, his pants pressed. I've never seen him without a tie.

His hair is slightly disheveled, as if he just woke up.

"Why are you here? Did my mom call you?" I look behind him, hoping she'll appear in the doorway. But she doesn't. "How sick am I?"

I try to sit up but he stops me.

"Just relax, Kate. You need to stay still."

"Why?"

And then I'm hit with an image. Headlights, a crash, and me trapped inside my mother's car. I'm fighting the images off but I'm breathing so fast I start to feel dizzy.

"What happened to her?"

John catches my hand before I pull my blankets back.

"You're alright, Kate," he says. He grabs my hand and holds it in his.

"Stop saying that. I know I'm alright. Where is my mom? What happened to her?"

The woman is back. She appears just over John's left shoulder. In her hands she holds a needle. A shot. The same thing she gave me before.

"No. I don't want that," I say. "Please, John. I don't want to sleep anymore. I just want my mom."

I don't realize I'm crying until John reaches up and brushes my tears away.

"Kate," he says.

And I know. He doesn't have to say the words. I know.

I close my eyes just before he whispers, "She didn't make it."

I feel my heart explode into a thousand sharp pieces that spread throughout my body and then get lodged inside my throat. The pain is so much that I know if I could bring myself to cough I'd cough up blood. I can almost taste it filling my mouth, my stomach, my head.

I'm flailing my one arm at John and screaming. Lunging for his chest, slapping his face.

He just watches me. The nurse touches his shoulder and when he shakes his head she leaves the room.

"I'm sorry, Kate," his mouth says. But I can't hear him. All I hear is me or what has to be me, even though I don't recognize the sounds.

He pushes my hair back from my face and stays with me until I'm reduced to whimpering and nothing more. Then he slips out of my room.

He doesn't hear me when I whisper, "Why her? Why her and not me?"

But the man sitting in the corner of my room does. He's been watching since the moment I woke up, perhaps longer. He doesn't take his eyes from me. At first I thought I was imagining him, that he was a side effect of whatever drugs are inside my body. But when he moves his chair next to my bed and takes my hand I figure he's real. His hair isn't blonde, nor is it dark. His face is handsome. I don't care that he's witnessed this moment. I don't care about anything at all.

"You're going to be alright, Kate. You will survive this," he says, and the way he says it makes me think he may be right. He sounds so sure of himself.

"No," I say. "I will never be alright."

I close my eyes. I can't think of a reason to keep them open.

"You and I, Kate," he whispers just before I fall asleep. "*We* will survive this."

Six

There is no place where death won't find you.

Even in my dreams she's gone. I watch her slipping away, her hands reaching for mine until they fall with the rest of her into the darkness. Where she disappears. Forever. And when I wake misery coats my skin like a layer of dirt, making me wish I could shower it away.

Death.

How does one survive death?

John's been sleeping in our guest room. He comes in and checks on me, and so does his nurse. Her name is Ruth and I've found she never comes empty handed. Food, pain medicine, water. She shovels each item into my mouth if I won't do it. And I mostly won't do it.

"You have to eat," she says. "How will you ever get better if you don't eat?"

When she asks me this I never have a response.

I've learned that in the accident I broke both my legs, my right arm, some ribs and, well, I stopped listening after that.

"It's a miracle you survived," Ruth says.

"Lucky," she calls me.

She watches John shine a light into my eyes to check for a concussion. She's convinced he should find one. And John keeps looking, even though I suspect he knows the truth.

He's covered my legs and my right arm in plaster. It's hot, heavy and unnecessary. But I don't complain. As long as there is air moving through my chest, I shouldn't complain, right?

I haven't seen the man again. Not since that night. I asked John about him once but it made him uncomfortable, I could sense it, and caused Ruth's lips to purse. I didn't ask again.

I'm beginning to think he was a hallucination.

The funeral is Friday. John said he didn't know how to contact my mother's friends, since he'd never met any, so he announced it in the paper.

I said that was a good idea. He doesn't need to know we've never really had any.

I keep my bedroom dark. I can hear the ocean from just outside my windows but I don't want to see the sun. It feels wrong to see light when all I feel is dark inside.

I don't sleep much, although I pretend to. John and Ruth both try to get me to talk about the accident. They ask me questions about what happened or if I remember anything in particular. The police have also been by a few times to ask the same questions.

"I don't really remember," I say, because it's easiest. I don't want to think about the things I yelled at my mom or how disappointed she was in me. I don't want to remember how it felt to hold her hand and fight off death while she couldn't.

Lefty rarely leaves my side, other than the occasional trips to feed himself, but he always returns. He touches his left paw to my hand and with his yellow cat eyes asks me where my mother has gone. I can't bear to tell him.

"Kate?"

John hovers in my doorway. He's dressed in scrubs again.

"I have to head over to the hospital but I should be back by morning." His eyes move around my room and then dodge the portrait of my mom resting on top of my desk. "Ruth should be here soon," he says. "She's running a bit late."

I nod my head to show him I've heard, but he doesn't leave. He shifts his feet in my doorway and then clears his throat.

"You may have a visitor tonight. His name is Andrew and he. Well, he knew your mother." John clears his throat again and then looks at me.

I look back.

"This isn't the first time he's visited. He was here that night. The night you woke up."

"I remember," I say.

"Right. Well, I'll be off then."

"See you later." I don't know what to say to John. I know he's hurting, he loved my mom, but now that she's gone I can't imagine I'm enough to keep him around.

"Kate." I look up and find he's still standing in my doorway.

"Yes?" I say when his pause goes on too long.

"I just want you to know, you have other options." He nods his head once as if he's said all he needs to say and then walks off down the hall.

Ruth arrives a few minutes later. She brings me French onion soup she made at home and some French bread she picked up on her way over here.

"Eat, Kate. Please eat," she says. She watches me take a few bites of the bread and then leaves my room looking like she just won a battle.

I take one last bite of the bread and then push it away. I'm not hungry. I'm never hungry.

All I want to do is sleep.

The doorbell rings just as I'm closing my eyes. I hear Ruth shuffle down the hall and then seconds later someone's knocking on my bedroom door.

When the man enters my room he turns on the light. For a moment I'm blind. I've been living in the dark for what seems like weeks but could only be a few days.

"Hello Kate," he says. His voice is rich, not exactly friendly, but neither is it intimidating. He pulls my desk chair over to the side of my bed and takes a seat.

A smile lifts the corner of his mouth when he catches me studying him and then he crosses his arms against his chest.

"How are you feeling?"

"I'm great," I say, and his eyes narrow a bit at the tone of my voice.

"Do you remember me? I was here the other night."

I nod and wish I could sit up more. He has a look about him that makes me nervous, like he's about to drag important information from my mind, stuff I didn't even realize I knew.

"So how long before you get out of bed?"

The question catches me off guard.

I glance down at my plastered body. "I kinda have to be able to move first."

"Right," he says. "You're lucky you get to recuperate here at home. Hospital food is a bitch."

"Yeah. Lucky," I say.

He doesn't react to my sarcasm. Instead he tilts his head an inch to the right and asks, "And why is it again John has you here instead of in a hospital?"

"I- He's the doctor. Ask him."

"I just might do that." The way he says it makes me think he already has.

"Would you like to sit outside?" he asks.

I open my mouth to answer and then close it.

"I'll help you get out there. It's still light out, and the breeze coming off the ocean may help clear your mind."

"I... I'm not." I stop and shake my head. I don't want to leave my room. If I stay in here I can pretend that my mom is somewhere else in the house, cooking or folding laundry, anywhere but the city morgue. I open my mouth to explain and then just shrug.

He shoots me that look again, the one where he's about to ask me a question that he already knows the answer to and then says, "You must love living here."

"I do," I say. "I did."

"You did?"

"I love California."

"Hmm." He sits back and studies me a bit longer. "So? What do you think? Are you up for a change of scenery?"

I blink back at him. For a moment I wonder if we're still talking about going outside.

"Perhaps another day," I say.

"Alright." He rises to his feet and I realize he's much taller than I first thought. I watch him walk around my room looking and yet not looking at what fills my personal space. When he notices the photo of my mom and me on my desk he stops and lifts it with hesitation.

"John said you knew my mom." My words are soft and yet they crash against him like a tidal wave. He holds the frame with shaky hands, like he's trying to keep from breaking it.

"Yes," he says. He places the frame back where he found it and turns away. When he looks up again his eyes are composed. Or rather, emotionless.

"When?" I ask. "When did you know her?"

"Another lifetime ago," he rubs the back of his neck and then takes his seat again.

"Have I met you before? Like when I was younger?"

"No."

"So then, why now?" I ask.

"What happened to your father, Kate?" The question comes at me so fast I almost can't think of the answer.

"I don't have a father."

"How about John? Would you consider him your father?"

I pull the blankets back off my legs. I can't tell if I'm warm or just nervous, either way I'm uncomfortable.

"My mother and John haven't been dating long. I've only known him for a year or so."

"A year's a long time for most people. Was she in love with him?"

"No." I don't need to think on this one. I know now why she picked John over all the other men who pursued her. "He's convenient," I say.

He sits forward in his chair with his elbows resting upon his knees. "How so?" he asks.

But I don't answer. If he hasn't figured it out already, I'm not about to tell him.

"Who are you?" I ask instead.

"Andrew," he says. "My name is Andrew Shore."

He's on his feet again. He moves toward my windows and I close my eyes in anticipation as he pulls each curtain back, bathing my room in sunshine.

When I don't hear him return to his chair I open my eyes.

He's watching me from across the room. I can't make out his expression because he's backlit, but something has changed. The room feels smaller, like he's filled it up with questions he's about to throw at me.

Strangely enough I'm ready for them.

"We met in London. Did you know she lived there most of her life?"

"Yes."

This sets him back. He perches his hip on the side of my desk and crosses his arms.

"What do you know about her childhood? And your grandparents. What did she tell you about them?"

"They're dead. We don't have any other family." I suck in a breath and say, "It's just us." Was just us.

Andrew moves back to his chair and when he takes a seat, for the first time, I can see him clearly. His hair is dirty blonde, his skin smooth except for a thin scar that stretches from his hairline down toward his right temple.

My hands are shaking as I pull the blanket back over my legs. My body is suddenly so cold my teeth almost start to chatter. I clench my teeth together, trapping the tiny gasp of surprise that rose up from my chest the moment I caught a glimpse of his eyes. Blue eyes. Just like mine.

"Do you want to talk about your mother?"

"Not really," I whisper.

"It appears she was a bit of a liar."

I open my mouth to object and then stop when he leans in toward me.

"Do you recognize me Kate?" His voice is strained like he's barely holding himself together, like I am.

I shake my head. My chest is rising and falling so quickly I'm starting to feel faint.

"We have something in common you and I. Have you noticed?"

I squeeze my eyes shut and continue to shake my head, no.

"She never told me," he says. "Do you know how that makes me feel?"

I cry out when he grips my shoulders.

"Look at me, Kate! Please look at me!"

"No!" I yell back. "You're wrong!"

I hear footsteps racing down the hall and then Ruth appears in my doorway. "Kate? Is everything alright?" She glares at Andrew, who is now sitting back in his chair, his expression relaxed. He smiles at her and asks if she'll bring me some water.

When she glances my way I nod my head.

"Thanks, Ruth," I say once she's returned.

She watches me drink half the glass and then closes the door behind her.

Andrew reaches out to take it from me but I shake my head. I hold the glass in front of me like it's a shield I can hide behind.

"What did she tell you about me?" he asks.

I stare up into his dark blue eyes, eyes I can't turn away from or lie to. Eyes I see in the mirror every day of my life.

"She told me you were dead," I whisper. "And that we were better off without you."

Seven

Jonah Selby could find her house with his eyes closed. After all, he's been haunting her street for the last few weeks.

From his hiding spot in the neighbor's yard he watches as the tall, blonde man walks outside Kate's front door to make yet another phone call. He waves his hands around and paces back and forth. But he doesn't raise his voice.

And Jonah hates him for that.

It sure would be nice to hear his conversations. Perhaps he could figure out just who he is.

It's been seven days since he last saw Kate. Seven days since the Jigsaw Club burnt down. Only once in that time did the light go on inside her room, but even though he hasn't seen her, he's convinced she's there.

She has to be.

The blonde man finishes his call and slips his cell phone back into his pocket. For a moment he appears to be enjoying the night air.

And then he turns and looks right at Jonah.

He can't see me. There's no way he knows I'm here.

Jonah holds his breath. He doesn't even dare blink.

The man takes a step and then another until he's so close Jonah can make out the logo on his baseball hat. Seattle Mariners. The tall, blonde man must be a fan.

The bushes Jonah hides behind are tall enough to conceal him, but if the man comes any closer he just might be able to make out the top of his head.

Jonah hears a faint buzzing noise and then releases his breath when the man pulls out his cell phone and moves back toward Kate's house.

Who is he?

Before the fire it was just Kate and her mother. Two women he could keep track of but now there's "Scrubs," the man who drives the Jag and has to be a doctor, his nurse, and the tall, blonde man. Three new arrivals. And they're making him nervous.

Where is Kate? Why hasn't he seen her? He used to watch her run every morning and night. Always alone, at least she thought she was. And always in the dark. It's been seven days now without a sighting, not a glimpse through her window. Not once has she left her house.

Something's wrong. He can feel it.

A few hours later Jonah turns the inside latch on his hotel room door and waits to see if his Nanna will stir. Nothing. With a deep sigh he slips off his shoes in the dark and crawls into bed. But he doesn't close his eyes. Every few minutes his Nanna wakes herself with bouts of coughing but then immediately falls back to sleep.

She's dying here. Dying in California — where she begged him to bring her.

Jonah's eyes are still open when the room fills with the colors of another gorgeous sunrise.

When Nanna demanded they visit California his first thoughts had been Disneyland, Dodgers and boogie boarding but his Nanna had other plans. Now he's spending his days counting Nanna's dying breaths and his nights searching for Kate.

"Jonah? Jonah, honey, are you there?"

"Yes, Nanna?" Jonah rises to his feet and hurries to her side. Her thin face and nearly colorless eyes are a weak background for her radiant smile. If only he could get her to eat. Even his threats to drag her back to Vegas aren't working.

"What's your plan, Jonah? Tell me again," she whispers and Jonah sighs.

"School, Nanna. I'll go back to school."

"Classes begin in a few weeks. You should call today and make sure they have you enrolled."

"Yes. I'll call today."

"And you'll take the money? You'll use it for college, won't you, Jonah?"

"Yes. A good school near here."

"Yes, near here. You must live close."

"Yes. Now how about some breakfast? I can have them send up some eggs."

"No. I'm not hungry just yet. Let's talk about it again." When Jonah rolls his eyes, she adds, "Please."

"I promised, Nanna."

"Yes. You promised. And you won't forget?"

"Never."

"And you won't wuss out?"

Jonah chuckles, as he usually does, when she tries to use his words. "Nope. No wusses here."

"Good, Jonah. Good."

"Now how about those eggs?"

But his suggestion is lost on her. She's already fallen back asleep.

Eight

The sky opens up the day Olivia Triumph is buried.

I watch from my wheelchair, two legs and an arm in casts, with John and Andrew poised on either side of me. They each hold an umbrella above my head, but occasionally a raindrop slips through and taps me on the shoulder.

John planned the entire thing, asking me questions here or there about flowers or music. I tried to help but with each answer I gave it was like giving up any hope that she may still be alive.

It's cold for mid-September, at least that's what everyone keeps saying. The weather, the flowers and how sad it is to lose someone so young, are the topics of conversation floating around me as I stare off over the cemetery.

It's a small group of mourners, a few work-related acquaintances of my mom's and a few friends of John's.

And there in the back, where he thinks I can't see him, stands Gabe.

At first I was surprised to see him and then I remembered he's too nice to miss something like this. Of course he brought his girlfriend. They travel as a pair now. And that's okay, I guess. I stopped caring two years ago.

It's funny how one day you're allowed to touch somebody, run your hands through his hair, kiss his lips, and then after a few words are exchanged, or some terrifying encounter shared, all of that changes. I used to stare at the back of Gabe's head in Bio class, my fingers tingling. All I wanted to do was reach out and feel his soft brown hair. Now only Shelley is allowed to touch him.

And I'm okay with that also. It took me a few months but I was eventually okay.

The mourners begin to shift about and I realize the service is over. Some of them place a flower on my mom's casket before moving off to find their cars. A few attempt to make eye contact with me while most pretend I'm invisible. And perhaps I am.

It would explain why I feel nothing.

The lifeless haze that welcomed me this morning surrounds me still. It hangs off my black dress and even my hair, which is pulled off my face in a tight bun.

"Would you like a moment alone, Kate?" John asks.

When I look up at him he gives me a halfhearted smile. His eyes are red, reminding me I should be crying. His throat swallows back the anguish he'll wait to release once he's alone.

I nod my head and he walks off, leaving me with a silent and very still Andrew.

We haven't talked much since the day he came to visit me. But he and John talk. I hear them late at night, when they think I'm asleep. I can't make out what they're saying but I'd bet money they're talking about me.

And then there's Gabe. He watches me from a few feet away while his girlfriend, Shelley, plays with her iPhone. I notice her dress is wrinkled and wonder if she was a last minute invite. Perhaps he hadn't planned on dragging her to her boyfriend's ex-girlfriend's dead mother's funeral. But in the end she begged to go.

My mother never liked Gabe, even though she pretended to. When he first started coming around she'd shoot me these worried glances, which I would of course ignore.

"Be careful, Kate. Please, be careful." Even now I can still hear her words.

And I was. I always am. But some things you just don't see coming.

When I look up I notice Gabe is staring at my casts with that familiar look of confusion. He never quite worked it out. When he catches my eye he mouths, "I'm sorry. I'm so sorry, Kate."

I nod my head and then look away, even though I've heard these words before I feel my throat tighten and my eyes well up. It's funny how it only takes one person to get under the armor. Strangely enough that one person is Gabe — someone who really never meant anything to me, other than in the physical sense. Touching Gabe was like running for me. It made me feel like I had power. The way he'd react to me, the way that would make me feel. For a while there I was addicted to it. To him. Until I realized it could never be. *We* could never be. Not with my secrets always a threat away.

Gabe is still watching me now. He appears distressed once my tears start to flow. It's the first time he's ever seen me cry. He whispers something to Shelley who opens her purse, digs around inside, and then shrugs.

His expression turns frantic. He taps the shoulder of the person walking by just as Andrew hands me Kleenex.

"Do you need me to stay, Kate?" Andrew asks.

"I'm fine," I whisper.

"I'll give you a minute," he says and then he leaves me.

And soon after so does Gabe.

In the end they all leave.

My mother's casket is covered in flowers. Purples and blues, bright pinks and reds — the flowers scream despondently at the dark gray sky weeping upon them.

I chose the flowers. "No white," I told John. My mother was too vibrant to be surrounded with the usual funeral-white flowers.

The only flower missing today is her favorite: the pink orchid. She always loved them for their simple beauty and graceful shape.

"They dance when no one's watching," she'd said about the orchids.

I left them off the list. Dancing orchids are more than I can handle today.

The light rain landing on my umbrella mimics a heartbeat and all at once I remember being plagued with nightmares at the age of five and how my mom would hold me against her chest until our breathing matched.

"The nightmares can't hurt you, Kate," she'd say. "No one can."

I try not to think about how her heartbeat is now silent. Or how she will never hold me, sing to me, or comfort me again.

A flash of anger moves through my chest. It's dull, not the usual fire-red hue but it's definitely there.

My eyes scan the cemetery and then glaze over when I notice the burial crew. Like vultures waiting for their prey to die, they hunker down in the distance.

I feel the blood drain from my face right along with the stirrings of rage and once again became numb.

A light footfall in the grass alerts me to Andrew's return.

"Is it time to go?" I ask.

"That all depends, Kate," an unfamiliar voice responds. "Where exactly did you have in mind?"

Just over my left shoulder is a man I don't recognize. His hair is brown with a light sprinkling of gray. His eyes are small and dark and when he smiles at me his eyes almost disappear.

"Hello, Kate." He reaches his hand out toward me but I ignore it. "My name is Dr. Dolus. I knew your mother."

"Dr. Dolus?"

"Yes." His eyes move from the top of my head down to the bottom of my casts where my ten bare toes twitch nervously from such blatant attention.

"She never mentioned you."

"Really?" His mouth turns up in a forced smile. "We go way back."

The rain has stopped but a light breeze moves across the cemetery. When it reaches me I watch my skin respond with tiny goose bumps. But I feel nothing at all.

"Lovely weather we're having," the doctor drawls. "So fitting, yet strange for California this time of year." He pulls his long, dark coat closer. His eyes roam over my casts. "Good thing you're all bundled up today. Although, a wet cast can be such a drag."

I shift in my wheelchair but I remain silent.

"How long does John think it necessary to hide you like this?"

"It depends on how—"

"Quickly you heal? But of course." Dr. Dolus leans down toward me and whispers, "shouldn't be too long now, should it?"

"Two months," I say.

"Yes." Dr. Dolus smiles and one of his tiny eyes disappears in a wink. "That sounds about right."

"You said you knew my mother. Was it from the Shoppe?"

"No." He reaches into his chest pocket and hands me his card. "My office is in Seattle. In fact that was the last time I had the pleasure of seeing your mother. She came to see me last week."

"Last week?" I sit forward in my chair. "You must be mistaken—"

"Afraid not, my dear. Your mother definitely paid me a visit." He cocks his head sideways and lifts one dark eyebrow. "It was an interesting meeting. She mostly wanted to talk about you."

"Me?" I glance down at the card in my hands. *Dr. Luke Dolus,* it reads, with his address and phone number underneath. The one thing it doesn't tell me is exactly what kind of doctor he is.

"Your mother was concerned for you, Kate. She had many questions."

The breeze returns. It lifts a stray hair from the back of my neck and excites the chill that has just begun to move throughout my body.

"Who are you?" I say.

Dr. Dolus smiles. "Now we're asking the right questions." He squares his shoulders and stares off across the cemetery. "We both know you're unique, my dear." His eyes return to mine and his smile widens. "A success, I'd call it. Before your mother paid me a visit I was unaware of my own accomplishments."

I can feel my heart begin to race, but I manage to keep my expression blank.

Oh, Mom. What did you do?

Dr. Dolus opens his mouth to say something more and then his eyes lock on to something directly behind me. Andrew. Even without looking I know he's on his way back.

With a look of annoyance Dr. Dolus gauges the distance between himself and Andrew and then shoves his hands deep into his jacket pockets.

"My condolences, Kate." He nods once and then turns back toward the parking lot.

"Stay in touch," he calls over his shoulder. "We have a lot of catching up to do."

"Are you ready, Kate?" Andrew asks from behind me.

I nod my head as I watch Dr. Dolus climb into a dark chauffeured car.

I glance back at my mother's casket.

The rain is falling harder now, shedding tears for the woman who died too soon.

And the girl who is now alone.

It's not real. She isn't really in there.

A slight shuffle in the grass reminds me of Andrew's presence.

"I can't—" I stop and focus on the raindrops sliding down her casket.

"Kate?" Andrew leans around so his face is close to mine. He slides his sunglasses off and I get a peak of what my eyes must look like. Red. Swollen. And heartbroken.

"I can't let her go," I whisper. "I can't leave her here. In the ground. It's not right."

Andrew reaches out and wipes a tear from my cheek and then stares down at his hand as if he's surprised at what he's done.

"She isn't in there, Kate," he says, and for a moment my heart fills with joy. My eyes are wide with hope until he says, "She isn't really in there. Just her body."

And then it hits me all over again. She's gone. Forever. And I'm alone.

I close my eyes.

I love you, Mom. Please don't leave me. Please.

Andrew reaches out and takes my hand. For the moment it's just the two of us, the rain and a long brown box.

With a heavy nod I allow myself to leave the cemetery grounds.

"Who was that man you were talking to?" he asks.

I grip the business card in my hand. "Just another man my mom knew but kept from me."

Andrew doesn't respond. He pushes me toward the large black car John has rented for the service and then once I'm safely inside he climbs into the front seat. His eyes are hidden behind dark sunglasses that, when he turns around to check on me, reflect my vacant expression.

John reaches across the seat to squeeze my hand while Andrew watches me in the rearview mirror from the front seat.

"Kate? Did you hear me?" John says.

I blink up at him in answer.

"I asked if you knew that man."

"Dr. Dolus?"

"Who?" John's eyes narrow as if he recognizes the name.

"I don't know him," I say. But something tells me I should.

Nine

Back at the house Andrew and John help me out of the car and instead of carrying me to my bedroom they place me on the couch in the living room.

I notice Ruth isn't around.

"Kate," John says, "Andrew and I would like to speak with you for a moment."

"I gathered that." I lean back against the couch and close my eyes. "Does it have to be right now? I thought I might lie down for a while—"

"I'm leaving in the morning, Kate," Andrew says. "I need to get back."

"Back?" My eyes snap open. "Where is back?"

"Mercer Island," he says. "It's in Washington State."

"I know where it is." But I hadn't until just recently when my mom pointed it out on the map in our Seattle hotel room.

"It's the only place more beautiful than San Diego," she'd said, and I'd wondered how she knew.

"So you're leaving then?" I focus on the photo of my mom smiling down at me from the wall. She's wearing Mickey Mouse ears and her clothes are still wet from Splash Mountain. One of the many day trips we took when life got too difficult, and laughter felt more important than school.

"I have to," Andrew says.

There is a hole inside my stomach that expands when I think of Andrew leaving. I shouldn't care — I don't know him — but having him around has made me feel a tiny bit less alone.

He's my father. Someone I should know, but don't. Someone who should be dead. But isn't.

I haven't said the word father out loud and neither has he. I think we're both afraid if we put it out there, someone might take it away. At least, I am.

"I want you to come with me, Kate," he says. "To live with me."

I open my mouth to speak but John interrupts.

"And I would like you to stay. Your mother and I talked about marriage, as I'm sure you know. If this horrible thing hadn't happened we would have married next spring." John leans forward on the couch, blocking out Andrew and the smiling photograph of my mom up on the wall. "You don't have to leave everything you know. Your home, your school, your friends. You can stay here with me." His eyes are locked onto mine. "I want you to know you have options. You don't have to leave."

I stare at John, the man who loved my mom more than anything, would have done anything for her.

But she didn't love him back.

I remember the day I demanded to know where my father was, like he was a lost jump rope or a doll.

"I'm sorry, Kate. Your father died before you were born," my mom explained, and that's where the story ended. No matter how many times I begged for the story to be told differently, the ending never changed.

So I created him. Black hair, blue eyes — that matched my own, obviously — and tall, mysterious and attentive. He traveled the world buying me presents that no one else had even dreamed of. That was why he was never home. He was too busy shopping. I knew one day he would show up with moving trucks filled with gifts that would make up for the fact that he'd never been around.

When I grew out of the need to be given countless presents, my mind started going in a new direction, a direction that changed my mom's story into a lie. My father couldn't be dead. If he were anything like me, that wasn't possible.

Across the room from me are two men; one who I've known for a short amount of time but I know, because of my mom, would do anything for me, while the other is a complete stranger. One my mom pretended to love while the other…what? Broke her heart? Or did she break his?

Either way she kept him from me.

I close my eyes and try to get inside my mom's head. What would she want me to do? When all I hear is silence I open my eyes.

"I want my casts off," I say.

John rubs the back of his neck and sighs. "Are you sure?"

"Yes."

"Wait! What do you mean?" Andrew pushes off from his position against the wall. Back and forth his eyes travel from me to John and then back again. "You're removing her casts?"

"So you've decided then," John says. His brown eyes are heavy, barely open. He pinches the bridge of his nose with his right hand and I wonder if he's even slept in the last few days.

"Kate?" Andrew says.

"When did she tell you?" I ask, ignoring Andrew completely.

John leans back into the couch. "She told me just before you left for Seattle. She said it was important that I know." He shrugs and says, "I guess because I'm a doctor. She wanted, no, needed someone she could trust."

"Told you what?" Andrew asks.

I shake my head in confusion. My mom always told me never to tell anyone and here I come to find she couldn't keep my secret. First John, then Dr. Dolus. Who else did she tell?

"She loved you, Kate," John says. "Very much. She would have done anything for you."

"Why'd she keep Andrew a secret?" I turn and direct my questions at the source. "Why didn't she tell me about you?"

"I can't answer that, Kate."

"Can't or won't?"

Andrew just shakes his head. "She must've had her reasons."

"Reasons you won't share with me? How am I supposed to trust you when you won't answer my questions?" When he just stares back at me I add, "And why do you want me to come with you anyway?"

Andrew's voice is gruff when he answers, "You're my daughter," three little words that don't amount to much but do enough damage just the same. "You're my daughter, Kate. Give me a chance."

I want to believe in him, I really do. I want to pack my things right now and pretend I'm off on a new adventure and when I return my mom will be waiting, excited to hear all about my trip. I want to. Desperately. And the strength behind that want terrifies me. "I don't know," I whisper. All around me are my mom's things; knickknacks, furniture and photographs. She's all around me.

"You can stay here, Kate," John says. "I told you, you don't have to leave."

But I do. One look at Andrew and I've made my decision. I can't stay here, not when so many unanswered questions will follow him onto a plane tomorrow morning.

"Please John, I want them off," I say.

"Now?"

"Yes. Now."

John gets up from the couch and walks down the hall to the spare bedroom. He returns with a cast saw.

"Are you sure?" he asks again, but this time it means something different.

John still doesn't believe.

"Remove them," I say.

"What's going on?" Andrew moves across the room toward us. His mouth is drawn, his hands clenched. "What do you think you're doing?"

"It's okay, Andrew, I'm ready."

"You're ready? Just like that, huh? You decide?" He turns on John. "Aren't you the doctor?"

"Kate?" John holds the cast saw in his lap. His eyes tell me what I already know to be true.

I have to tell him.

"Andrew, there's something you should know about me."

"Especially if she's going to live with you," John adds.

Andrew's eyes pin me to my spot on the couch.

"I'm different," I say. "My body heals at a much faster pace than, well, everyone else."

Andrew leans forward and asks the question I dread the most. "How much faster?"

"I don't need the casts, Andrew. I never did." I look at John and he nods his head. "It was all for show."

"What are you talking about?" Andrew turns on John but John holds strong.

"It's the truth, Andrew. I didn't believe it at first but when I arrived at the hospital and saw it for myself I knew I had to get her out of there."

"I don't believe this," Andrew says. "You can't possibly be thinking of removing those casts. I saw photos from the accident. She's lucky to be alive!"

"Whether or not you believe it doesn't change anything." A knot is forming inside my stomach, twisting and turning until it fills it completely. "It doesn't matter." Like a mantra I repeat it a couple more times inside my mind. *It doesn't change anything. It never will.*

"Please John," I whisper. "I want them off."

John stands up and moves toward me. For a minute I think Andrew might try to stop him but then he moves back to his spot against the wall. From there he can see us clearly, aloof and yet supervising.

The saw is hot and loud but the air that hits my skin, once the casts have been removed, feels wonderful. It's like I'm being dipped in a pool of cold water.

John runs his hands up and down my legs and arm until he's convinced I'm healed. "You may feel a bit wobbly at first," he says, and then he helps me to my feet, holding on to my hand as if I'm learning how to walk for the first time. After a few solid steps I drop his hand.

"Or not." His eyes are filled with wonder when he looks at me, like he's seeing the real-life Santa Clause, or Superman himself. "It's amazing," he whispers. "You're amazing, Kate."

But I don't pay him any attention. My eyes are focused on Andrew.

He's watching through narrowed eyes, his expression unconvinced, as if this is some elaborate trick we're pulling.

"I guess this means we don't share this ability?"

"What exactly are you asking, Kate?"

"I always wondered," I pause and look down at the new skin covering my right arm. "I can't be the only one."

Andrew doesn't answer right away. I can almost see the wheels in his mind turning. He doesn't want to believe. He can't believe. But like he said, he saw the photographs. No one could have walked away from that accident. And even if they had, they shouldn't be walking right now.

"No, Kate," he says. "I guess I'm not that lucky."

Lucky. I really hate this word.

"There's nothing lucky about it," I say.

"How do you feel, Kate?" John is studying me. His doctor senses must be tingling right about now.

"Thank you for taking care of me, John." I walk across the room and pull him in for a hug. "She loved you," I lie. Suddenly it's very important that he believe this. I don't want him to come to the same conclusion that I have, that my mom used him to keep me safe.

John squeezes me tight and then drops back onto the couch.

Andrew is still watching me. If skepticism were paint he'd be dripping with it. But it doesn't matter to me whether or not he believes. Truth is, it changes nothing. "Before I agree to go with you I have a few questions," I say.

"Of course," he answers softly.

"Why'd she leave?"

His chin drops and he slowly nods his head. "That's an important one."

I cross my arms and wait for his answer. The skin on my right arm and my legs feels moist and sweaty from the casts but altogether brand new. I can hear John's steady breathing from the couch and for a moment I think we've lost him to exhaustion but when I glance his way I find he too is waiting for Andrew's response.

"When your mother and I were married, no, change that. When I met your mother I was at the height of my career," Andrew begins.

"And what was that?" I ask.

His eyes meet mine and then they drop to the framed photo on the table of my mom and me on my twelfth birthday. "Security. I worked in security."

"You mean like a bodyguard?" I ask and Andrew smiles.

"Not exactly."

"Well then, what exactly?"

"I was in charge of keeping certain objects safe."

"Like people or things?"

Andrew's smile widens. "Both."

"Who did you work for?"

"Anyone who could afford me."

"Well that explains everything," I say with a roll of my eyes.

"Good," Andrew smiles.

"That's all I get?"

"For now." Andrew glances at John and I get it. For now.

"Okay." I nod my head for him to continue.

"Well, my job involved a lot of traveling."

"To London," I say.

"And other places."

"You mentioned you met my mom in London," I say when he doesn't continue.

"Yes." He's still studying the picture of my mom and me resting on the top of the coffee table — two auburn-haired, fair-skinned girls with only each other to count on.

"Why did she leave you, Andrew? Why did she tell me you were dead?"

"Perhaps she wanted it to be true." His eyes are clouded with the same pain and confusion I've been carrying around since the day I learned of her death.

"Why?"

"Like I said, I worked a lot. Traveled a lot. She rarely saw me."

"That's no reason to wish you were dead," I say.

"She wanted more."

"What?" John asks. "What was it she wanted from you?"

"Early retirement." His eyes are heavy as he admits to this. "It hurt her that I chose my work over her, Kate. She never understood."

"And so she left," I say.

"Yes. She left."

His eyes drop back down to the photograph and I wish I could get inside his head, see into his memories.

"You loved her," I say. It isn't a question because even if he tried to deny it I'd know it was a lie. But Andrew doesn't deny it. When he looks at me his eyes tell me everything I need to know.

"And now?" I ask.

"Now what, Kate?"

"What do you do now?"

"Any damn thing I want," he says with a smile.

When I raise an eyebrow he adds, "I'm retired. I have been for the last six months."

"You don't look old enough to be retired," I say. And he doesn't. He appears to be in even better shape than Coach Elton who runs eight miles every morning and night. At the age of thirty-eight.

"Thank you." His smile widens and I feel something stir inside of me, that familiar connection my mom and I shared. That need to be loved and accepted for who I am. Unconditionally.

I want this. I need this to be real.

"Last question, Andrew."

"Yes?" He hasn't moved closer, neither of us has, and yet I feel as if he's close enough to touch. Or merely a decision away.

"How do you feel about cats?"

Ten

She's back. He'd only seen her once since the night of the fire — briefly through her bedroom window — but once was enough to ease Jonah's fears and confirm his suspicions. She's alive.

Jonah shifts his position in the driver's seat of his rental car and ignores the rumblings in his stomach. The late lunch he'd scarfed down hours ago seems like a figment of his imagination now. The neighbors have an orange tree in their backyard but when he'd gone searching for a ripe piece of fruit he'd almost had a heart attack when their sensor lights switched on.

Kate's house is still. Almost too still. Only two rooms appear lit through the thickness of the blinds. The amount of activity isn't enough to keep his heavy eyes from falling so instead he entertains himself by imagining what her life is like.

Full, he decides. Her life is full in comparison to his. Her days are filled with friends and sunshine, family and love. Everything Jonah lacks. Well, Las Vegas has its share of sunshine but it isn't the good kind. It isn't served on a beach with a light breeze. No, Las Vegas sunshine is like everything else in Vegas: flashy, overproduced and stifling. And as for friends? Jonah's only friend is a ten-year-old boy named Oscar, and while he's a better friend than any other prospect he's ever had, he's ten. Too young to take to the casino and too young to understand Jonah's need to leave Las Vegas behind.

Oscar has recently stopped asking why Jonah is always at the casino. It isn't like Jonah has an answer anyway. How do you explain to a ten-year-old that it isn't the money you're after but the pain? Jonah likes pain. Or rather, Ricky the Harrods bouncer, likes inflicting pain and Jonah is more than willing to morph into a punching bag.

The first time he and Ricky met was a night Jonah couldn't forget if he tried; otherwise known as the night his suspicions were confirmed. And the game began.

The table was high stakes poker. Big money. Top players. Jonah could feel his fake-I.D. taunting him from his jeans pocket but the take was too high.

"All in," Jonah dared to the only other player left in the game.

"You sure you want to do that, boy?" the cowboy to his left whispered in his ear. "You know who you're up against, right?"

And Jonah knew. Playing cards with the casino owner's son wasn't the smartest thing he'd done in his life but how do you say no to two tens staring back at you in your hand while two more are showing on the table.

"I'm gonna make this real easy on you," Ricky begun soon after. "You stay out of my casino and I won't give your family a reason to wear black." The beating that preceded his words hadn't been too bad until Jonah decided to fight back.

Because, hell, why not?

The taxi ride home had been interesting. While the driver chatted to his fellow cabbies on the radio Jonah watched his cuts and swollen knuckles disappear by way of the bright lights of the Las Vegas Strip.

The next night when he returned for more, Jonah answered Ricky's challenging sneer with a slow wink and a smile of anticipation.

Over time Jonah's game grew into an experiment of sorts. The pain was becoming tolerable, almost subtle at times, and the battle wounds never lasted longer than the cab ride home.

Why it's important for Jonah to continue the game is something he'd yet to figure out. Perhaps it's the sense of empowerment he feels when even Ricky's best can't bring him to beg for mercy. Or perhaps it's the euphoric high he experiences afterwards when he watches his body erase the violent residue of the evening. Either way Jonah knows one thing. He needs to get the hell out of Vegas before the game leaves him without any feeling whatsoever.

The front door opens and Jonah slides back into the shadows. A man comes out and closes the door behind him. Jonah watches as the man's shoulders drop and his head soon follows. He takes another step and lowers himself down onto the front step and rests his head in his hands. Jonah feels a stirring of sadness for the man who manages to keep his crying silent. He would recognize the tall, blonde man anywhere.

After a few minutes the man's trembling shoulders are still and he rises to his feet. He reenters the house as quietly as he left it and after ten minutes Jonah watches another room go dark. The far window at the back of the house remains lit and Jonah knows Kate is still awake. He can feel it. If she's anything like him she doesn't sleep much lately. If she's anything like him, she never has in the first place.

When the neighbor's sensor lights flicker on once again, Jonah rests his head back against the seat and tries not to think of the plentiful oranges just a few feet away. His eyes are so heavy and his back aches. He would have missed the movement if he hadn't been staring directly at the car parked across the street from Kate's house. At first he thinks he may have imagined it but when the shadow moves again, Jonah's body tenses. It appears he isn't alone in his stakeout tonight. He watches for the next hour hoping to catch some movement but the shadow stays relentlessly still. The only sign of life is an occasional glow from a cigarette being lit followed by a smoke signal. Jonah's tired eyes beg to blink and without food or water he knows tonight will be torture. On any other night there'd be no doubt that Jonah would fall asleep. But tonight that isn't an option. Tonight, the rules have changed. You can't slack off on a stakeout when you know you have company.

It's close to dawn, long after Kate's window finally goes dark, when the shadow breaks the silence of the quiet neighborhood and drives off. Jonah doesn't hesitate. Keeping the sedan in sight, he follows it for the next twenty minutes until it pulls to the side of the road.

Jonah is torn. It isn't that he's afraid to approach the car but he really hoped to gain information by following it somewhere. Somewhere other than a deserted highway. In frustration he keeps driving until he comes to a gas station about a mile down the road. For the next ten minutes he broods with regret until his screaming bladder forces him to get out of his car and move toward the restroom. He's washing his hands when the door creaks open and a tall, bald man walks in.

"I really hope you got a good reason for tailing me, kid."

Jonah grabs a paper towel and casually dries his hands. "I'm pretty sure I do." He tosses the balled-up towel in the trashcan and leans back against the sink. "Why are you watching her house?"

The bald man's face doesn't react as he spreads his arms wide and fills the doorway. His long, dark coat opens and Jonah tries not to stare at the large silver gun tucked into his waistband. "I'm sure I don't know what you're talking about. And I'm even surer that you won't be following me again. You see I've got real sensitive eyes and your grandmother's rental car has these bright lights that, well, they give me a headache."

"I'm sorry to hear that," Jonah replies. He's been aching to have it out with Kate's shadow but now he's not so sure. Two things are keeping him from provoking him any further: the shadow's mention of his Nanna and the shiny, silver gun. Jonah can take a good kick or punch from the best of them but he's never messed with a gun.

"You know it's getting real late, kid. You should probably get back to your hotel."

Jonah nods and moves toward the doorway. "Yeah. I think you're right." A slight chill begins to make its way down his back. He's desperate to discover exactly who this guy is but something tells him not to push his luck.

"On second thought," the bald man mutters, and Jonah feels a quick blow to the back of his head. And then nothing.

Eleven

"I saw you run."

We're taxiing down the runway when Andrew shares this confession.

I'm not sure if my next question should be when? How? Or how fast?

I settle on, "When was that?"

"At the nationals. That's how I discovered you." When he turns to me I can make out another faint scar just above his left eyebrow. "My neighbor runs track for the school you'll be attending. I was at Husky to watch him compete."

"Oh yeah?" I'm not sure which is more startling; that I never thought to ask how he found out about me, or that I'm going to be attending a new high school, one where even my father already has a friend.

"He and his brother were talking about you after the race. Not too many Triumphs around. It got me curious."

"So you were there?" I know we've already established this but I refuse to ask him the real question burning my tongue, *what did you think of my race?*

"Yes. I always try to make his meets." Andrew sits back in his seat as the plane starts to ascend. "Was you mother there?"

"Yes." My mind is spinning. Andrew was there! And he saw me race.

"I thought I saw her," Andrew says. "I went to grab a drink at the concession stand and I could've sworn I caught a glimpse of her through the crowd."

"Really?" My voice sounds calm, but I'm anything but. We're sitting so close there's no doubt Andrew would notice if I began to hyperventilate. How is it possible they missed each other? And did my mom see him? Or better yet, what would she have done if she had?

"She was wearing green that day, right? A tad overdressed for a track meet but she looked nice."

"Yes." I place my hand on my chest, willing my heart to settle down. "She had a meeting just before." I think back to what she told me. "With the buyers." No. That's not right. She told me in the car that she'd met with a doctor.

And then it clicks. Of course. She met with Dr. Dolus.

"She always looked great in green." Andrew's eyes are closed. This conversation isn't having quite the same effect on him apparently. After a few more minutes it appears he's fallen asleep.

I reach down and grab my backpack at my feet. Lefty hears me rustling around and lets out a loud mew. I pat his soft fur through the holes in his kitty carrier and soothe him with promises of treats to come.

Once he's settled I search inside my backpack for the lavender smelling journal I stole from my mother's room last night. I crept into her room looking for something to take with me to Washington, anything to help me remember her. I left with a suitcase filled with her favorite clothes, perfumes, soaps, and one lavender smelling journal I didn't even know she kept.

I'm not prepared for her handwriting. It swims in front of me. The letters smooth and graceful, just like my mom. And the words. All at once I hear her voice as if she's reading it aloud. Some of the pages are filled with details of the Shoppe; issues with clients, worries about shipments. I remember how crazy the hours leading up to our trip to Seattle were and it's obvious by the few lines scribbled on the last page that she didn't have much time to indulge in journal writing.

Then I see it. His name.

I've made an appointment to see Dr. Dolus. Can't believe he was able to squeeze me in last minute. Still unsure, but I can always cancel. My heart races just thinking of the trip but Kate's so excited to compete I can't disappoint her.

We'll be in Seattle for less than forty-eight hours. Kate wants to stay longer but I don't think it's a good idea. She thinks it's because I can't stand to be away from John. She doesn't know he offered to come. It's only forty-eight hours. Forty-six to be exact.

But what would Andrew do if he saw Kate?

What would he think of me?

I'm not sure why I care but the idea of being in Seattle after all this time...

I can't stop thinking about him.

I close the book with a snap.

But not before Andrew sees it. His eyes move from the journal in my hands to me. From the look on his face I can tell he has read each and every word.

I scramble for something to say, but I've got nothing.

Andrew continues to study me. When the flight attendant comes by to ask if we'd like a beverage, without looking at her, I tell her I'd like a ginger ale. Andrew eyes the tiny bottles of alcohol she has stashed in her pockets, but with one last glance at me he asks for a cup of water.

"See if you can get Lefty to take a drink," Andrew says once she's brought us our drinks. He hands me his cup of water and I thank him. His concern for my cat surprises me. I'm not sure what I expect from him after reading my mom's journal entry, but it definitely isn't kindness.

"I think you're going to like Washington, Kate," he adds.

I open my mouth to say something, I'm not quite sure what, when the flight attendant swings by and says, "Please fasten your seatbelts. We'll be touching down real soon."

Andrew drives at a breakneck speed. I don't know much about cars but apparently his fancy, silver sports car only comes in fast.

Aside from a few general explanations such as, "it rains here a lot" or "people around here don't know how to drive when it snows" Andrew doesn't say much. His silence fills in the spaces between us, which is far more welcoming than useless chitchat. Neither one of us is capable of pulling it off anyway.

I gaze out the window at Andrew's world; it's green and damp, but beautiful.

"Is this where you lived? You and my mom?"

We're at a stoplight. I peek over at Andrew when he doesn't immediately answer and find the man in the next car eyeing Andrew's car. When the man catches my eye he smiles and mouths, "nice car."

I don't know how to respond so I just look away.

"We lived here for two years," Andrew says. "Just after we moved to the States."

Two years!

"Two years?" I say.

"Yes."

"And was it always in the same house? I mean, the house we're going to now?" Andrew turns to me. "Yes." His blue eyes flicker past my face, out the window and then back to me.

"This is Mercer Island," he says, just after we cross a bridge.

And my mom was right. It is more beautiful than San Diego. If San Diego were an elegantly dressed woman, Mercer Island would be her younger, more beautiful cousin. From the country.

It feels private, like a secret island no one should know about. The houses are tucked neatly between tall pine trees like they're afraid to be noticed. Every once in a while I catch a glimpse of water through the trees. Andrew slows down. I'm not sure if he's dragging out the inevitable or if he feels he can relax now that we've reached the island. He maneuvers his car through the windy streets like we're coming to the end of a roller coaster ride. At the end of an especially narrow road — which I later realize is his driveway — is Andrew's house.

"It's beautiful," I say, but that doesn't do it justice. The house is rather modern in its design, like it could be off the pages of *Architectural Digest*. It has large windows that reach above the trees and straight edges that cut into the natural flow of the environment. It definitely doesn't blend in like the rest of the houses in the neighborhood. If it wasn't surrounded by trees it would definitely stand out.

Andrew gets out of the car and goes to open the trunk. He's already pulled my suitcases out and is moving up the stone path that leads to the front door before I can even climb out of the car.

When he realizes I'm not following him he turns back and waits while I catch up. We're a few feet from the front of the house when the front door swings open and a boy about my age comes charging out.

"Took you long enough, old man! Since when do you drive the speed limit?"

"Hello to you too, Brandon," Andrew says, and then steps aside as the boy rushes past him and stops directly in front of me.

"Hey Kate. Welcome to Washington!"

"Thanks," I say, drawing out the word.

Brandon towers over me with a wide grin. His hair is California blonde, his eyes blue. It isn't his good looks that make me uncomfortable it's the way he's smiling at me. It seems as though he already knows me.

"Kate this is Brandon," Andrew says with a knowing grin. "Occasionally he lives next door."

"I can't tell you how excited I am to meet you!" Brandon reaches for the kitty carrier in my hands and Lefty lets out a howl of protest. "Hey kitty." He holds the bag up so he and Lefty are eye to eye.

Lefty lets out a hiss.

"If you get too close he might swipe at you," I warn, reaching for the kitty carrier. "He doesn't really like people."

"Sounds like Andrew," a new voice says.

I take a breath in, completely surprised, when I glimpse a set of familiar gray-green eyes.

Just behind Brandon is the boy who tried to help free me from the janitor's closet. And judging by the expression on his face he is better prepared for this moment than I am. My heart does this little fumble-beat-beat-fumble thing causing me to frown. *This can't be good.*

"Hey Kate," he holds out his hand and I glance down at it. "I'm Zack. Brandon's older brother." And then we're touching — his hand in mine, our fingers squeezing and then letting go. I can still feel his hand long after he's pulled away.

"I'm Kate," I say, and he smiles.

Oh, yeah. He already knows that.

I look from Zack to Brandon to Andrew and then back to Zack. There are four of us on this playground and yet it feels like I'm the only one wearing a blindfold.

"You were there," I say. "You were at Husky."

"Brandon runs on the Mercer Island High track team. Remember, I told you on the plane?" Andrew comes up behind me and I find between Brandon, Andrew, Zack and the trees, I'm surrounded by tall.

"That's how I found out about you. Brandon and Zack were talking about you after the race."

"You were amazing, by the way," Brandon says.

"Yeah. Amazing," Zack agrees, and yet when he says it I feel something flutter inside my stomach.

Where Brandon is blonde and sun kissed like a Greek god Zack is dark and haunted. His deep gray eyes lock onto mine, making it difficult to look away. And when he smiles I feel embarrassed. For no reason at all.

"Let's get you settled in." Andrew rests his hand on my back and moves me past Zack.

Andrew's house is bright and clean yet very masculine with its dark furniture and giant flat screen television mounted on the wall of the living room. I'm immediately drawn toward the deck where I can see water sparkling through the window.

"That's Lake Washington," Andrew says from directly behind me.

"Your house is…very pretty." I stop myself before I say "beautiful" again.

He smiles and looks back out over the water. "It's your house now, Kate. I want you to feel comfortable here."

"Andrew has the best toys," Brandon says as he vaults over the side of the couch clearing it in a way that suggests he's done this many times before. "And speaking of toys… Did you show her yet?"

"They just arrived, Brandon. I doubt he's had a chance." Zack is leaning against the back wall half in the living room and half inside the kitchen. It's as though he's distancing himself from Andrew and me, unlike Brandon who has jumped right into the middle of the fray.

"Show me what?" I pull my attention away from Zack and glance about the room. Andrew's artwork is perfectly displayed, each clearly lit with a tiny museum light. All about the room there are carefully arranged sculptures and artifacts. From the look of it either Andrew has traveled a lot or he's trying really hard to make it appear that way.

I remember the first time I visited John's townhouse — with its nautical theme and country blue kitchen — I asked him who decorated it and he'd told me that it came fully furnished. "One day, when I have some time off, I'll pay someone to come in and redecorate. Or perhaps, Olivia?" He'd turned and smiled at my mom. And she'd smiled back.

But John never took time off, and the paintings of boats at sea still sailed his walls a year later. It seemed now he was stuck with them.

When the silence cuts into my thoughts I look up and find I'm the main focus of all three men in the room.

"Show me what?" I ask again.

"Andrew bought you a red jeep!" Brandon explains. His eyes are excited, so excited I find I don't need to be. I turn to Andrew in disbelief.

"What if I'd decided to stay in San Diego?"

"I would have driven it down to you."

But I don't believe him, and neither do Brandon or Zack. They share a laugh that Andrew chooses to ignore.

"I noticed you didn't have one," he says.

"A Jeep?" I say with a laugh. "Is that a prerequisite in this state?"

When Andrew doesn't answer I glance down a bit embarrassed. "I never needed one."

"Well you'll need one here," Brandon explains. "And of course I'll be needing a ride." He winks at me from across the room, and I hate his confidence. I hate it so much, but mostly I'm jealous of it.

"You can borrow it, of course. Anytime you need to." The words are said to the ground as I lift Lefty in his carrier and move toward the spiral staircase.

"Sure," Brandon says after a moment of silence. "That works too."

"I should really get Lefty situated before he puts up a fuss," I explain, but the truth is I can't handle this conversation right now. I'm used to feeling uncomfortable, but this is a whole new level for me. My father bought me a jeep? *My. Father.* The man a week ago I believed was dead.

"Of course." Andrew ushers me upstairs to my new room, following close behind.

"I tried to think of everything you might need," he says from the doorway, "but if I forgot anything just let me know."

"You did this?" I ask, looking around at a room that almost completely resembles my own back in San Diego. Purple bedspread, black desk, even the walls are painted the same shade of lilac.

"I didn't do it personally," Andrew explains. "Brandon and Zack helped out while I was with you in California."

"It's perfect. Thank you."

And it is, all except for the awkwardness lingering in the air. But that follows me everywhere.

"Why don't you take some time to rest?" he says and then backs out of the room. "We can continue the tour later."

Rest? I just got here.

But I nod my head and say, "alright."

Andrew closes the door with a faint snap and I'm left alone. I let Lefty out of his cat carrier but he chooses to go back inside. I promise him treats if he'll come out, but he just continues to smell the air as if he's anticipating a challenge, perhaps another three-legged cat hiding in the bathroom.

I don't mean to fall asleep, only to test the softness of the bed, and the pillows, but when I open my eyes my new room is dark and there is rain falling softly outside my window.

Out in the hallway I'm greeted with the familiar sounds of dinner being prepared. It smells Italian, whatever it is, and my stomach reacts immediately.

"Are you hungry, Kate?" Andrew asks when I appear in the kitchen.

"Yes." I can't remember the last time I ate.

"Good thing. Andrew cooked for half the neighborhood." Brandon tosses a piece of garlic bread my way and I catch it, barely.

"The neighborhood? Really?" my eyes narrow on Andrew.

"Don't worry, Kate. Andrew isn't exactly one for social gatherings. It's just the four of us tonight." But when Zack says this, it isn't the idea of the neighborhood dropping by that alarms me. It's him. There is an energy about Zack, like he's about to leap at me at any moment. I can't help but eye him warily while he smiles in an annoyingly relaxed way.

"How's Lefty holding up?" Andrew asks.

"I managed to talk him out of the kitty carrier, but now he's under my bed."

"Sounds about right. He'll adjust sooner or later."

Or perhaps I'll join him, I think. Looking around at the happy, smiling people in the kitchen makes me think Lefty may have the right idea.

Over dinner it becomes obvious that Andrew has known Zack and Brandon pretty much all their lives.

"Our fathers were friends," Zack explains, and I recognize that word, were. It's part of my new vocabulary: was, used to, and of course the never to be forgotten isn't. As in she isn't living any longer.

I watch the three of them play off each other the way my mom and I used to. They finish each other's sentences, and laugh before the punch line. It's a new side of Andrew. One I never got a chance to see that week he lived with John and me.

As the meal continues he opens up a little bit more. And I shut down. It's not that I'm jealous of their relationship. I'm not sure what I expected when I chose to come here with him, but I definitely didn't expect him to already have a family.

I watch the three of them from my chair, slightly pulled back from the table, but mostly I watch Zack. His smile, his eyes, the way they work together in a way that comes off as confident, self-assured. It works well on him. Too well. I wish I could paint his confidence on me, a splash of color to bring out my eyes or elevate the pink in my cheeks.

Anything to help me appear more alive.

Occasionally he talks with his hands, casting them up in the air to help complete a sentence or finish a thought. And I like his hands. When they reach for his glass or his fork I find I'm jealous. To be touched by those hands. How would it feel? I wonder. And that's ridiculous. I know it's ridiculous. But it's the truth.

A few times he catches me watching him and each time it happens he smiles, but I don't smile back. I pretend to be studying the other objects in the room, like the ceiling fan or the copper pots and pans hanging above the gas range.

But I'm not fooling anybody. Not him. Not me.

"So when did you meet Zack?" Brandon asks when the conversation hits a lull.

I look up from my barely touched plate of pasta. "What do you mean?"

"While you were sleeping, Zack told us how the two of you met at Husky, but he wouldn't give any details."

"We didn't exactly meet," Zack explains.

"No." I shake my head, unwilling to fuel the story along.

"Kate was, well, I'm not quite sure what you were doing..." Zack raises an eyebrow in challenge and I shake my head.

"It was nothing," I say. "A bit of a misunderstanding, I guess." I take a bite of pasta and chew slowly, what was delicious before suddenly has no flavor.

"What kind of misunderstanding?" Andrew asks. "I admit I'm intrigued, mostly because Zack never mentioned anything about this until now."

"It was nothing," I repeat. "I was locked in a closet, Zack tried to get me out but he didn't have a key so I kicked the door down."

"You kicked the door down?" Brandon chuckles. "Pretty intense, Kate."

"You were locked in a closet?" Andrew's fork hovers over his plate of pasta. His eyes are narrowed upon my face.

"Yes," I say. "But it was nothing. No big deal, really."

Zack leans back in his chair. I can tell from his expression he's not about to let this drop. "Why were you in that closet?"

"It's a long story. A rather uninteresting story. Believe me."

"I find that hard to believe considering I'm so interested," Andrew drawls. He's stopped eating and his hands are folded in front of him as if he has all the time in the world.

"Yeah, well." I twirl the pasts around on my plate.

"Kate?" Andrew says.

"It's really not a big deal. I got locked in. You know, to keep me from running. Not a big deal."

"You mentioned that." The look in Andrew's eyes is so intense I drop my fork. "Who locked you in?"

"Just some kids from another school," I say. And their coach. But I'm pretty sure I shouldn't bring up that little nugget of information right about now.

"Has this happened before?"

"Not exactly."

"Kate." Andrew closes his eyes for a split second and takes a breath.

"I mean, I've never been locked in a janitor's closet before if that's what you're asking."

"It's not."

"Well, then yes and no. It's just stupid intimidation. All athletes do it." When my words fall upon silence I turn to Brandon and say, "You know what I'm talking about, right?"

"Can't say I've ever been locked in a closet before."

"Okay, perhaps that was a bit extreme but you can't tell me you've never been tripped? Or had your gator aid spiked?"

"Tripped, yeah, but who spiked your gator aid?"

"I think the better question is, with what?" Andrew asks.

I glance up and find he isn't exactly enjoying this conversation. His mouth is tight and the look in his eyes reminds me of Lefty when someone gets too close to his food.

"The first time it was—"

"The first time?" Zack interrupts.

"—an over the counter sleeping pill," I continue. "But don't worry. I didn't drink it."

"Oh, I'm not worried," Andrew says. "And the next time?" His hands are resting on the table, he appears calm, but one of his fingers is twitching.

"It only happened twice."

"Well that's refreshing," he says.

"What did they give you the second time, Kate?" Zack asks. He's watching me from across the table, his meal forgotten.

"GHB," I say.

"You mean GHB, the date rape drug?" Brandon throws his hands in the air and almost knocks over his glass.

Zack just frowns.

I steal a glance at Andrew who has grown quite still. He appears to be studying the knife in his hands, counting each notch along the serrated blade.

"I'm pretty sure that's not what she had in mind when she slipped it into my drink."

"She?" Zack asks.

"Who?" Brandon says at the same time.

"No one you'd know," I explain. "Just some girl who used to be on my team.

"And did you drink that one Kate?" Andrew asks. He's still playing with the knife.

"No." I pause a moment and then say, "I let her drink it."

"What!" Brandon exclaims.

"Why?" Andrew asks me.

"Why what?"

"Why'd you let her drink it?"

He's watching me now, the knife forgotten in his hands.

"Because, why not?" I stare into his eyes, eyes that narrow the same way mine do. "Don't worry. I kept her in sight until she passed out. And I told someone soon after."

I get up and carry my plate to the kitchen sink. I can feel their eyes watching me as I rinse my plate. But I don't care.

"No one ever messed with me again after that," I add. "Until Husky."

"Well, damn, Kate. I wouldn't mess with you either," Brandon says. His smile is back, perhaps a little bit forced.

"Thanks for dinner, Andrew." I push my chair in at the table and grip the back of it with my hands. "And it was nice meeting you two." I nod to Brandon and Zack. Brandon winks at me but I'm not sure what Zack does, I can't look at him. *Won't*, actually.

"It was nice to meet you, Kate," he says. It sounds sincere, but I'll never know.

I leave the kitchen to a chorus of goodnights, and when I look back, just before I reach the stairs, three pairs of eyes are watching me leave.

So, alright. I lied. I didn't actually let her drink it. I gave it to Coach who alerted the authorities and she was disqualified from the meet.

But I wanted to. Damn, I wanted to.

I mean, why shouldn't she feel what I would have felt had I drank it?

The dizziness. The nausea. The loss of control.

But in the end I couldn't do it.

I had to lie at dinner. After all these years pushing people away comes easy.

But it's a lot easier when they don't like me.

Twelve

Las Vegas

"Where have you been, Jonah?" Oscar's perpetually sad eyes lift to Jonah's face and then shift self-consciously to the road. "I haven't seen you in weeks."

"Away, Oscar. I've been away."

"Well, what does that mean? You said you'd be gone for a couple of days but it's been over three weeks, not like I'm counting, but it has." Oscar's tiny ten-year-old mouth forms a pout that looks more like a kiss than anything else. "Mom says I shouldn't ask but I'm askin'. Where is away and why did it take you so long to get back? There's only a few more weeks left of summer."

Jonah sighs. Without opening his eyes he shifts his position on the soft grass and stretches his arms above his head. "I was in California."

"Well, why didn't you say so? I know where California is. I'm not stupid. Why didn't you just say, 'Oscar I'm going to California and I'll be back in over three weeks.'"

Jonah opens one eye and smiles. "Oscar, I had to go to California for over three weeks."

Oscar plops down on the grass beside him and groans. "Geez, Jonah! Was that so hard?"

Jonah chuckles. "I guess not."

"Are you back now?"

"It appears so."

"I mean for good? No more trips away?"

Jonah sits up and rubs his stinging eyes. When was the last time he'd slept? He'd spent all night at the casino avoiding Nanna's ghost, which strangely enough had followed him to Harrah's. She always loved to play cards and she'd been the one to secure him a fake I.D. in the first place.

Ricky had caught wind of Nanna's death and had given him "the night off." Jonah didn't have much fight in him anyway.

"Well you can't leave again," Oscar continues. "School starts in a few weeks!"

"So it does."

"I mean you're going to school, right? Mom says you've got to graduate and stuff. You can't make a living being a professional poker player."

"Is that what Mom says?" Oscar's mom always seemed to have something to say.

"Yes, Jonah, it is." Oscar pauses and his sad eyes focus back on the ground. "I'm sorry about your Nanna. Mom's been crying for days."

Jonah nods and rolls to his feet.

"You wanna play ball or something?" Oscar asks, following Jonah toward his house.

But there is no "something" with Oscar. It's either ball or nothing. "Maybe later, kid. I've got to get some sleep."

"It's 2 o'clock in the afternoon, Jonah! No one sleeps in the middle of the day!"

Jonah moves toward his Nanna's house and slides Oscar a backward wave.

"Why don't you wait and sleep tonight? Like everyone —"

Jonah closes the door on the rest of Oscar's words and moves toward his Nanna's bedroom.

It was only about a month ago when everything changed.

They'd been arguing over a call for the hundredth time that day. It was Oscar's turn to bat and just before he'd pitched him a fast one, Jonah had turned and waved at his Nanna. She had the best view of the game. She'd spent hours watching them play. It was one of the few moments in the day when her TV was off.

"Jonah, honey," she'd yelled from her window. "I think I'd like to get out a little today."

"Sure thing, Nanna. You want to move lunch outside?"

"No, dear. I want to go into town."

Jonah's mouth had opened to respond and then closed again. This was a first. Nanna hadn't left the house since she was put on bed-rest seven months previous. "What is it, Nanna? I can take care of it for you."

"No, Jonah. It's something I need to do. Can you be ready in an hour?"

"Of course," he'd responded.

And he had.

The temperature had been a cool eighty-two degrees that day. A refreshing change for Vegas, especially in late July.

"Alright, Nanna. What is this secret mission? You got a date downtown?"

Nanna had smiled at her grandson. Holding her purse tightly in her lap she'd looked out the window like she was seeing the world for the first time. "Park in front of the Savings and Loan, Jonah. There," she'd pointed, "there's a spot. See where that white car is pulling out?"

Jonah's hands had tightened on the wheel. Something wasn't right.

"Good afternoon, Mrs. Selby. Jonah. It's so good to see you again." Mr. Hayes, the bank manager, smiled when they walked into the heavily air-conditioned bank. "Please, have a seat in my office. I've got the paperwork ready for you. Just give me a minute to gather it all up. Would you care for some water while you wait?"

Jonah had helped his Nanna sit in the dark blue upholstered chair and then had taken a seat himself.

"I'd love some water, Bill. This new medication I'm on dries up my mouth."

Mr. Hayes nodded and smiled in acknowledgment before turning his attention to Jonah, who turned down the water even though his throat was feeling tight.

When the man left the room, Jonah pounced.

"Nanna, what is this all about? Are you getting a loan? If you need more money you should have told me. I can make a go of it down at the casino."

"No, Jonah. I don't need money and I'm not getting a loan."

"Then what, Nanna? Why are we here? Dr. Gray's gonna be furious when he finds out you were out this long." Dr. Gray wasn't just Nanna's doctor; he was her close friend, and he was almost as over-protective as Jonah.

Mr. Hayes entered the room again and Nanna looked up at him in relief. Closing the door behind him he moved to his desk with a stack of papers. "Alright, Mrs. Selby. If you could just look over everything and make sure it's all correct."

Jonah's eyebrows drew together in concern as he watched his Nanna flip through a stack of papers so thick it looked like they wouldn't make it home before dinner. He tried peeking over her shoulder but her discouraging scowl sent him away in frustration.

"It all looks right to me."

"Wonderful." Mr. Hayes smiled, took the papers from his Nanna's hands and looked up at Jonah. "Would you like me to explain everything, Anna?"

Nanna turned and stared into Jonah's eyes and he felt his world begin to crumble. Her eyes were strong and bright. Her face determined. *This isn't good.*

"Bill, can you give us a minute."

The bank manager whispered, "of course" and moved out of the office. When she'd heard the door close softly behind him, Nanna sat up a tiny bit straighter. Her eyes were clear.

"I've been saving money, Jonah, since before you came to live with me." She reached for his hand and squeezed tight.

Jonah took a deep breath.

"My plan was to leave it to Sara — your mother— but well, she's old enough to get into trouble on her own dime." She paused and Jonah watched the familiar cloud of disappointment his mother's name usually created cross her face. "Mr. Hayes has been helping me throughout the years. He lets me know what's best for my money and he'll help you as well." Nanna's eyes welled up and one tear slipped out and made its way down her wrinkled face. "It's your future, Jonah, your peace of mind, and mine. I want you to go to college. Somewhere away from here — perhaps California. I hear they have lots of good schools there. But wherever you go, you will be strong, Jonah. You always have. You —" She stopped. Letting go of his hand she opened her little white purse and began digging around until she found a tissue. With her right hand she held it up to Jonah's face and wiped away his tears. "It's not going to be much longer that I'm here. Dr. Gray says I've beaten the odds already. I wanted to do this before I got any worse. I need to know you'll be alright, Jonah. I need to know you won't feel —" Her face fell and she whispered the last word into her chest: "abandoned."

Jonah couldn't speak. The tears were falling fast and his Nanna's wet tissue was doing more harm than good. "You're gonna be fine, Nanna. You're going to recover." Jonah reached for her hand, his grip firm. "With this new medicine Dr. Gray gave you, he says you could make it another year."

Nanna shook her head. "It's not true, Jonah. That's what I wanted you to think. I was hoping you would go back to school in the fall but I underestimated your stubbornness. I know I don't have a lot of time and I need to know that your future is taken care of."

Jonah pulled his hand away and jumped to his feet. He towered over her, his body shaking. "*I'm* not going to give in that easy, Nanna. We'll use the money to find another doctor, try another treatment — anything. There's got to be something more we can do."

His words sounded strong but when he looked into his Nanna's eyes his shoulders dropped. She was telling the truth. There was nothing left to do but watch her die and hope that it would happen peacefully.

Nanna was silent. The tears were running down her face too now and Jonah flinched in pain. He'd never seen his grandmother cry. She was too strong to cry. She was the source of his strength. "I'm sorry, Nanna. I didn't mean to make you cry."

"Promise me you'll be alright, Jonah. You must promise me."

He let the air fill his lungs and fought for strength. "I promise," he breathed.

With a shaky hand Nanna signaled for Mr. Hayes to come back into the room. When he entered he was carrying a box of tissues and a pen.

Jonah watched his Nanna sign her name over and over again, noticing how each signature grew weaker and weaker. Each S less confident and more like a straight line. His Nanna was disappearing right before his eyes.

Just like his resolve.

The ride home had been quiet. Even the outside world didn't seem to exist.

"I want you to plan a trip for us, Jonah." His Nanna's voice was soft and yet her firm manner left no room for argument.

"A trip? Dr. Gray will never allow it."

"He already knows. He's arranged for three weeks' worth of medication."

"Three weeks?" Jonah's eyes widened in disbelief.

"Three weeks. Hopefully it's enough time."

"Where is it you want to go, Nanna?" Jonah asked softly.

"California. San Diego to be exact."

"Hey, Jonah!" Oscar had yelled when they'd pulled up the driveway. "Do you want to finish our game?"

"Maybe later, okay?"

"Sure." Oscar watched from the street while Jonah helped his grandmother from the car. Her steps appeared heavy as her feet dragged along the ground. When they got to the front door she turned and rested her face against Jonah's chest.

They stayed like that for a few minutes. One trembling hand clutched his shoulder while the other rubbed circles on his back. Slowly his Nanna pulled away and steadily moved through the door.

He'd buried his Nanna in California. He'd watched her body take its last breath and felt like he should join her. With Nanna's death, everything felt different. Jonah no longer had anyone to watch over, and no one to watch over him. As for Kate, she was gone. He'd checked in on her the night before he'd left and her house was in darkness, the kind of darkness that had pushed his already melancholy heart into a serious depression.

The night he'd awakened on the floor of the gas station rest room after his run-in with the bald man had been one of the last nights his Nanna had been alive. Her breathing had worsened soon after. Her color turned almost gray. Jonah wouldn't leave her side. Kate and her mysterious shadow were no longer his priority. The letter he'd written and slipped inside her mailbox was the best he could do under the circumstances. Hopefully it would be in time.

And now he only had a few more days in Vegas. Enough time to pack up his stuff and move on. He had a promise to keep.

"Promise me, Jonah," she'd said. His Nanna's final words had been about yet another promise. "Promise me you'll heal the heart I helped break."

And Jonah had promised. He'd promised that and more. But first *his* heart had to heal.

Thirteen

Mercer Island

The next morning I awake to rain.

The house is silent when I tiptoe downstairs. I'm not sure why I'm so intent on being quiet. I'm pretty sure I heard someone moving around when I was putting on my running shoes. To me running is like everyone else's morning coffee. I need it before I can face the world.

I slip out the front door and make sure not to lock it behind me. Andrew hasn't given me a key yet and the last thing I want is to get locked out in the rain.

Once I'm outside the early morning mist hugs my body close like a protective cover. My footsteps are the only sound on the silent streets.

It doesn't take long before I'm lost in the momentum. The ground races by, blurring into a fuzzy mass of rocks and road.

I feel like I'm flying, like at any moment I will soar above the trees.

I was thirteen the first time I realized I was fast. Growing up in one city after another didn't give me much elbowroom, so it wasn't until that day in the park that I truly realized what I could do.

I'd been watching them for over an hour while my mom met with a client across the street. In my eyes the family was almost too good to be true, in their matching outfits and combed hair. They appeared to have just walked off a photo shoot, some advertising campaign selling the all-American dream.

The dad was pushing the oldest child on the swings — a girl with long blonde braids — while the mom changed the toddler's diaper in the grass. No one noticed when the stroller started rolling down the hill.

No one but me.

I was at least sixty yards away. Half a soccer field. And the baby was sleeping, she wouldn't have put up a fuss.

I didn't think about it, I just ran. When I caught the stroller just before it hit the river, the mom looked up, her face as white as the diaper in her hands.

No one saw me get there; at least no one said anything. And it didn't take long before I wanted, no needed, to feel that speed again. And again. And again.

When my mom arrived I was sharing their lunch next to a large tree that blanketed the entire family— myself included— in shade. I remember she smiled at me, commented on the weather and then pulled out one of the many excuses she carried with her, reasons why we needed to move along.

I never planned to tell her about the baby. I wasn't sure how she'd handle it, drawing attention to myself in that way, or possibly risking an injury in such a public place.

But the mom couldn't wait to spill the entire story. She hugged me again — three times total— and then hugged my mom. She still had tears in her eyes.

As we walked away my mom reached out and took my hand.

"You did a good thing today, Kate," she said. "A very good thing."

The next day when I asked to go back to the park we didn't leave our car by the playground, instead I wanted to visit the public running track on the opposite side of the Green.

"I want to go running," I said. "Do you mind?"

"Of course not, Kate." She'd packed some snacks and a book to read and she was all set to soak up some sun. For the next few hours she watched me run around the track, cheering and clapping each and every time I raced by, until we were the last two people there.

And then I showed her just what I could do.

Now, as the rain picks up, I take it slow. I'm not used to the wetness of the road, the slick gravel under my feet. I concentrate on the neighborhood around me, memorizing each street sign I pass so I can find my way back to Andrew's house. But soon the fog moves in, swallowing first the houses and then each and every last street sign. It closes in on me like a cocoon of white and my chest tightens with alarm.

I have no idea where I am. Or how to get home.

I pull my cell phone out of my pocket but it's dead. I forgot to charge it last night.

I'm cursing my stupidity when just off in the distance I hear it.

Footsteps.

I turn around and wait for a figure to arrive — hopefully someone who might know where Andrew lives — but the footsteps stop.

All I can hear is my breathing and a bird chirping somewhere in the neighborhood.

I take a few more steps and when I hear them echo back I pause again.

Tiny tingles of unease trickle down my back but the fog continues to keep its secrets.

I wait for the footsteps to catch up, still convinced they're helpful rather than dangerous. They're moving slowly, almost hesitant, as they close the gap between us.

I have to admit as much as I want to see whoever is out there, the idea of someone breaking out of the fog so close to me kind of freaks me out.

I start walking faster this time, almost a jog, but with each step I take, the footsteps echo back twice. Finally, when our steps are in sync I stop and peer through the fog.

"Hello? Is anyone there?" I call out. I grip my arms around me, suddenly cold.

But no one answers me.

I imagined it. That's the only explanation. I shake it off and start running again, my pace much slower than normal. Then I stop. Nothing. I take four more steps. Silence. A couple more. More silence.

I take a deep breath and relax. This was a stupid idea, running in fog. Next time I'll know better.

Something sharp is poking my foot from inside my shoe and when I bend down to investigate I find a small white pebble has wedged itself between my shoe and sock. It only takes a second to dig it out and toss it into the road, but when I straighten up I hear it again.

Footsteps. Slow at first and then they quicken to a run.

Are these footsteps new? Or are they the same ones from before? I decide to wait it out before I start moving again.

A twig snaps directly behind me and then the footsteps stop.

I spin around. Nothing. No face, no motion in the fog.

I open my mouth to call out once more but something tells me to stay silent.

A low guttural laugh breaks through the fog directly behind my right ear and my heart stops altogether.

I take off, faster than I've ever run before. Even when I hit a subtle incline, my legs race up it as if it's nothing but a flat road.

At the top of the hill I can see a slight clearing in the fog. The neighborhood doesn't appear familiar but I move toward it decidedly. A figure appears through the fog and my body trembles with relief. Brandon is running toward me.

"Hey Kate. You're up early."

It's everything I can do to keep from hugging him.

"I'm lost," I say when he comes to a stop in front of me.

His welcoming smile widens.

"Well, it's a good thing I changed my route today. How long have you been out here?"

"I'm not sure, exactly." I turn around, searching the neighborhood I just left, but the street is empty. "Perhaps an hour or so?" I say.

"Really? You haven't even broken a sweat."

And I haven't, although, the footsteps left my body clammy with fear.

"Can you help me get back, Brandon? I think I've had enough of this fog."

"Sure thing," he says and starts jogging back the way from which I just came.

"Can we go a different way? I'd love to get a feel for the neighborhood. You know, so I don't get lost again."

It's everything I can do to keep my voice from sounding hysterical.

"That works for me," he says. "In fact I'll point out some landmarks along the way so you'll remember for next time."

"Thanks, Brandon." I turn around one last time to make sure we won't be followed. No one is there.

"So, Kate…"

"Yeah?" I match Brandon's pace as we run along the street.

"You were planning on running for our school, right?"

"I hadn't really thought about it."

"Yeah, I know. You've kinda had a lot going on lately." His smile is a hint apologetic, but I'm not sure why he's apologizing.

"You see, I kinda set up this impromptu track practice today."

And there it is.

"The whole team's going to be there."

"Oh, Brandon, you shouldn't have." And he really shouldn't have. I'm not sure I'm ready to start back on a team just yet. What would my mom think? What would my mom think of *me*?

"Well, Coach is pretty excited to meet you. He's gonna pretend he's not, you know so the rest of the team doesn't get all bent out of shape, but when I told him you were coming—"

"And when was that?"

"When was what?"

"When did you tell the coach I was coming?"

"Um. Last week, I think. When Andrew called from California."

"When last week?" I only just made up my mind two days ago.

"The day after Andrew left for San Diego. He called and had a list of things he needed me and Zack to do for him."

"What kind of things?"

"Well, there was your room, of course. And the Jeep. He wanted me to set up some kind of welcome party with all my friends."

I stumble slightly at this announcement and Brandon grabs my arm just before I fall.

"You okay?" he asks once I've got my footing.

"Yeah, thanks."

"Don't worry," he says taking in the concerned look in my eyes. "He called me back and had me cancel the party a few days later. He wanted to give you a bit more time to adjust before my friends got their claws into you."

"You're friends have claws?" I ask lightly.

Brandon laughs. "Only a few. But don't worry. I've got your back."

I follow Brandon through the rest of the neighborhood and when we near the home stretch he begs to race.

"Come on, Kate. Consider it a warm up for later today."

So I decide to let him win — it's the least I can do after he rescued me in the fog. But when he jumps around Andrew's driveway like he's just won a marathon I decide, never again.

"Kate? Is that you?" Andrews's anxious voice greets me when I walk through the front door. I find him standing behind the kitchen counter with his hands firmly placed at his sides. "I didn't know where you'd gone, Kate."

"I went running."

"I can see that. Now." Andrew's frustration should worry me, but I have to admit, I'm excited to see how this new father-daughter scene will play out.

He pulls down a gallon of orange juice from the top shelf of the refrigerator. "Maybe next time you can leave me a note," he says while he pours himself a glass.

He grabs another glass down from the cupboard and then he hands it to me.

"Does that work for you, Kate?"

"Yes, of course."

"Fine." His shoulders drop and his face relaxes. "Are you hungry?"

"I was just going to take a quick shower."

"And what are your plans after that?"

"Brandon wants me to meet the track coach, but if you need me—"

"That's great!" Andrew says. His smile is encouraging, something I've yet to see while talking about coaches or track meets.

"Yeah. So. I should be gone a while, I guess."

"Alright." Andrew is still smiling. "Why don't you take the Jeep."

"The Jeep?"

"Yes." He tosses something in the air and I catch it with my right hand.

"The Jeep," I say, staring down at a set of shiny new keys. My keys.

"Good luck today, Kate," he says as he walks out of the kitchen. "Go give them hell."

.   .   .

The wet grass soaks through my shorts while I watch the Mercer Island track team warm up. Periodically Brandon turns and smiles in my direction and each time he does some different girl I don't know watch him do it. The girls on the team appear welcoming, they always do in the beginning, but to me they're just a gaggle of hoodies and running shorts. I know from experience that if I feign disinterest they eventually leave me alone.

A petite blonde with a heart-shaped face walks toward me. Her smile is bright and her make-up distracting. The amount of glitter applied to her eyes shimmers back at me. If the sun were out this girl would sparkle like a diamond.

"Coach Abrahms says he's ready for you," she announces. "He's giving us a much needed break so that he can spend some time on his new favorite track star."

I flinch inwardly at the girl's words but when I look up I find only humor in her eyes, not the usual disdain or jealousy I'm so accustomed to seeing.

"No worries, Triumph. We all know you're faster than us," the girl continues. "To be honest it's a bit of a relief. Now we don't have to worry about him planting steroids in our food. Can't make it on America's Next Top Model if you've got hair growing on your chest."

"At least you've got your priorities," I say.

"Damn straight," she replies. "Once I graduate I ain't running nowhere. Not even if I'm chased. I'm only on this team for the extra-curriculars."

It takes me a minute to realize the conversation has lulled. I'm too busy staring at the purple glitter embedded to the girl's eyelashes. She's almost pixie-like in her appearance. She reminds me of the faerie drawings my mom used to create for me when I was younger.

"My name's Emily, by the way." She sticks out her hand with an impish smile and says, "Emily Cooke."

I can't help but notice when I take Emily's hand that today's date is written on top in bright red marker.

"I forget things," Emily explains. She blows a large bubble of her gum and lets it pop with a loud snap. "It's a little bizarre actually. I could recite the TV show I watched last night verbatim but if you ask what month it is or what I had for breakfast I'd have to plead the fifth. My mom calls it selective memory but I'm not so sure who selects it for me. Every day is different."

Was she serious? I stare up at her, my eyes narrowed in disbelief in case she suddenly yells, "just kidding!"

"So, anyway," Emily continues with a smile, "we're really excited you happened upon our team, Triumph. Now get your ass off the grass and go make nice with the track."

"Make nice with the track?"

"You know," Emily explains, "where you run around real fast-like and you make the coach forget we exist long enough for me to get some texting in." To emphasize her words Emily pulls out a sparkly pink iPhone from her back pocket. With a loud crack of her bubble gum she moves away.

Coach Abrahms takes a look at me, points to the starting line and then aims his stopwatch in the air. "I know about your recent record, young lady, but *everyone* tries out on my team."

I open my mouth to explain how I'm not sure I really want to be on the team but he cuts me off.

"You race the 400, right?"

"Um, yeah, but I—"

"You like our track?"

I look around at the newly constructed track and nod. "It's great but—"

"Brandon! You ready with the gun?"

"Sure thing, Coach." Brandon aims the starter pistol in the air and I instinctively take my mark. I can't help it. It's like Brandon is Pavlov and the starter pistol his bell. And of course that would make me the dog in this scenario.

"Go!" Coach Abrahms yells.

The shot of the starter pistol reverberates in my head and for a split second I'm lost. My mind is back at the track meet. Luckily my feet know what to do. I take off while the memory of my mom's voice yells encouragement all the way to the finish line. But even when the race is over the memories continue. In surround sound.

Bleachers filled with bodies, a cheering crowd. The cadence of charging feet as my fellow racers come up from behind. My mom's face captured in the headlights of an approaching car. And then screaming. Nothing but screaming.

Even with my eyes closed and my hands over my face I can't keep out the nightmare.

"Kate, that was amazing!"

"Great job, Kate!"

"Welcome to the team!"

I pull my hands from my face and take in my surroundings. I'm not at Husky Stadium. I'm at Mercer Island High.

And my mom is still dead.

Brandon's face blends with the rest of the team as one by one they converge on me. Their hands reach out to welcome me with sportsmanlike slaps and pats. All I can think about is leaving. The race has ripped the band-aid off my fresh wound.

"I've got to go," I whisper to no one in particular and hurry off the track.

Fourteen

Andrew's front door is locked, and of course he doesn't use a key like everyone else. No, he has some fancy keypad where you have to type in a number, a number he told me twice and made me repeat back twice before I left. But, of course, I forgot. I'm convinced there's a 6 and an 8 but the last number isn't 0 or 3 like I thought and I only get one more chance to type in the correct code before the alarm triggers and the cops arrive.

I definitely don't want the cops to arrive.

I'm standing outside in the rain, second-guessing my memory, when the door magically swings open.

"Hey Kate." Zack's barefoot and smiling, his hair slightly messy as if he's been running his hands through it. "Andrew was afraid you'd forget the code."

"I didn't forget all of it." I take a step toward the doorway and stop. Zack is filling the doorframe and for me to enter the house I'll have to get entirely too close to him.

"I only forgot the last number," I continue from my safe position on the front porch.

"Did you want to come inside?" His eyes tell me he's aware of my discomfort and he finds it amusing.

"No. I like the rain," I say as another large drip slides off the roof and hits me in the eye.

"Right." He steps back, just enough for me to enter the house.

"Thanks," I say and brush past him.

"How were tryouts? Did you make the team?"

"I guess. I didn't really stick around to find out." I strip out of my soggy sweatshirt and head into the kitchen.

Zack follows me. His eyes take in my nearly wet t-shirt and my running shorts and by the time he looks back up I find I'm out of breath. Why is he here anyway? And why does he have to be so attractive? I can handle cute. Gabe was cute, while Zack is a whole new breed of sexy.

"What do you mean you didn't stick around? Did something happen?" He pulls up a seat at the counter and watches me gulp down a glass of water.

"Nothing happened. I ran, coach timed me and then I left."

"What?" I say when Zack raises an eyebrow.

"You seem a bit upset."

"I'm not upset. I'm cold. And wet."

"I noticed." He pulls his long sleeve shirt up and over his head and hands it to me, but not before I notice his stomach is as alluring as his eyes. "Put this on," he says, standing in front of me wearing only a thin, white t-shirt and jeans.

"I'm okay." I move to the sink for another glass of water. I don't want to wear his still-warm shirt that probably smells like pine trees and fresh air, everything healthy and male, because then I'll smell like him.

And I'll lose my mind if I smell like him.

So instead I concentrate on drinking my water.

"We get a lot of rain here," he says as if he's explaining away my wetness.

"You think?"

"What we lack in sun we make up for in rain."

"They should put that on the license plate." I finish my water and put the glass in the sink. "Thanks for letting me in."

"Kate?" Zack calls out to me just as I'm about to hit the stairs.

"Yeah?" My right foot moves to the first step while my hand grips the railing. I look like I'm poised to race someone up the stairs.

"I was thinking we could chat for a minute before Andrew   gets   home."

"I'd really love a shower," I say.

"Well, I think it's a little soon in our relationship for that, but, okay," he drawls.

I whip around and find him leaning in the kitchen doorway. His arms are crossed in front of him and he's laughing at me. At least his eyes are. The rest of him appears relaxed and too damn sexy. "It's just a chat, Kate. I'm not asking for anything more than that."

But I don't believe him.

"Alright," I say, and when he doesn't immediately respond it's my turn to raise an eyebrow. "What did you want to chat about, exactly?"

"You." Zack smiles when he notices my frown. "What? I thought all girls loved to talk about themselves."

I shrug. "I'm not exactly up on what other girls do."

"Yeah, I kinda guessed that about you." He moves into the room and sits on the arm of the big black couch. "I'm not sure if Andrew has told you or not but Brandon and I lost our parents a few years ago. Brandon was fourteen and I was sixteen."

"He didn't tell me."

"Yeah, well, Andrew's not much of a talker."

"Neither am I," I say.

Zack's eyes narrow and then he smiles.

"You'll get along fine then."

When he doesn't say anything more, just continues to stare at me with those eyes of his, I say, "what happened to your parents?" I didn't want to ask but I get the feeling if I don't contribute to this conversation soon he'll just continue staring at me until I melt into a puddle right here on the stairs.

"My parents were killed in a small plane accident down in the Caribbean."

"I'm so sorry." I know it's the proper response. I've heard it enough lately to know it by memory but it feels strange coming from my lips.

"Thanks."

"I can't imagine losing both parents. That really sucks."

"Yeah. It does. You're lucky to have Andrew."

"Yeah, lucky."

"You disagree?" he asks.

"Sorry. I just really hate that word, lucky. It implies that life is occasionally fair, and you and I both know that's not the case."

"Why, because we lost loved ones?"

"That's one reason."

Zack shakes his head. "That isn't why I told you, Kate."

"You mean you didn't want this to be one of those bonding moments when two people realize they have something in common and suddenly a friendship is born?" I shrug my shoulders and take another step up the stairs. "I'm sorry about your parents."

Zack slowly gets to his feet. I watch him take one step and then another until he's standing right below me.

"No, *I'm* sorry, Kate."

"About what?"

Zack's eyes are narrowed on me now. The friendliness replaced with something else entirely. Something I can't place. "I didn't realize you thought I wanted to be friends." His eyes drop to my mouth and hover there, until I'm so self-conscious I pull my bottom lip in and bite it nervously.

"Okay, so you don't want to be my friend," I say.

"No."

"Then you won't mind if I go upstairs now?"

"Actually I do." He grips the railing on either side of me and leans so close our foreheads are almost touching. It's way too close for me but I refuse to be the one to back away first. "Is this what I have to do to get you to look at me?" he asks.

"You mean invade my space?"

Zack's smile turns into a smirk.

"What's your problem?" I ask when he doesn't move away.

"That's funny," he says, and his breath tickles my eyelashes. "I was just going to ask you the same thing. I get that you're sad. It sucks to lose someone. Believe me, I know. But I don't think that's what this is. This, I don't give a damn, persona of yours. No, I think this is something else."

"I don't care what—" I stop talking when his eyes drop back down to my lips.

"What, Kate? Am I too close for you?"

"Yes."

"Am I making you uncomfortable? Asking too many questions?"

"Yes!"

"Would you rather I stay on the other side of the room, maybe stop looking at you altogether?"

"Yes, I mean, I don't really care what you do."

"Really? I find that hard to believe."

"Why?" I say far too softly.

Zack has me trapped on the stairs, my body bent backward to keep from touching him, but his eyes are like bands around my wrists, holding me in place. They burrow their way into my mind so that even when I blink all I can see are his gray-green eyes.

"What do you want, Zack? I'm tired and wet and I'm not really enjoying this game of yours."

"*My* game?" he says with a laugh. His white teeth flash at me and then his lips cover them with a smirk. "You must have me mistaken for someone else. I don't play games."

"Okay. You don't play games. So this," I point my finger back and forth between the two of us, "this is what you'd call chatting?"

Zack just smiles.

"I admit games are fun sometimes, like when you and I can't keep our eyes off each other at dinner and then later you pretend I don't exist. That one is always a party favorite."

"I don't know what you're talking about," I say.

"Don't you? Let's try something then." I feel his hand slide up my arm until it's resting along my collarbone. "You tell me when to stop and I'll stop." His fingertips are soft; they send a rush of warmth up my back, which eventually leads to a shudder. His eyes follow the path his hand makes up my neck and into my hair. And then his other hand arrives. It skims along my hip to my waist and then brushes up and down the small of my back.

"What are you doing," I say, but it comes out all breathy and faint. "Why are you doing this?" I add with more force.

"That's not how you play, Kate. Remember, all you need to do is say, stop. Do you want me to stop?"

"Yes," I whisper, nodding my head slowly while his hand moves through my hair.

"Then say stop, Kate," he breathes against my neck. "All you have to do…" he moves his mouth so close that each word tickles my skin, "is…" his lips hover near my ear, "say… stop," he whispers.

I open my mouth and the word is right there on my tongue, but when his eyes fall on my lips I can't think. I can't speak.

It's one little word, Kate. Say it!

But I can't.

I know what I want. I know exactly what I want. My eyes close as I lift my mouth to his.

"Kate? Are you here?"

Andrew's voice is like an electric shock. Zack and I spring apart like we've been pushed. I fall back on the next step, landing hard on my butt, while Zack jumps down to the floor.

"We're in here, Andrew," he calls out, and it kills me that his voice sounds calm and unaffected.

104

"Who the hell do you think you are?" I hiss once I've regained my senses.

Zack's eyes are dark, almost charcoal in color with tiny specks of emerald fire.

"Don't you know? I'm the one who's getting under your skin, Kate. Pretend all you want with everyone else but now we both know with me it's just an act."

I stare up at him for a minute and then shake my head, no.

"Hey, Kate. How'd it go?" Andrew says.

"What?" I say and much to my embarrassment I can feel my face fill with color.

"He wants to know how tri-outs went." Zack walks over to the coffee table and picks up a textbook, something science-related, and then flops down on the couch.

"Oh. Right. I have to take a shower," I say and then blush again, remembering Zack's earlier comment. And of course my second blush doesn't go unnoticed. I can hear Zack chuckle under his breath as I make my way up the stairs.

"Did you make the team?" Andrew calls out to me when I reach the top of the landing.

"Yes."

"And are you going to run, Kate?" he asks.

I turn and find Zack still watching me from the couch. He's holding his book up as if he's reading, but his eyes are on me.

"Yes," I say. "I'm going to run."

Andrew is making dinner again. Apparently he enjoys cooking and is rather good at it. When I walk into the kitchen after a long and drawn out shower I find he's lined up his ingredients on the counter as if he's on a cooking show.

Zack and Brandon are here again. I heard their voices as soon as I left my room, which left me about two minutes to get my game-face on. Apparently they eat dinner here every night. That is when they're around.

I manage to avoid Zack's eyes, but not for long. He draws me into the conversation, asking me question after question until I'm forced to glare at him, while he just smiles.

My mom was never really into cooking. She didn't have a lot of extra time at night, so we ate out a lot. Or ordered in.

Andrew slices the peppers and onions as if he's been doing this all his life. It's mesmerizing watching him. If it were me I'd have sliced all of my fingers off by now, but Andrew hasn't even nicked one.

"So that pretty much explains Coach," Brandon says, and I realize I haven't heard a single word he's said.

"Right," I say and smile at him distractedly.

"Are you excited for school tomorrow, Kate?" Andrew asks.

"I'm not sure excited is the word."

"Oh come on!" Brandon laughs. "It's high school! Senior year! How can you not be excited?"

"Do you want the short list or the long one?" I say.

"Alright," he laughs. "I admit being new sucks. But you've got me, Kate. I'll show you around, introduce you to everyone."

"Everyone?" I say. Oh boy.

"Yes, everyone," Zack chimes in. "Didn't Andrew tell you? Brandon is senior class president. And he takes it all very seriously. Not a soul escapes his notice."

"Great," I say.

"Good luck tomorrow," he says. His smile is sympathetic but it changes into something more when I don't look away.

"And what about you?" I say. "Where do you go?"

"U-Dub," Brandon says.

"The University of Washington," Zack explains when I look blankly back at him. "I'm a sophomore," he adds.

"I see."

"He should be in Boston," Brandon pipes up, "solving our world's most complicated problems with all those other elite M.I.T. minds but instead he's studying molecular biology at a state school."

"Brandon," Zack says.

"What? You know I love having you around. Just wish things could've been different."

"Well, M.I.T. is hard to get into," I say.

"Who said he didn't get in?" Brandon steals a pepper off the cutting board and pops it into his mouth. "He got accepted, he just chose not to go."

"Brandon," Zack says again, this time with feeling.

"Brandon, why don't you throw some plates on the table," Andrew suggests.

"And shut up," Zack says.

"Oh come on, Andrew. You know you wanted him to go just as badly as I did. I mean it's your alma mater."

"Wait, what?" I say. "You went to M.I.T.?"

"All four years," Andrew says.

"And you graduated?"

Andrew laughs. "Isn't that generally the idea?"

"In what?"

"Biological engineering," he says.

"So... okay," I choke. "Whatever will you do with that?"

Andrew looks up from the cutting board and laughs. "Well, I have to admit. It didn't help me get my first job."

"And what was that?" I ask.

Andrew continues chopping for another minute until all of the red, green and orange peppers are in tiny bite-shaped pieces. "The Army," he says. "I was in the Army."

"Oh." I watch him scoop the peppers into a skillet, listening as the oil welcomes them heartily with a loud sizzle and pop. "And how long were you in the Army?" I can't look at him while I ask these questions. I can't look at the man I know nothing about.

"Long enough," he says, and just like that the conversation is over.

Brandon jumps in with more questions about school, like when I have lunch and how I *have* to sit with him. It almost feels timed, like he's so used to Andrew's elusive answers he's sparing me the frustration.

Zack gets up and begins pouring water into each glass on the table. When he leans over to fill my glass his hand rests lightly on my shoulder.

His mouth is entirely too close when he whispers, "Keep asking, Kate. Questions are good."

"I will," I whisper back, once I find the words.

After dinner I offer to clean up while Brandon, Zack and Andrew move into the living room. I'm just about to turn on the dishwasher when Brandon calls my name from the other room.

"Come watch, Kate. I'm about to make my TV debut!"

The three of them are scattered across the couches, all of their eyes glued to the large flat-screen TV mounted on the wall.

"This reporter stopped by track practice last week, wanted to interview me for their local interest story," Brandon explains.

"That's great," I say, but my eyes are focused on the picture on the screen.

"...and a familiar face is back in the news again tonight. If you've been downtown recently, you'll recognize the newest addition to Seattle's skyline. This big glass building behind me, is home to Dr. Luke Dolus, the controversial scientist involved in the latest..."

108

"I'm not sure this is the right station. Which channel is WTSE, Andrew?" Brandon asks and then the photo disappears and the Simpsons appear.

"Wait! Turn that back!" I cry out.

But it's too late. By the time Brandon gets us back on the right channel the newscaster has moved on.

"What was it, Kate?" Andrew asks. He looks up from his lounging position on the black leather loveseat.

"Nothing. I just thought I recognized someone. But it was nothing."

"Goodnight," I say, making my way to the staircase. All I can think about is getting upstairs to my computer.

"Wait!" Brandon calls out. "You'll miss it!"

"Oh, right." I hover near the back of the room for the next twenty minutes, all the while hearing the newscaster's words over and over again in my head.

Controversial. Scientist.

Dr. Dolus.

Once Brandon's brief five-second clip ends I hit the stairs running. I only stop to call out goodnight.

"Hey, Kate! What about tomorrow?" Brandon yells up to me.

"Tomorrow?"

"Yeah. I usually catch a ride to school with my girlfriend, Marnie, but I thought you might like me to ride with you. Help you check in and stuff."

"Tomorrow?" I say again. I can't figure out what Brandon's talking about. All I see is Dr. Dolus and a big glass building.

"Yeah. Tomorrow. You remember. It's the first day of school for a special someone I know."

"Oh. Right. School."

"So? You want me to ride with you?" Brandon's smiling up at me, in his expression is a promise of friendship.

"That's alright, Brandon. I've had plenty of first days. I wouldn't want Marnie to have to ride alone."

"She won't mind. I promise," he says. "She'll be totally cool with it."

"I—"

"Seriously, Kate. I won't take no for an answer. I don't want you to—"

"I can handle it, Brandon," I say. And just in case the message isn't clear I add, "I'll see you at school." With my eyes staring straight ahead, so as to avoid all three pairs of eyes looking up at me, I mumble, "goodnight."

Up in my room I begin Googling the good doctor. Most of the current articles I find online describe Dr. Dolus as being involved in cloning research. "Regenerative Medicine" they're calling it. I guess the term "cloning" has negative connotations. I find one brief article, written over sixteen years ago, about a class action suit filed against him. Apparently quite a few women who'd sought him out for fertility treatments had either miscarried or given birth to stillborn babies. When I dig deeper I discover that the case was later thrown out.

Why would my mom schedule an appointment with a cloning/fertility specialist? And now that they've met, why is he seeking me out?

I click through a couple more links, more articles that tell me nothing more than I've already determined.

And then I see the photo.

Dr. Dolus is an attractive man who in most of the photographs is either smiling into the camera or at someone just out of view. But it isn't his charming smile that catches my eye. It's the man standing on the sidelines. It appears Dr. Dolus is rarely alone. Whether he's exiting his building or leaving a charity event, lurking in Dr. Dolus' shadow is a man dressed in black. He's tall, about a foot taller than the doctor, stocky in build, as if he works out by lifting small cars above his head, and he's bald, just like the coach from Husky.

Lyla and Todd's coach. I close my eyes and try to remember his name, but nothing comes to me. Staring at the photograph I'm not so sure it's even important.

It's hard to know if it's really him, considering when I saw him, the coach was at least twenty feet away. And it was just the one time.

But it could be him.

It looks like him.

The real question is, why?

"Kate?" Andrew knocks on my door and when I call out for him to enter he peeks his head into my room.

"Are you busy?"

"Um. No?"

"When you get a chance can you come down to my office? I'd like to talk to you."

"Okay."

After he leaves I print out the photo of Dr. Dolus and the bald man and tuck it into my backpack. Something tells me I should keep it with me.

Lefty is hovering around his food dish. He still refuses to leave my room, so before I head back downstairs I fill his bowl with food and replace his water.

"It's the coward's way out, cat. You know that, right?"

But Lefty ignores me. He just crunches his food and twitches his tail.

"Come in and take a seat," Andrew says when I knock on his office door. He's sitting behind a dark, wooden desk, rummaging around in the top drawer. "I wanted to find you the spare garage door opener. I'm not sure where I hid it...it's been a while since I needed both of them."

It feels rather personal being in Andrew's office. It's not quite as personal as say, a bedroom, but close. He does seem to spend a lot of time in here. There are a few built-in bookcases along the far wall and a long black leather couch that reminds me of the kind of couch you'd find in a psychiatrist's office. I make my way to the bookcase, curious to see what kind of books Andrew reads. The first one I come to holds a selection of American classics, such as Moby Dick and The Great Gatsby and then stacked across the top is a selection of sociology textbooks. My fingers brush the spines of each one like they're absorbing bits and pieces of a puzzle. I'm not sure what to make of the man who places To Kill A Mockingbird next to a weathered copy of Popular Sociology Today.

On the top of the last bookcase is a small photo inside a metal frame. I reach for it but my fingers can't seem to grasp it, they're shaking too violently. A much younger version of my mom rests inside the frame. She looks happy and in love. If it weren't for the fact that she looks so much like me I'd barely recognize her. The man in her arms is Andrew. While she smiles into the camera he smiles at her.

"You loved her," I whisper, afraid I'll startle the euphoric couple in the frame.

When I get no response I turn, thinking he didn't hear me.

"I'm actually trying not to hate her." Andrew is watching me from behind his desk. His hands are still buried inside the top drawer but he's stopped his search for the moment.

I glance back down at the photograph. "She loved you." When Andrew remains silent I continue, "Truly. I've never seen her look this happy. Not with John. Not with anyone."

"She didn't know me, Kate."

"And why's that?"

"She didn't stick around."

"So it's her fault? I was wondering when this would come up."

"I never blamed her for leaving," Andrew says. But the words are left dangling in the air as if one by one they'll fall off the edge of a cliff.

"So what is it exactly? That she never told you about me?"

"How many schools have you gone to, Kate?"

"What? Why?" The abrupt change in topic throws me even though I'm beginning to notice there's a pattern to Andrew's way of communicating. You think you're in control of the subject matter and then "POW!" he hits you with random.

"You told Brandon you've had many first days. What did you mean?"

"We moved around a lot. Different cities, lots of new schools."

"Why'd you move so often?"

"Well, there was the franchising. My mom wanted to get her name out there. She managed to get her jewelry sold in fifteen separate stores across the country."

"But she wouldn't need to move to do that."

"No. She wouldn't."

"So then, why?"

"I shouldn't have to spell it out, Andrew. You know I'm different."

"And is that why you're pushing everyone away? Because you're different."

"I wouldn't call it pushing," I say.

"Brandon and Zack want to be your friend. Don't you see that?"

"I'm not sure—"

"You can trust them. Believe me. They'll never hurt you."

"I'm not afraid—"

"Aren't you?"

I pause and take a breath. "I was going to say, I'm not afraid of them hurting me."

"Well, good then." Andrew smiles at me and starts digging around again inside his desk drawer. "Then there shouldn't be a problem with you hanging out with them. Right?"

"Why is this so important to you? Brandon is class president and captain of the track team. I can only imagine he has a collection of friends all vying for his attention. Why is it so important that he be *my* friend? And Zack. Well, he's a good-looking kid. Seems friendly enough."

"Kate?"

"I mean some might find him cute. He's not exactly my type but—"

"Kate."

"Yeah?"

"I found it." Andrew tosses me a small black box and I catch it with my right hand. "Don't leave it in your car. Carry it with you."

"Okay." I stare down at the small garage opener. Of course it isn't just a button, no, that would be too easy. This little black box has a keypad for which I'm confident I'll need to learn another code just to get it to work.

"Zack and Brandon are good kids. They've been through a lot, like you, and will put up with a lot. You can trust them."

"I don't trust anybody," I say.

"And you shouldn't." Andrew narrows his eyes and adds, "Unless I tell you to." He walks around his desk and when he stops in front of me he's smiling, as if a smile can lighten the conversation. "This is how you use the keypad. He types in four numbers and the screen changes. And then he types in four more. "If you forget, Zack knows all the codes and carries a spare."

"How trustworthy of him." I take the garage opener from Andrew and notice he has tiny white scars along the top of his hand. "Did you get those from cutting vegetables?"

Andrew looks down at his hands in confusion. "What?"

"Those scars on your hand. You're very fast you know. When you slice... vegetables. Did you, um, cut yourself?"

Andrew stares at me for a minute and then says, "No. I've never cut myself."

"Alright then, did someone cut you?" I ask with a laugh.

But Andrew doesn't find it amusing. He turns back to his desk and returns with a small envelope. "This came for you today."

"Thanks." I study the envelope. My address in San Diego is handwritten across the front but I don't recognize the writing, mostly because it's almost completely covered by the forwarding address label.

"We're going to dinner with Brandon and Zack tomorrow night," he says. "Kind of a welcome/first day of school celebration."

"Alright," I say, still staring down at the letter in my hands.

"I made reservations for six o'clock. Does that work for you, Kate?"

"Sure. Six. Goodnight, Andrew," I say on my way out of his office. "Thanks for the garage opener. And the Jeep. I don't remember if I said thank you or not." I turn the letter over in my hands, my eyes on the floor. "I really appreciate all you've done for me."

"You're welcome." Even without looking I can feel his eyes holding me to my spot in the doorway. "I'm glad you're here, Kate," he says.

Hearing these words has a strange effect on me. I feel like I'm being strangled, the pain in my throat so intense I might scream. I still don't know how to feel about this man, but I do feel something.

"So am I," I answer, and then quickly make my way out of the room.

Lefty's already asleep on my bed when I get back upstairs. He lets out a soft mew when I sit down beside him and rolls onto his back. I reach out to pet him and then stop. My fingers hang in mid-air while I read the letter Andrew gave me.

Kate,

I'm sorry for the directness of this letter but I would never forgive myself if something happened to you.
Someone is following you.
I can't explain how I know this or why, just that it is the unfortunate truth.
I wish I could tell you more, but it's all I know so far.
Hopefully one day I'll have the opportunity to tell you everything. Until then watch your back and try not to be alone. Oh, and keep a change of clothes on hand. You never know when you might need it.

There's no signature. No return address. The postmark is from San Diego, and for some reason that makes the whole thing even creepier. I keep trying to tuck it back into its envelope, but my hands are shaking.

When I close my eyes I hear footsteps following me in the rain, and the faint sound of sinister laughter.

Fifteen

Las Vegas

Jonah drops his backpack on the backseat of the greyhound bus. For a little over eight hours he'll be trapped here with two drunks, a screaming baby and his new best friend, insomnia.

The bus driver climbs aboard, positions himself in his ripped and deflated seat and maneuvers the bus onto the road. With a sigh, Jonah stares out the window. It's four hundred and twenty-six miles to San Diego. And upon arrival those four hundred and twenty-six miles won't feel nearly far enough from Las Vegas, his past or the empty home he's left behind. But he made a promise. It's San Diego or bust.

With a jolt the bus comes to a stop and Jonah grips the seat in front of him while the drunk near the front slides to the floor.

"Get up!" yells the bus driver. "This isn't the Holiday Inn!"

The drunk slowly drags himself back into his seat.

Jonah's hands are still gripping the seat. His skin is lighter than normal for this time of year but he's been spending a lot more time indoors lately. Bright sunny days are Mother Nature's cruel gift of torture for those who spend their nights grieving in darkness.

Last night was an exception. He'd gone to Harrah's to say his goodbyes.

"When you gonna get enough of this, Kid?" Ricky asked.

Slowly Jonah picked himself up off the ground in time to receive another uppercut to the face. "When you admit your true feelings for me, Ricky," he replied, spitting blood from his newly loosened tooth.

"Ah, Jonah. I just don't get it. You could go to any casino on the strip to play cards. Why do you always have to come to mine?"

"Because you'd miss me." Jonah lunged forward just in time to guarantee a quick kick to the abdomen.

"Drew wants it to stop," Ricky admitted as he watched Jonah fall to his knees. "But I keep telling him, I'd rather be the one to beat the crap out of you. Those other goons down the strip won't be as nice as me." He leaned down and pulled Jonah to his feet. "Have you had enough, kid?"

Jonah spit again and noticed the floor was much cleaner tonight. Ricky was definitely taking it easy on him. With a well-timed kick he could change that right now.

Which he did.

Ricky grabbed himself in agony and Jonah smiled. "What do you think?"

"You know what I think, Jonah?" Ricky moaned. "I think you're sick. I think any kid who looks for this kind of attention has something really wrong with him."

"Sick? Maybe. Or maybe I'm just looking for love in all the wrong places."

"Go home, Jonah." Ricky rose to his feet and moved toward the exit. "I don't want to play anymore." And the door closed behind him with a loud crack.

Jonah took a minute to push his hair back off his face and straighten his clothes before he slipped out the backdoor into the alley.

If only all his goodbyes could have been that easy. Telling Oscar he was leaving felt like losing his Nanna all over again.

"So when do you think you'll be back?" Oscar stared down at the dirt he'd been kicking at his feet for the last fifteen minutes.

"I don't know. But I need you to do something for me, alright? I need you to hold on to all of the baseball stuff. I won't be able to take it with me. I'll need it back though. Can you keep it safe?"

Oscar nodded but he still wouldn't look up.

They sat like that on the sidewalk in front of Oscar's house for a few more minutes. Oscar was sad but Jonah knew it was time to move on. He'd walked the halls of Nanna's house long enough. A week. Seven straight days of sadness. Seven straight days of his Nanna's ghost reminding him of the promises he'd yet to keep.

It was time.

Across the street, a moving truck pulled up in front of a house. Jonah watched two men climb out.

"I bet Matt's a great catcher."

Oscar kicked a rock under his mother's car. "Who's Matt?"

Jonah smiled. "The new kid across the street. They got here yesterday from Chicago. Matt's your age. I bet he could toss a ball good too. You know Chicago — lots of baseball."

Oscar finally looked up and his curious eyes studied the house across the street. "You think he likes the Cubbies or the White Sox?"

"Don't know. Have to ask him."

Oscar swiveled around on Jonah in horror. "You didn't ask him? You know his name but you didn't ask him what team he likes?"

Jonah laughed. "I only talked to his mom. He was out shopping with his dad so I didn't get to meet him. Just heard he likes baseball."

"Hmm." Oscar glanced over at the house again just as a young boy raced out the front door.

"That must be Matt. Oscar, why don't you go ask him yourself?"

The boy shifted slightly but he didn't get up from the sidewalk. "Nah. He looks busy."

Jonah snorted. Matt wasn't busy. He'd noticed them sitting on the curb and was watching curiously. Jonah stood up and waved. "Hey Matt. I hear you like baseball."

Oscar elbowed him in the knee. "Whatcha gotta do that for, Jonah? Now he's never gonna let me be. He'll be wantin' to play ball every single minute of the day!"

"So?" Jonah laughed. "Sounds like someone else I know. Go talk to him, Oscar. You remember how you felt when you were the new kid on the block?"

Oscar kicked the dirt one last time and then stood up. "Well, I at least gotta find out what team he likes before I agree to let him play."

Jonah watched him walk across the street before turning around to walk to Nanna's front door. The taxi was coming to pick him up in an hour and he still had some last minute things to do.

"The Red Sox!" Oscar's cry of outrage could've been heard from a block away. "Did you hear that, Jonah? Matt here likes the Red Sox!"

Jonah chuckled and walked through Nanna's front door for perhaps the last time. Oscar would be fine.

Now he was sitting on the bus, with all his worldly possessions locked up in storage and a single duffle stored above his head.

He'd stalled long enough.

It was time to find Kate.

Sixteen

Mercer Island

The next morning Andrew surprises me with an enormous cheese omelet. I take two bites and decide high school is best served on an empty stomach. When I begin shifting the food around on my plate Andrew watches from above his morning newspaper.

"Nervous?" he asks.

I push the food until it no longer resembles its previous shape. "A little."

Andrew folds the paper and places it down on the kitchen counter. "It's just high school, right? Nothing life threatening or dangerous?"

I eye him skeptically. "How long since you were in high school?"

Andrew laughs. "Longer than I care to admit." He stands up and takes my plate of mangled omelet to the sink. "It will be nice to already know someone, right?"

"Sure."

"Kate?"

"Yeah, I know. Be nice to Brandon and Brandon will be nice to me."

"Or there's the alternative," Andrew says.

"What's that?" I ask, even though I'm pretty sure I live it.

"Be alone," he says.

"Right." And who'd want that?

I grab my backpack off the floor and make my way to the garage.

"Good luck at school, Kate." Andrew is smiling as he leans against the sink.

"Thanks, but luck has nothing to do with it," I mutter under my breath.

"I feel like I should offer up some words of advice or a quote of some sort."

"A quote?"

Andrew shrugs his shoulders. "Yeah. When I was young my father used every opportunity to spout out a quote or two."

It hits me how bizarre it is that I don't know anything about Andrew's family. Or his life, for that matter. "And did it work — these quotes?"

"Not really. But I think it made *my father* feel better."

"My mom had a zillion quotes and they all revolved around facing your fears..."

Andrew smiles. "Is that what you're going to do today? Face your fears?"

"That all depends on how many spiders cross my path." *Or if anyone at school tries to stab the new girl with a knife.*

Andrew laughs. "See you tonight, Kate. Drive safe and — oh, I've got one. " He moves past me and brushes the top of my head with his hand, "Forgive your enemies, but don't forget their names."

I stare after him thoughtfully. "Is that something your father would say?"

"Nope, I learned that my first day on the job."

I overestimate the drive to Mercer Island High School and when I arrive I'm early enough to sit in my car and study it from a safe distance. It looks nice enough, bigger than I expected, which is good. I'm hoping for a large pool of students. A smaller crowd makes for a dramatic entrance and, as usual, I'm all about blending in.

When I walk through the doors I realize this could be any of the last three high schools I've attended. It smells the same and the students most likely defend their territories the same. After all, high school is an overpopulated wood filled with hungry wolves vying for the respected and coveted position of the alpha.

I keep my head down — never make eye contact — and concentrate on the brightly colored lockers that eventually lead to mine, or home base, as I like to call it. Andrew took the time to get my class schedule worked out as well as my locker assignment. He even went to the trouble of drawing a color-coded map of the school — my classes are in green, restrooms in blue, the cafeteria is a light orange and each exit is brightly shaded red. He clearly has way too much time on his hands.

"Hey Kate!"

All of the eyes watching from the shadows widen with greater interest when Brandon walks toward me. "You made it."

He's bouncing with the uncontainable energy of a puppy. I have to resist the urge to soothe him with softly spoken words or a light stroke of the ears. "I made it," I say.

"Come on, I'll show you around."

"I have a map," I say and hold it up for him to see.

"Who needs a map when you've got me?"

I open my mouth to answer and then decide against it. *Be nice. I'm supposed to be nice.*

But being nice is the complete opposite of what I've always done in these situations.

As we walk down the hallway together it doesn't take long for me to discover how popular Brandon actually is. The girls strategically laugh and flutter their eyelashes when he gets near while the guys reach out with a strange compelling need to slap his palm.

Brandon is the alpha male.

And I'm in trouble.

I mean, how easy would it be to dance in the pulsing lights of Brandon's strobe-like popularity? Easy. Very easy. Until it became complicated.

Luckily my schedule doesn't match up with Brandon's and so for most of the day I'm on my own.

Until lunch.

Brandon is waiting outside my Spanish class, leaning confidently against the red lockers. "You hungry?"

"Not really," I say.

"Well then you can keep me company while I eat." He falls into step right beside me.

"Listen Brandon, I appreciate—"

"Kate." He pulls us into a nook between lockers. "We're going to be friends. Do you understand? Andrew is like a father to me, which kinda makes you my sister."

"Sister?" I say with disbelief.

"Yes. Sister."

Huh. If Brandon and I are brother and sister than that makes Zack…

Gross. Well, there's one way to keep my thoughts clean.

"I know you've been through some stuff lately and I understand your need to be alone but I really want us to be friends."

"Friends?" I say.

"Yep. Friends," Brandon replies. He throws his arm around my shoulders and steers me toward the cafeteria.

Friends. Can this actually happen? Can Brandon and I be friends? Andrew says I can trust him, but Andrew doesn't completely believe in my ability. I'm debating the merits of a friendship with Brandon when we walk into the cafeteria.

Once I see how many people are waiting for him at his table, I've got my answer. Brandon's friends spill over each other like plates of food at an all-you-can-eat buffet. Their confidence dictates the noise in the cafeteria.

And then right in the middle of the chaos, sitting pretty with her bean salad and ice tea, is Marnie. At least it has to be. She notices us the moment we enter the room and her eyes light up when she spies Brandon.

"I want you to meet someone," Brandon says, and he turns us so we're headed in her direction.

But Marnie doesn't wait for us to make it to the table; instead she hurries to Brandon's side as if their hips are magnetic.

"You must be Kate," she says.

"And this is my girlfriend, Marnie," Brandon laughs. "Not sure if you can tell how excited she is to meet you."

Marnie's cheeks fill with color but it only heightens her beauty. Her hair is dark and short, the kind of haircut only pretty girls can get away with, and her brown eyes are so friendly and open I can't help but smile back.

"It's nice to meet you," I say.

Do I shake her hand or hug her? I'm not sure what to do in this situation. The way she's looking at me makes me think she's expecting a hug... but I can't know for sure.

Marnie makes the decision when she wraps her arms around me like we're best friends. "I'm so glad you're here for Andrew," she whispers right before she takes a step back.

"Thanks." My smile slips off a bit when I look up and notice the rest of Brandon's table watching us like we're the afternoon movie.

It's definitely time for my escape.

"Brandon. I forgot I have to talk to Coach. I'll catch you later."

But Brandon doesn't give in that easily. He grabs a bag of chips and a fruit drink— something in the red family— and walks with me, his arm draped around Marnie's shoulders.

"Kate Triumph," Coach Abrahms says when we walk into his office. "I was just thinking about you."

"Were they happy thoughts?" I ask.

"That all depends." Coach narrows his eyes at me and they almost disappear. "Are you ready to break some track records with our team?"

"I'm really not about breaking records..." I begin, but when Brandon chokes on his drink I stop.

"Really, I'm not—"

"Listen, Triumph," Coach interrupts. "I'm seen your scores. You don't have to be modest here. We're all about achieving your best on this team."

"Alright," I say. "I guess that's fine."

The words are barely out of my mouth when Brandon whoops with joy and Coach Abrahms welcomes me with an overly aggressive handshake and a smile. "Practice is after school on Monday, Wednesday and Friday. Our first meet is this Saturday. Any reason why you wouldn't be able to make it? Tell me now, otherwise you're signed up."

"Can't think of one," I answer. But that's a lie. With the help of my mom's voice inside my head, I can think of a million.

"Great. Good to hear it." He nods once and turns back to his clipboard. "See you tomorrow at practice. Reeves, make sure she doesn't miss her next class."

And I don't. But I'm punished anyway.

Mr. Miller, the stiff and aloof-sounding English teacher makes me stand up in front of the class and introduce myself.

"Hi, I'm Kate Triumph from San Diego," I say, and make my way to the only open seat in the back of the room.

"What brought on your move to Washington?" Mr. Miller asks without the slightest speck of interest on his clean-shaven face. He's too distracted by his apparent love affair with the chalk in his hands as he writes out our reading assignment for the week.

When I don't answer he doesn't seem to care, and neither does anyone else in the class. They're all too busy holding off the food coma that always seems to hit right after lunch.

"Want a piece?"

I turn to find my fellow teammate, Emily, offering up a metal tin containing a buffet of chewing gum.

I smile and shake my head. "I'm good, thanks."

Emily blows a bubble so large that when it pops it nearly covers half her face. I take in her 'Smurfs, An Endangered Species' t-shirt and her rainbow colored fingernails, and when she catches me staring she smiles the smile of someone who's used to being stared at.

"I saw you run, you know. At the track meet — at Husky," she announces as we make our way down the hall after class. "My mom told me to watch out for you."

"What did you say?" We'd just reached my locker and I'm having a difficult time hearing her words through her chomps. It also doesn't help that the hallway is filling up with stampeding students rehashing the gossip of the day.

"My mom — she said you were going to win before you even began the race. She's got some pseudo psychic ability that she pulls out of her bag of tricks every once in a while. I think it's her secret desire to write the horoscope column in the local paper, but she believes it's real."

"Interesting," I glace down at the cheat sheet I've been carrying around in my pocket. Between the house code, garage opener code and my locker combination I'm in jeopardy of forgetting my own name.

"So she's sitting in the stands reading her *Barely Dressed* books and —"

"Her what? Embarrassing books?" Emily talks so fast I only catch certain syllables.

"Her *Barely Dressed* books," she repeats slowly. "And yes, they're embarrassing books as well — the couples are groping each other's naughty parts as if they're cannibals or something." Emily shudders like she's been hit with a bucket of ice water.

When I just stare back she adds, "You know — Livonia Locke and Henrietta Blossom? Romance novels."

I continue to blink at her blankly.

"You've never heard of Livonia Locke?"

"Can't say I have."

"Well, anyway," Emily continues, "she was reading — which she always does at track meets. She feels it's her way of supporting me even though the characters in her books could probably tell her more about my race than she could. I'm convinced she goes purely for the male attention she gets when she walks up and down the steps of the bleachers in her mini-mini skirt. My mom, she's got her own flavor of milk shake. I like to call it the 'I was fat in high school but now I'm not, so I'm gonna dress like a teenage girl whose parents don't give a damn' shake."

I grab my last book and close my locker door. "The point, Emily. I'm going to graduate before this story ends."

Emily smiles and blows another large pink bubble. "She knew. She knew you were going to win and she tried to get me to go up and talk to you — you know, find out who you were and stuff — but you seemed kinda busy."

"Busy? Busy doing what?" I drop my book-laden backpack to the ground. Emily's story doesn't seem to be anywhere near finished and it appears every teacher at this school believes I need to spend some quality time with my textbooks tonight.

"You were busy winning and I was just glad my karma was in good standing that day and I didn't have to race you. You intimidated the hell out of me, Triumph, but now that you're on my team...I think this track thing might not be so bad."

"I'm not intimidating. I just enjoy running."

"You think?" Emily smiles at me with amusement. "That part's pretty obvious. Anyone with half a wit can see that. In all honesty I'd rather just watch you compete." Emily sweeps her matching braids back off her face and sighs. "Meets can be *so* exhausting."

I laugh. "Yeah, what with the running and all."

She tilts her head to the side and grins. "You're my new hero, Kate Triumph. Just like my mom said." She deepens her voice and stands up a little taller. "'Everybody needs a hero, Emily. Without them we're just a bunch of simple-minded fools.'"

"Is your mom a man? What's with the deep voiced impersonation?" I ask.

"She just got a Laryngectomy. You know where she breathes through a hole in her neck?"

"Oh geez, Emily! I'm so sorry!"

"I'm kidding, Triumph. She just has a deep voice."

I shake my head and pick up my backpack. I can't keep up with this girl.

"You think I'm a bit odd, don't you?"

"I wouldn't exactly call it odd..." I say.

Emily laughs. "It's okay. Personally, I prefer quirky. It makes me sound cute as opposed to weird. Not that weird's bad. You seem to pull it off alright."

My eyes grow wide and I laugh humorlessly. "Weird? Really? Is that what they're calling me these days?"

"Weird, snob, recluse. Yeah, I've heard things. But you know what I'm calling it? Selective. And that's a person I can get behind. See you tomorrow, Triumph." Emily backpedals down the hall and I notice her arms are empty. No books, no backpack. Just a large giraffe-shaped purse containing what I envision to be the world's largest assortment of glitter and gum.

.   .   .

"Shore, party of four."

I look up as Andrew, Zack and Brandon start making their way to the hostess stand and then follow slightly behind. The hostess leads us to the back of the restaurant where it's less crowded and apparently the ability to see your fellow dining companions is less of a priority.

"I'm starving," Brandon announces. His head is buried in the menu.

"Kate, I hear the Fettuccini Alfredo is great here," Andrew says. He winks at me over the menu and I can't help but smile. That he remembered that Fettuccini is my favorite pasta dish is sweet. It's such a daddy/daughter moment I'm not sure whether to cry or smile.

"That sounds good," I say, and even though my meal is decided I keep my menu up. It's the best way to study Zack while he studies the menu.

We haven't had a moment alone since that incident on the stairs — the incident that keeps me up at night. I know it's natural for me to get caught up in boys my age, but the way Zack seems to affect me is different.

I remember the first time I hooked up with Gabe. It took him awhile to approach me, and I definitely didn't make it easy. He sidled up to me and said, "Hey."

And I said "hey" back.

Our conversations always began with a couple of "heys."

But Gabe was nice and sensitive. He always worried about my feelings, while I worried about letting him get too close. I never realized how important he was to me until the day he disappeared from my life. Disappeared as in he didn't follow me around anymore.

It was the night after our first kiss. A kiss so soft I didn't feel it at first. It was as if he was hovering just over my lips, blending our breath before he dared to touch me.

Finally out of sheer curiosity I kissed him, threw my hands around his neck and pulled him to me. And it was nice. Sweet.

Nothing like how I imagine Zack and my first kiss could be.

"So, how was school?" Andrew asks. He's already asked this twice but both times my "fine" wasn't a good enough answer.

"Kate's on the team," Brandon says. He hands his menu to the waitress and sits back with a smile.

"Was there ever a doubt?" Zack asks, and when he catches my eye he gives me a look that tells me he knows I've been watching him. Or perhaps I just feel guilty. Either way I blush.

"So when's your first meet?" Andrew asks once the waitress leaves with our order.

"Saturday."

"Can't wait." He rubs his hands together with anticipation.

"We're going to kick some ass! Right Kate?" Brandon exclaims.

"Right," I say, and there's a smile on my face when I take a sip of my soda. It's hard not to like Brandon, his enthusiasm for life, his all-encompassing attitude. He's growing on me. Or perhaps I'm letting him in.

Either way it's trouble.

Brandon smiles at me from across the table and I realize I feel different.

I feel relaxed. Alive. And I'm not sure how to feel about that.

During dinner I learn that Andrew has a boat. Apparently right now it's in the shop, but when it's not, it's practically his second home.

"Do you fish, Kate?" he asks.

"Um, no," I say. "I never have."

"Well, we'll have to change that." There's excitement in his eyes. They sparkle and flash like a neon sign that reads, "I get to teach my daughter how to fish!"

And I get to have a father. A *father*. I have a father.

Around the table are smiles, and they're all directed at me.

Brandon's smile says friendship, while Andrew's is more pride with a hint of happiness.

And Zack? I'm not sure I can read his exactly. Or perhaps I'm not ready to.

"Excuse me," I say, and get up from the table.

"Is everything all right," Andrew asks and I nod.

"I just have to use the restroom."

A convenient excuse, I know, but I can't help it. I have to walk away from the happy. My mom's been dead less than two weeks, and I'm feeling the beginnings of a good mood.

It doesn't feel right to feel happy. As much as I want to, I just can't.

Hidden back by the bar, I notice the ladies room has a line so I wait by the bar and watch the weather report on the TV mounted to the back wall.

Covering the days of the week are clouds and raindrops signifying more rain.

Is this some kind of joke? Meteorologists in Washington? I mean, what's the point. Why don't they just post the word, September, and then cover it with raindrops?

"Well, hello, Kate," a voice purrs.

I turn and find a dark-haired man sitting in the back corner of the bar reading a newspaper. "Strange how we keep running into each other." He gets up and walks toward me.

The lights are low in the bar but it only takes me a minute to recognize Dr. Dolus. His suit is perfectly pressed, his face clean-shaven, but it's his scent that's permanently fixed in my memory. He smells clean, too clean, like rubbing alcohol or Lysol.

"You haven't called," he says with a pout. "I was beginning to think you didn't miss me."

"I've been busy."

"Ah, well. This works out nicely then. I hear the food is great here."

I don't answer. Something in the way he's watching me forces me to take a nervous step back. I feel as if he's trying to dissect me with his eyes.

"Come now, Kate. You shouldn't fear me. Dr. Dolus only wants to help you."

"*Kate* doesn't need any help," I reply.

He raises an eyebrow and smiles. "Oh, Katie. Can I call you Katie?" he asks. "Don't you want to know why your mother came all the way to Seattle to see me?"

"Of course you do," he adds when I don't immediately respond. "It's been eating at you since the first time we met." With a smug smile he leans back against the bar as if he has all the time in the world. "Go ahead, Katie. Ask away."

"My name's Kate."

His smile widens but he stays silent, waiting for me to bite.

"Why?" I finally ask, but Dr. Dolus only raises his eyebrows in challenge. "Why," I begin again with a sigh, "did my mom come and see you?"

"She realized what you and I already know — that you're different from everyone else and well, your mother was a little frightened of that." With a shake of his head, his eyes peer down at me. "Kids can be so cruel."

I clench my hands into fists to keep them from shaking. Fear is a difficult thing to hold down. "I don't know what you're talking about," I say. "There's nothing wrong with me."

Dr. Dolus chuckles. "Wrong? I never said there was anything wrong. That was your word." He shakes his head. "Girls — such a lack of confidence. No, there's nothing *wrong* with you, just something very right. I created you. I'm the reason you exist. Your mother couldn't get pregnant and came to me for help. You see, it's my specialty." He smiles. "At least it was. Now I've moved on to bigger and more lucrative things." When I remain silent, he continues. "Your mother wanted us to meet. She knew how busy I am and so she came to set it up with me first. When I heard about your situation I was immediately concerned for you." He leans forward. "Tell me, how is high school these days?"

My jaw tightens. "What did my mother tell you?"

"Your secret," he smiles.

My stomach drops and I look around for an escape.

"She was going to talk to you about coming to see me but I guess she never had the chance." He takes another step and I glare up at him. The sympathy in his eyes is making me nauseated.

"What do you want with me?"

He chuckles once again and gazes down at me appreciatively. "I do like a girl who gets to the point." He leans in and I notice his eyes appear even tinier up close. "I want to help you, Kate. This ability you have could truly harm you if anyone were to find out. Think of what they'd do to you. Different isn't the new pink, as they say. And I can only imagine how hard it would be for a young girl like you. It's so important to fit in at your age. I feel it's my responsibility to make everything better — for you and for your beautiful mother. May she rest in peace knowing her daughter is just like everybody else. Ordinary." His mouth turns down when he says this word as if it's tastes foul or something and then his expression changes. "Don't you think she deserves that?"

I take a deep breath. I have to run. I have to get away.

"I only need you for a few short months," he explains. His voice sounds far off like I'm falling into a hole. "It shouldn't take very long to fix you," he says and then he laughs, causing his eyes to disappear completely. "Fix you! As if you're broken."

My mouth is watering like I'm going to be sick. "I'm not—" I stop and choke on the word "broken."

"You would be paid quite handsomely for your time, of course. Think of all the money you'd be able to spend at the mall with all of your friends. Oh, wait," he pauses for effect. "Your mom did mention something about how you like to keep to yourself." He reaches out and his cold hand touches the top of mine. "Isn't that a bit lonely, my dear?"

"I have to go," I say and I'm proud that I manage to get the words past my trembling lips.

"Wait! Think of all the people you could help. Do you know how many patients die of Cancer every year? If we explored your ability to heal — we could cure Cancer. HIV. Alzheimer's." Dr. Dolus pauses dramatically. "You would be a hero, Kate."

"And you would be a very rich man."

"Don't you think you owe it to your mother?" he continues. "She was so concerned, why just talking about you made those beautiful green eyes of hers tear up."

I flinch, just like he wants me to. "Stop," I say. "I'm not interested."

I turn my back on Dr. Dolus. Only ten long strides back to my table.

"Kate!" he calls out.

I stop and debate whether or not to turn around. His tone has changed. He no longer sounds sympathetic and kind. A note of impatience has entered his voice. "You may as well come now, before they know."

I turn, my face tight with annoyance.

"Do you honestly think they'll never find out?" He gestures around the restaurant. "How long, Kate, before the rest of the world discovers you? A few weeks? A month?" He moves closer like he's on wheels and when I look down I see his shiny shoes are sliding on the carpet. "Accidents happen, my dear. What if something happened during a race? Isn't that what your mother feared the most? All those bleachers filled with carefree and excited onlookers." He closes his eyes as if he's picturing it. "It's a beautiful day for a race, proud parents and smiling, students all waiting for the show to begin." His eyes shoot open and flash at me. "Oh, and what a show they're going to see. It's only a matter of time before they point at you, screaming in fear, while your body heals itself in front of their very eyes." And then suddenly he's upon me, his face in my face, his wild eyes filling my vision. "How long, Kate? How long before your secret is out?"

My feet won't move. I'm lost in the picture he's painting. It's not like I haven't seen it before. Me covered in blood, running, racing from the eyes that within minutes will widen with horror.

"John protected you last time," Dr. Dolus whispers. "Oh, yes. I know about his little trick. Clever. Very clever." He reaches out and grips my arm. "Is he here *now*, Kate? Will he always be around?"

I stare up into his beady eyes and take a breath, but it's shaky at best. "I don't know what you're talking about. You must have me confused with s-s-someone else," I stutter.

But my brave stutter only makes him smile.

He leans in close and I can almost taste the glass of wine he was drinking. "I applaud your acting skills but I don't have time for this silly game, my dear. The truth is you need me as much as I need you. Before your mother paid me a visit I was certain those years were a complete and utter waste of time. And now I come to find I was a success. A brilliant success." His fingers dig into my arm. "I need this. I need to understand exactly what went right."

"What do you mean? It was some kind of experiment?" His fingers are hurting me but I don't pull away. I'm caught up in his words. "Did my mother know?" I whisper.

"She got what she wanted."

"She wanted a baby," I yell and then quickly lower my voice. "What did you do to her?"

Dr. Dolus doesn't respond.

"There were others, weren't there? You experimented on those poor women and they lost their babies."

"You shouldn't believe everything you read, my dear."

"That's funny," I snap. "My mom used to tell me I shouldn't believe everything I hear."

His eyes narrow and then his thin attempt at a smile returns. "You must take after your father. Your mother never disrespected me this way."

"Perhaps if she were still alive…?" I force my gaze away from his sickening smile and look up at the TV directly behind his head. The woman on the screen is smiling and overly excited that she's successfully removed a dark stain from her white shirt. She holds up two shirts, one that is clean and one with a large stain across the front.

Blood. The stain resembles blood.

"I'm pretty sure we have nothing more to talk about, Dr. Dolus, I think it would be best if you left me alone."

I have to get out of here. I take a step toward the restaurant and then feel his cold hand once again grip my arm.

"Kate—"

"I'm not a science experiment!" I hiss and jerk my arm away.

He opens his mouth to respond and then slowly closes it. His eyes are communicating everything he wants to say but can't. Luckily their meaning is lost in the dim lighting of the bar.

The walk back to my table is longer than I remember. Perhaps it's the heaviness of the conversation with Dr. Dolus still resting upon my shoulders. I don't look back even though I know he's watching me.

Please, just go away, I silently plead. And. Leave. Me. Alone.

Seventeen

"You're awfully quiet tonight. Was the first day that bad?" We're on our way home from dinner and Andrew's still digging for answers. Can't fault him for his perseverance.

"Really, Andrew," I say with a forced smile. "The first day wasn't that bad."

It could have been worse. Much, much worse, say if Dr. Dolus had shown up at my school with a pack of attack dogs.

"You're just so quiet, and you barely touched your food." Andrew isn't going to let it go.

"Just thinking about my mom a lot today," I say.

"Right."

And... cue silence.

But the truth is I can't get Dr. Dolus' voice out of my head. *Secret. Fix you. Freak.* The last one I added. It's always a good fit when talking about myself. I don't need anyone to say the word aloud.

So was my mom aware of Dr. Dolus' plans? Or did she go in hoping for a baby and instead came away with a healthy bundle of weird? No. It's not possible. Not my mom. She never would have signed up to be a lab rat.

"Did you enjoy dinner?" Andrew asks. He's watching me from the passenger seat; in his lap is a white Styrofoam box with my Fettuccini inside.

"Yes. The food was great." That is what I ate of it.

After my rendezvous with Dr. Dolus I had the chilling sensation I was being watched, but when I looked up all seemed normal in the restaurant. Normal amount of laughter. Normal amount of dishes clanking. Normal amount of conversation. One would think if evil were lurking there'd be some kind of warning, or at least the background music should change. But the music in the restaurant was soothing and soft.

"Your turn is coming up," Andrew announces just as I notice the Walgreens on the corner. I hit the right hand signal and then headlights bounce off my rearview mirror, blinding me. The car behind me is flashing his brights, not in an exasperated "I want to go faster than you" way, but in a "You better move now or get run down" sort of way.

"Does he want me to move over?" I ask Andrew. "I'm already in the right lane."

Andrew turns around in his seat. Suddenly the Jeep lurches forward and my fingers grip the steering wheel with alarm. The car nudged me from behind.

"Keep going, Kate. Step on the gas and keep driving." Andrew's voice has an edge and I instantly react to it. My foot stomps on the gas and we shoot forward.

"Did I cut him off? Is that why he's being so aggressive?" No sooner do I say the words when the car races up from behind and once again bumps the back of the Jeep. My eyes fly to my rearview mirror and Andrew spins back around.

I step on the gas. The Jeep isn't handling the speed and neither am I. Both are shaking from a combination of performance anxiety and lack of experience. Not to mention I feel like I'm reliving a nightmare.

"Andrew? What's going on?" My eyes are wide with fear.

"I want you to listen to me very carefully, Kate, and do exactly as I say. Okay?" His voice is calm, much calmer than I believe he should be. The car is pulling around into the left lane and it's much too close to the driver side of the Jeep. I turn the wheel instinctively to the right and swerve toward the shoulder.

"Kate!" Andrew grips my right arm. "Listen to me."

"What?" My eyes are fixed ahead, my face tense. The past is blending with the present and I'm becoming hysterical. It's as if we're back on the PCH and any moment now I'll hear my mom scream.

"Kate." Andrew's voice is close. He's facing me — his seat belt no longer on — while he coaxes me soothingly. "I need you to listen very carefully. I'm going to take the wheel and slowly move my foot down to the gas pedal —"

"What?" I turn toward him and my quick movement causes the Jeep to swerve.

"Listen to me!" His eyes shoot to the road in front of us while I right the Jeep once again. "I've done this before. It's going to be fine. See, my hand is taking the wheel —" My eyes shift between Andrew and the road. "Now I'm going to move my left foot toward the gas pedal and as I edge closer to you you'll sit up slightly so that I can slide underneath. Do you understand?"

"No, I can't. This is insane. I —" My voice rises in alarm and the Jeep swerves again when I pull his hand off the steering wheel. "No. I'm driving. *I'm* driving. You can't just take the wheel while I'm driving!"

The road in front of us is morphing rapidly into the PCH and my mind is conjuring up images of the smiling man behind the wheel.

"Kate. You have to trust me. I can get us out of this. Do you understand?"

The car pulls up alongside of us again and I step down hard on the gas. But the car is much faster.

"We're not going to be able to outrun him. The only option we have is to let me drive. Trust me!"

I turn then and look at him. The intensity in his expression slices through my recurring nightmare.

"Alright." My breathing is fast and I force down a steadying breath into my lungs. "What do you want me to do?"

This time when Andrew explains everything I sit up and listen. Slowly I ease my foot off the gas and Andrew's foot moves in underneath. His hands move to the steering wheel and I release my hold. I push up off the seat with all my strength and allow him enough room to slide underneath. I end up in his lap.

Without obscuring his view, I roll to the vacant passenger seat. I've just reached the seat when he turns the wheel hard to his left and the Jeep spins into oncoming traffic. I scream at each car that whizzes by.

"Put your seatbelt on, Kate," Andrew orders. He punches the gas and the Jeep races down the highway in the wrong direction. Andrew's expression is calm and steady — just like his hands. He doesn't appear phased when the oncoming cars honk and swerve out of our way.

I don't think fast enough to cover my eyes; instead I watch in complete and utter amazement as Andrew navigates the Jeep in between each car like a pro.

It feels like a lifetime that we're fighting for room on the crowded highway but it's only seconds before Andrew pulls off the main road.

The car that was following us is long gone and my heart is desperate to return to its normal pace. I focus on breathing while Andrew takes the long way home.

"I need to make sure we aren't followed," he says.

And even though his words sound like a foreign language to me right now, I nod.

I sit back as we ride through unfamiliar neighborhoods. My eyes are frozen on the road. I can feel Andrew's occasional glance but I'm too busy willing us home safe to look at him. I'm still gripping my seat; my fingernails are imbedded in the soft upholstery.

"Are you alright, Kate?" Andrew's words are spoken softly but I still jump in response.

"Yes."

"You did great, you know. You were terrified and yet you didn't let it get to you. You were very brave."

When I turn toward him my expression is calm, almost unfeeling, just like his. Andrew's eyes narrow upon my face. "Kate? Are you sure you're alright?"

I peel my hands from the seat and relax my fingers. "I'm fine."

The road is dark. It continues to conceal our location until I begin to recognize some familiar landmarks: the house where I first heard the footsteps, the hill where I met up with Brandon. Three more blocks. Three more. I take a deep breath and lean back against my seat. I'm relieved when our neighborhood finally reveals itself.

When Andrew's hands tighten on the steering wheel I whip around with a soft whimper. The headlights are back, speeding toward us once again.

Andrew floors the gas and the Jeep takes off, but the sedan catches up with us easily. I watch in horror as it pulls around us in preparation for another round of bumper cars.

"This guy needs a new trick," Andrew growls, before he stomps on the brake and turns the wheel hard to the right. Suddenly we're in the woods. The scratching sound of trees clawing at my window confirms it. I grip the dashboard, watching the branches whizz by while we bump along a dirt path.

I'm praying our assailant doesn't dare follow us into the woods but within seconds I can see the same set of headlights bumping along behind us. He's determined to get to us. I glance over at Andrew. He's wearing a menacing smile.

"Andrew?"

The smile quickly turns to concern.

"It's alright, Kate. He can't go very far along this road. I don't know if he's stupid or just committed. Either way it's only a matter of time before he gets stuck."

He. Who's *he*?

"What does he want? Why is he following us?"

I'm not sure who I'm asking, Andrew or myself, but neither of us responds.

The Jeep delves deeper into the woods and I hold on tight while Andrew continues to display a clear knack for reckless offroading. The car is still behind us, its headlights growing faint as it decreases its speed. It's no match for the forest closing in.

"Hold on," is all the warning I get before Andrew uses the side of a hill to change direction. As the Jeep climbs, its engine roars with determination. Fighting against gravity I cling to my seat. My eyes are squeezed shut. But after three deep breaths, the world rights itself and the Jeep lands back down on all fours.

"That was fun," I say. My heart is racing.

Andrew flicks the headlights off and darkness swallows us. We're crawling toward the faint headlights of the car in the distance. We watch a tall figure jump out of the car and throw himself up against the hood. With all his might he pushes, but the small sedan appears to be stuck.

"Do you think he needs some help?" I say, my shaky voice betraying my act of bravado.

Andrew is waiting. For what, I don't know. His face is tense and resolute.

"Perhaps I should offer my services," he says.

This time it isn't Andrew's expression that chills me, but his tone. I'm relieved I can't see face, I'm convinced the look in his eyes would scare me.

The figure climbs back into his car and kills the lights, disappearing into the night. Andrew flips our headlights on, and the car is back. But it's too late. The driver's side door is left open, and the man is gone.

I reach over and lock my door, it seems silly at this point but it makes me feel safer. Andrew presses the button for the off road lights and the brightly lit trees began to dance like they're on stage. He reaches into the backseat and grabs a black duffle bag tucked underneath. I watch him pull out a small flare gun.

"If you see him coming out of the trees before you see me, aim it into the air. If he gets too close, aim it at him."

He places it in my hands and I gaze at him in shock.

"You're leaving me?"

"I'll be right back, Kate. Remember what I said." He leaps from the Jeep and creeps stealthily toward the abandoned car. I'm left to huddle inside the Jeep.

Andrew reaches the passenger side of the car and I feel like my heart is about to explode. My breathing is racing my heartbeat, creating a dizzying effect. Only the soft purr of the car's engine can be heard above my panic.

It's a trap.

Andrew sees it coming before I do. The car's engine roars to life but I don't have any time to react. Andrew is helpless on foot as the car charges toward the Jeep like a cornered animal. It hits hard — head on — and I'm thrown forward into the windshield.

I crumple to the floor as if I'm boneless. A few drops of blood trickle down my face. My head is pounding, the rhythm pulsing through my body.

And then I hear the car fly into reverse.

Not again. Please!

I start to climb the seats. I have to get out of here.

But this time the tires are spinning and aimed in a new direction.

"Andrew!" I yell, ignoring the pain splitting my head open. My father is illuminated in a blinding light that ricochets off a shiny object in his hands. Is it a gun?

He has a gun?

Two shots fire — and then a third. Andrew stands his ground and faces the car like a warrior, a warrior bearing down on a car-shaped dragon.

I don't see what happens next.

My head is pounding. When the headlights grow faint and darkness spreads toward me, I whisper Andrew's name. I'm falling. Did I climb out of the Jeep? I reach up to rub the moisture from my eyes. Is it raining again? Am I crying? I feel a large gash in my forehead and when I pull my hand away, it's covered in blood. There's a black fog moving in. It's so heavy it pushes my eyelids down. I hear more gunshots, but they sound distant and muffled.

"What do you mean, take her home? Are you insane, John?"

Throbbing. I awake to Andrew yelling and a whole lot of throbbing. It gradually dissipates while I feel my head diminish in size. The swelling is going down.

I'm used to the signs now. First the pain, then the numbness until everything feels brand new. It's the only way to describe it — like starting over or beginning fresh.

"I just called to find out what blood type she is, just in case they ask, and you're telling me to turn around and go home? You're a damn doctor, John! She's lost too much blood to just put a Band-Aid on it and—"

"A negative," I whisper.

"What?" Andrew turns toward me and I open my eyes long enough to notice we're still in the Jeep.

"My blood type. A negative. But I won't need any. Blood. John's right. Take me home."

The next time I open my eyes I'm in bed and Andrew's sitting at my side. Relief showers down upon me until I see Andrew's eyes. They're large and wild. His reaction to my healing is very familiar — it was always the same with my mom. The eyes always react first, and then the jaw slackens, which leads to the eventual, full-fledged openmouthed shock. After that, the image is complete.

Andrew is stunned.

I look down at my hands. They're already healed. No trace of the tiny cuts from the broken glass. Andrew reaches out and tenderly touches my forehead where the large cut was, stretching from the top of my hairline to my eyebrow. The deep and gruesome injury must have worried him when he carried me to my room but now my skin is smooth and flawless.

"I told you," I say. "You didn't believe me."

"Kate," Andrew whispers. "You're unbelievable."

I look away. "I'm weird."

He shakes his head in wonderment and I continue, "Have you ever been to the circus, Andrew?"

"The circus?" He searches my face for some sign of logic.

"Yes, the circus. You know — clowns and elephants and tightrope walkers?"

"You're not a circus freak, Kate."

"You mean you don't see the similarity between me and the bearded lady?"

Andrew laughs. "Well, maybe the hair."

I reach up in horror. My hair is matted to my scalp with dried blood. I look at Andrew. "Where is he?"

His eyes darken. "He's gone."

"Gone?"

"Yes, Kate. Gone."

"Not dead, but — gone?"

"Yes, unfortunately. Only gone."

I don't know how I feel about this. I remember a scene from earlier and my eyes widen. "You had a gun."

Andrew hesitates. "I always carry one as a precaution."

"Just like the flare gun and the duffle bag of emergency supplies?"

"It's important to be prepared."

"Prepared? Prepared for what?"

"Anything. You should always prepare for the worst. The element of surprise is better anticipated than experienced."

Another quote. I smile. "Is that something your dad used to say or is it another work related thing?"

Andrew's eyes are guarded. "Either way it's important."

I fall silent and begin twisting my ring around my finger.

"How long, Kate? How long have you had this ability?"

Our eyes meet and I sigh. "I don't know. I mean I know when I became aware of it but by my mom's stories it's been going on a lot longer than that."

"Take a guess."

"Since birth maybe? It wasn't anything crazy that happened. I was never hit by a car or shot on the street or anything like that." I steal a glance up at Andrew and then wish I hadn't. His expression is rather formidable. "I was two," I hurry to explain. "My mom said she had suspicions before then, like when cuts or bumps disappeared overnight or when she took me to get my ears pierced at eight months old —" I point to my hole-less ear lobes and make a face. "Really puts a damper on a girl's need to accessorize."

Andrew raises an eyebrow and I continue.

"I was very intrigued by the sliding glass door. My mom said she turned around for a mere second just to throw something in the oven and the next thing she knew I was screaming and blood was everywhere. It was a clean slice. I don't know how she managed to get me wrapped up and into the car when she saw the tip of my finger just dangling there. A pretty gruesome scene." I shudder. "She held me in her lap the whole way to the hospital while driving with one hand." I pause. This is my least favorite part of the story. But Andrew is hanging on every word.

"They rushed me in to a room, unwrapped my mother's makeshift tourniquet and much to their surprise found no reason for all of the blood."

"Your finger had healed."

I nod. "Like it was brand-spankin' new."

"In the matter of an hour?"

"Less than that. The hospital was only a five minute ride from our house and it was a slow day so they were able to get us right in."

When Andrew continues to study me I add, "I used to think it was my mom's doing. You know, kiss it better and all that." My eyes are suddenly stinging and my throat feels tight. "Any time I got hurt she was there, comforting me, kissing my scraped knee or bruised forehead." I glance down at my ring. "I was eight when I finally realized it was me." With a deep breath I force myself to meet Andrew's eyes and find he's watching me with concern. "It was just a simple bike accident," I hurry to explain. "I loved racing down this one hill. The loose gravel near the bottom only added to the rush, but on that day I hit it wrong and went flying. I didn't cry. I brushed myself off, ignored the blood trickling from my knees and hands and hurried home." With a shrug I finish, "You can guess what happened next." My eyes drop to my smooth hands. "My mom didn't even know I got hurt that day."

"And your casts, Kate?"

"Unnecessary."

"Then why—"

"Appearances, Andrew. It's always about appearances." There's no mistaking the bite to my tone. "Oh, and that reporter that kept calling. John was concerned he would show up to the funeral."

"What reporter?" Andrew asks.

I laugh humorlessly. "They wanted to do a human interest story on me. Can't you see it? 'High school senior wins world record and loses beloved mother in the same day.'" My hands fall limply onto the bed. "What a story that would make," I whisper.

Andrew curses under his breath. "Do you know his name?"

"No. John was the only one who talked with him. I never answered the phone."

"I see. And John? How long has he known?"

"I didn't know he did until after the funeral. I guess he and my mom had some kind of plan worked out." I pause. "Just in case."

"Is there…anything else, Kate?" Andrew asks after a moment of silence. "Any other abilities or…?"

"Just one," I whisper. Strangely enough this one is far harder to admit to.

"Your speed."

"Yes."

"And was your speed immediate or did it increase over time?"

"I've always been fast. I just didn't realize how fast I was until I began to push myself."

I know what's coming. I can almost see the words forming on his tongue.

"How fast are you, Kate?"

I smooth the blankets down along my legs and then meet my father's eyes. "My mom used to say I was too fast. Too fast and too inquisitive."

"And how fast is that?"

A slow protective fire spreads through me and the best word to describe it would be: pride.

"No one can catch me. That is, no one *I* know."

When Andrew doesn't say anything my confidence dwindles and I begin twisting my ring. He must have so many questions for me. How could he not? But he remains quiet. Truthfully, I feel a bit relieved that he knows. It's like someone else has joined the "I know the truth about Kate Triumph and I still like her" team.

"Your ring is beautiful."

I slip it off my finger and hold it out to him. "My mom made it. It's her design."

Andrew holds the ring gently in his hand and inspects it from every angle.

"My car!" My eyes suddenly well up. "He killed my car."

"Well, it's not dead, but it needs a lot of work." He studies me for a minute and then says, "Perhaps we should try something...bigger."

"Like?"

"How would you feel about a Hummer?"

I stare at him in disbelief. "An army vehicle? You want me to drive an army vehicle?"

Andrew smiles. "No?"

Eighteen

"I won't be around for dinner tonight, Kate. Will you be alright?"

"You got a date?"

It's possible. For all I know he's already got a girl tucked away in a townhouse somewhere. Andrew's a very attractive guy. The waitress at the restaurant last night made a fool of herself, batting her eyelashes and bringing our table extra food. By the time we left I was surprised, Holly — the all so helpful waitress — didn't offer to drive us home.

Without looking up from his breakfast, Andrew reads my mind. "I don't have a girlfriend, Kate. Not now, not before you got here. I'm going to Tacoma."

"Sounds fun. What's in Tacoma?"

"The car that followed us last night was stolen from a guy in Tacoma. I'm headed down there this afternoon to talk with him and see if he has any ideas on who may have taken it. I should be back before dark." He looks up from his paper. "You're sure you'll be alright on your own?"

"I'll be fine, Andrew." I spread my arms out wide. "See, all healed, inside and out." But my eyes don't quite tell the same story, and we both know it. Last night's off-roading has taken its toll. My eyes are as heavy and dark as Andrew's, but neither of us is willing to admit to it.

I take a sip of my orange juice "Do you think he's lying? Maybe reporting it stolen was just a cover."

"I don't think he's lying but I'll know more this evening. Kate, last night must have been terrifying for you. Are you sure you're okay?"

My armor slips a bit when I look up and see the concern in his eyes. But I know better. Show weakness and get locked inside my room. At least that was the way of it with my mom.

"No worries. I think the part that bothered me the most, well, besides the fact that he was trying to run us off the road and all, was seeing my mom's car."

Andrew looks up from his paper. "What do you mean?"

"The car that followed us — the Honda Accord — it's what my mom used to drive. Same make, same model, even the same exact color. I think that's why it got to me so much."

"Are you telling me that's the same car your mother was driving when she was killed?"

"Yes." I lean across the counter. "Do you think it's too coincidental?"

"I think," Andrew brushes the top of my hair, "we're going to be late getting you to school."

I groan and grab my backpack off the floor. "So, are you my new chauffeur?"

"Just for a little while."

"Until the Jeep is fixed?"

"Something like that."

"So tell me, Andrew. Where did you learn to drive like a cop?"

We're on our way to school in Andrew's silver sports car.

"Like a what?" he asks, pretending interest in the radio.

"You know all race car driver-ish with a hint of James Bond."

"James Bond, eh?" he says with a laugh.

"Uh, yeah! You didn't even seem freaked out. While I, on the other hand, was about to have a breakdown."

"You did great, Kate."

"So?"

"So, what?"

"Seriously, Andrew?"

"What?" he laughs.

"Where'd you learn to drive like that?"

"Would you believe me if I said the Army?" We pull up in front of my school and he hands me my backpack.

"Not really," I say, eyeing him suspiciously.

"Well, then." Andrew smiles at me and for a second I think he might lean across the car and kiss me goodbye, but instead he tousles my hair and says, "Have a good day, Kate. Play nice with the other kids."

•   •   •

Andrew's map was so helpful the day before that I leave it in my backpack and only once drag it out to find a restroom. Day two is very similar to day one with one exception — I'm just as sparkling new but now everyone knows my name. Oh, and that Brandon and I are friends.

If one more girl comes up to me and asks about his and Marnie's relationship I'm going to scream. Or bite. I haven't quite made up my mind. The only thing that gets me through is the promise of track practice right after school.

The boy's team is already warming up when I walk out to the field. I notice the girl's team is sitting in a circle stretching, so I head their way.

Emily introduces me to each girl, their names blurring together in a Stephanie-Ally-Lisa kinda way except for one girl, Heather, who appears familiar to me. When she catches me staring at her she smiles shyly and I have a flashback of her in red running shorts and a black tank top.

"You were at Husky?" I say and she nods.

"Heather came in second behind you, Triumph. Out of everyone here she's the one who's going to give you a run for your money. Get it?" Emily laughs at her pun while the other girls groan.

"It's not like that," Heather says. Her eyes are wide like she's just been startled and then she smiles. "I'm kinda a freak around here. They all make fun of me because I love running so much. But I don't care if I win, I just like to run." Her brown eyes flutter up to mine and then drop back to the ground, where she picks at the blades of grass, studying each piece as if out of nowhere they've become fascinating. "I know that's weird...but..."

"It's not weird," I say. "I get it."

Heather looks up and I find myself smiling at her.

"Triumph *totally* gets weird, Heather."

"Well no one's weirder than you, Emily," another girl — Sheila, I think— calls out and everyone laughs. Emily grins like it's a compliment. Today she's dressed in a bright purple jogging suit with Rainbow Bright on the front and her hair is braided like Princess Leia.

"We're going shopping Saturday after the meet. You in, Triumph?"

"Shopping?" I dig around in my suitcase of excuses but come up with nothing.

"And how do you feel about gaudy off-key attempts at popular music?" Emily continues.

"At the mall?"

"No, Triumph," she laughs. "Karaoke."

I wonder if I somehow missed the joke. The other girls are smiling and laughing right along with Emily.

And there's my answer.

"You see, Kate," she explains, "my karaoke parties are legendary. That is, they would be if we'd planned more than one last year. But I'm feeling truly inspired to throw one together in your honor."

"Don't do me any favors, Cooke," I say. Better to stop the insanity now.

Emily laughs. She appears nonplussed by my obvious lack of enthusiasm. "Just say you're in, Triumph."

"I don't think—"

"Great! We'll be leaving for the mall right after the track meet on Saturday."

Heather looks up and smiles at me sympathetically. "Sometimes it's easier if you just say, yes, and then come up with an excuse later. At least it works for me."

"But I don't think—" I begin again and then I'm cut off by Coach Abrahms' whistle.

"Alright, girls. Let's hit the track," he yells.

And I climb to my feet.

Aside from the will-not-take-no-for-an-answer shopping invitation from Emily, track practice goes off without a hitch. My body feels strong — stronger than it has in weeks — and by the end of practice at least half the girls on my team are smiling at me, and not in a menacing way. I'm not sure what to think of this place. I may have to steal someone's boyfriend to get these kids to hate me.

Or perhaps I could just roll with it. The thought comes out of nowhere and takes me by surprise.

"You ready, neighbor?" I stroll up to Brandon, my ride home. I might even be smiling.

"Oh, I forgot to tell you, Kate. Marnie and I can't take you home. There's an emergency student council meeting. Zack's going to take you. He should be out front by now."

"Actually I'm right here."

I whip around and there's Zack. He's dressed in a suit and tie, and I catch my breath. Damn you, Zack Reeves, for being so irresistible. Damn you to hell.

I wish my running shorts were a little fancier. Red with a white stripe up the side doesn't hold a candle to Zack's silky, polka-dot tie.

"Hey Zack. Thanks for taking over Kate-duty."

I glare at Brandon and the brothers laugh. "Kate-duty? Nice, Brandon. I'll remember that the next time *you* need a ride."

Brandon snorts in disgust. "A ride with you? No thanks. You've had that Jeep less than forty-eight hours and you've already destroyed it. I'd rather walk."

"I didn't destroy my Jeep, Brandon. Somebody—"

"Don't worry, Kate," Zack interrupts smoothly. "You know why Brandon doesn't drive anymore? He can't afford to. And it's not the price of gas keeping him off the road. It's the sheer amount of speeding and parking tickets he gets in a month."

"It wasn't a speeding ticket, Zack. I told you, it was a construction zone ticket."

Zack bursts out laughing. "Right, Brandon. You got a *speeding* ticket for *speeding* through a construction zone."

Brandon smiles sheepishly. "Yeah, that's right. I forgot about that."

"Hey, Brandon. I'm here to steal you away. Chaos is erupting in the student lounge." A tall brunette with laughing eyes and legs too long to be legal sidles up to Brandon and throws an arm around his shoulders. She doesn't seem put out by her mission, in fact, I'm pretty sure she volunteered. She appears to be the friendly type. But when her inquisitive eyes move on to Zack, I decide I don't like her.

"Gotta go, guys." Brandon shrugs the attractive girl's arm off his shoulder in a friendly yet forceful way. A solid demonstration of why Brandon is the alpha. Poise, confidence and a smile. He could be the poster child for the great American teen. "There's a war going on over the Homecoming dance," Brandon explains. "Something about global warming and temperature controlled rooms." He rolls his eyes and runs off with the brunette close behind.

I'm left underdressed and unprepared for my ride home with Zack.

"Ready, Kate?" he asks and I eye him uneasily.

"I wish you'd told me about the dress code. I would have shoved my evening gown in my backpack."

Zack laughs. "Yeah, sorry about that. I had an interview after my last class today and didn't have time to change." He bends down to grab my backpack off the ground and slips it over his shoulder. "I got here a little early and caught the tail end of practice. Do you feel ready for Saturday's meet?"

I try not to think about Zack sitting up in the stands watching me run. "You tell me, Zack. Do you think I'm ready?"

His beautiful eyes linger on my face and I have to turn away, or get trapped for good. "The first time I saw you run was at Husky," he says. "You were extraordinary then and you still are, Kate. So, yeah, I'd say you're ready."

Extraordinary. I like this word.

We walk up to a dark green Land Rover and Zack reaches in his pocket for his keys. On the side of the car painted in black is the name Defender.

"You named your car?"

Zack laughs at the horror in my voice. "No, *I* didn't name it. The manufacturer did. My dad just made sure everybody knew it. He was very proud of his car."

"I can tell." I walk around the car, inspecting it from every angle. Mostly I'm avoiding looking directly at Zack. "So now it's yours."

"Now it's mine."

"It's nice," I say. "It fits you."

Crap. Why did I say that?

Zack laughs. "I'll take that as a compliment."

"Okay," I say, and shrug my shoulders. My face evolves into my blank expression. I feel safer this way.

"I heard you were going to be all alone for dinner tonight? I was thinking pizza. You interested?"

"I'm not that hungry," I say.

"And do you plan on being 'not that hungry' all night?"

"Probably," I say.

We're driving toward Andrew's house and luckily Zack's car is pretty loud which makes conversation difficult.

"I'm spending the night with you Kate. I promised Andrew."

"You're—" My throat dries up and all I can do is blink.

"He doesn't want you to be alone, so you have two choices: eat out or eat in."

"Out," I say, while looking straight ahead.

I don't have to look at him to see he finds my quick response amusing.

I can hear it in his laughter.

Gourmet Pizza has thirty different types of pizza on their menu but after poring over it for more than fifteen minutes Zack and I opt for the extremely unoriginal, but always popular, pepperoni and cheese.

"So what was this interview for?" I ask when the waitress moves on to the next table.

Zack leans back in the booth. "A job."

"That's a fascinating story, Zack. Can I hear it again?"

He laughs and scoots forward in his seat. "Sorry. It's just that Andrew doesn't know about the interview so I don't really want to say anything."

I narrow my eyes in confusion. "And do you tell Andrew everything?"

"No, but if he knew I was applying for this position, I don't think he'd be too happy about it."

"I don't understand. Why wouldn't he want you to take this job? Is it dangerous?" I cover my face with my hands and gasp dramatically. "Is it some kind of secret job? Like a spy?"

I expect him to laugh but instead his face grows serious. "It's just something I've been wanting to look into.

And I didn't tell Andrew because I don't think he'll feel it's a good career move."

I sit back. "Well, what kind of career move would Andrew approve of?"

"He just wants me to finish school and become an engineer. Something practical and predictable."

"And what do you want, Zack?"

His eyes meet mine and hold. "Something else."

"Okay." I pull my drink closer and concentrate on drinking. "So tell me. Why *did* Andrew go to Tacoma? Don't the police usually handle these things on their own?"

Zack laughs. "Yeah. That's usually how it works. But not for Andrew."

"Why is that? Does Andrew know somebody in the police department?"

"Oh, he knows a lot of people..." Zack trails off but I'm still waiting for an answer. "I mean, yeah. He's got some friends on the force."

"Did you know Andrew owns a gun?"

The way Zack looks at me answers my question. "He owns a few. Does that concern you?"

"Should it?"

"A lot of people own guns. You know, the second amendment and all that."

"Uh huh. The second amendment." I use my straw to push the ice cubes to the bottom of my glass but they always pop back up.

"What exactly is bothering you, Kate? The fact that Andrew has a gun or that he used it on someone who was trying to harm you?"

I look up. "So he told you then."

Zack just nods.

"Did he tell you how I was driving and then I wasn't driving because Andrew did some crazy maneuver while the car was still moving?"

Zack smiles. "He didn't give me all the details, but yes. I would assume that could happen."

I stare at him a minute while he stares back. He knows something, something he isn't telling me.

"Andrew worked a lot?" I ask. "You know, before he was retired."

"Yeah."

"So he was rarely home? Mostly on the road?"

"Pretty much," Zack says.

"Do you know what he did, exactly?"

"What are you getting at, Kate?"

"I'm not getting at anything, Zack. It's just a question."

"He worked in security."

"Yeah, that's what I hear."

"And?"

"Well, he's a pretty good shot. Not to mention his impeccable driving skills."

Zack is quiet.

"It's not really something you just do, you know? Stay calm and drive like that…

"Why don't you ask *him* about it?" Zack says.

"Ask Andrew?" I repeat.

"Yeah. Why not? And besides," Zack adds after a period of silence, "he couldn't be that good of a shot. The guy got away."

"He wasn't aiming at him. He wanted to make sure his car wouldn't hit me again."

"He shot out the front tires," Zack says. It's not a question but I answer anyway.

"One shot each. He would've shot the guy next. I'm sure of it. But I distracted him. If I hadn't passed out —" I stop. I've said too much. There's no way he's told Zack *everything*. If that were the case Zack would be looking at me a lot differently right now.

"It must have really freaked you out," Zack says and I nod.

"Yeah." Let him think that.

Zack reaches out and takes my hand, and I can't help it, I flinch. "This ring you're wearing — I notice it every time you move your hand. It's really beautiful."

"Thank you," I reply and pull my hand away. "It's my mother's design. She was a jewelry designer."

"Yeah, Andrew mentioned something about that."

I look away and focus back on my drink. I don't want to talk about my mom with Zack. Or rather I don't want the subject to be changed.

"So... I saw his face," I say quietly.

"Who?" Zack glances up at me in surprise. "The person who ran you off the road?"

"It was a man. I know that for certain."

"How do you know?"

"Andrew thought the same."

"Was it perhaps his driving skills?" Zack muses and then bursts out laughing when I glare at him. "I'm not suggesting women can't drive. Just insinuating that men are more aggressive."

"Women aren't aggressive, huh? Well, once I get my Jeep fixed I'll gladly challenge that line of reasoning."

Zack laughs. "Touché."

I take a long sip of my soda and revel in my small victory.

"Do you remember anything else? Andrew said he got the license plate number but —"

"His eyes."

"You saw his eyes?"

"No. Not the man that followed us last night. The man from the accident. My mom's accident." I sit back and let the memory spill over me. Normally I try not to think about that night. Twice I've relived it in a nightmare but consciously I fight it off.

"What do you remember, Kate?" Zack's voice is hushed.

"He smiled at me. He looked into my eyes and smiled." When Zack remains silent I say, "Sick, huh?"

But he doesn't answer. He looks a little angry when he leans across the booth. I sit back.

"Did you tell Andrew?"

"No."

"Did you tell the police?"

"No."

When Zack's mouth stretches into a thin line I say, "I only remembered this a few days ago."

"You should tell Andrew."

"Okay," I say.

He tilts his head and his expression softens. "Is it that easy, Kate?"

"What?"

"I feel like I just won a battle." He sits back and the smile he gives me makes me want to run away and climb into his lap at the same time. "So what else can I get you to do?"

"One large pepperoni pizza." The waitress places the tray down between us and I feel like I should thank her for shattering the moment. Another second and I would have liquefied from that come hither stare of his.

"You got me to eat with you," I say. "Isn't that enough?"

Zack doesn't respond, he takes a large bite of his pizza, but the look in his eyes says it all.

Yep. Run, Kate. That's what you should have done.

The rain is coming down like a waterfall when we leave the restaurant. Zack tells me to wait inside while he gets the car. But in the few seconds it takes for me to climb into the passenger seat I get soaked.

"I don't know when Andrew will be back," I throw out into the silence. It isn't much but it's something to say.

"No worries, Kate. I'll keep you company until he gets home."

"I'm not worried," I say and stare out the window at the rain. But it's just another lie to add to my collection. I don't want to be alone with Zack. I want to go upstairs, close my door and forget about the way he looks at me. Mostly the way I feel when he looks at me.

"So you get to be my babysitter tonight," I say. "Lucky you."

"Babysit? No, I'm pretty sure I don't want to be called your babysitter."

I open my mouth but I can't think of a snappy comeback. Zack's smiling at me and there's humor in his eyes. He knows he makes me uncomfortable, and he's willing to use it to his advantage. I decide it's time for a new strategy. Zack plus eye contact equals speechless me.

I'm thinking about my escape when we pull up in front of Andrew's house. I could plead homework or perhaps a headache? That usually works.

We roll to a stop in Andrew's driveway and Zack's headlights catch something in the trees. Not something, more like someone. I'm not sure how it happens or even what I'm thinking but within seconds my car door is open and I'm racing into the trees.

"Kate!" Zack yells. But I don't turn back. Once my feet hit the ground I don't stop to think about where I'm going or even what I plan to do if I find him. The note warned me that someone is following me and up until last night I didn't want to believe it. But I can't wonder any longer. I can't keep waiting for him to find me. I have to find him.

I race toward the area where I saw the shadow. From behind I can hear footsteps crunching through the leaves and Zack calling out to me. When his voice doesn't seem to be getting further away I realize he's following me. The trees are growing thicker now and the falloff from the Defender's headlights is almost nonexistent. My hands are out in front of my body, blindly searching out trees and branches in my path. Or anything else I come across. I don't slow my pace until my body hits something solid and tall.

"What the—" Brandon's voice is close. Too close. I realize he's the one I've fallen on. His breathing is labored from the collision and so is mine. It feels like someone has reached inside my chest and stolen my remaining breath.

I gasp for air, just a little air, as two hands grab me from behind and drag me to my feet.

"Kate! What the hell were you thinking? Who—"

"I'm sorry, Brandon." My recovery is quick but my voice still sounds choked. My hands are shaking as I reach down to help Brandon to his feet. "I didn't know...I thought you were..."

"What, Kate?" Zack spins me around and I can tell from his tone, he's mad. "What were you thinking?" he yells.

"I saw a figure hide behind the trees and—"

"So did I. And I was about to back up and call the police — which is what we should have done — but instead you thought—" Zack stops and aims his anger at his brother who is slowly rising to his feet.

"And you! What the hell were you doing hiding in the trees, Brandon?"

"Geez, Zack. Settle. I was on my way here and heard your Defender. I thought it might be funny to—"

"To what, Brandon?"

"It was only a little scare, Zack. I was just going to jump out once you were near—"

"Well, obviously Kate doesn't like being scared. And neither do I." Zack takes a step closer and I think for a moment he's going to shove Brandon back down to the ground, but then he takes a deep breath and switches targets instead. "I don't understand why you'd do that, Kate." He pauses for another breath and then continues. "What were you going to do if you found someone who wasn't Brandon?"

"I didn't get that far."

"What do you mean you didn't get that far?"

"In my thinking, Zack! I didn't think about—"

"I guess not! You were too busy chasing after a shadow in the trees! Do you know how stupid that was? Do you know what could have happened?"

I cross my arms and glare up at Zack, but it's lost on him. The darkness hides all expressions and so neither Zack nor I realize that Brandon is smiling. Only when he starts laughing do we even remember he's there.

"Wow, Zack. You're really mad."

"What was your first clue, Brandon?" This time Zack does push his brother. But not nearly hard enough.

"It's just, I've never seen you so mad," Brandon continues, dusting himself off with a low chuckle to himself. "I thought it might be fun to mess with you guys. Didn't realize you were both so…tense." He turns and heads back toward the house.

Zack doesn't move and neither do I. His erratic breathing is close, almost on top of me. After a few more seconds of silence it returns to normal, in and out, in and out, while mine is still rapid and short.

"Are you alright, Kate?" His words are whispered. I almost don't hear them over my quick heartbeat.

"Yes."

He sighs and I feel it rustle my hair. "I'm sorry I yelled at you. I don't usually…"

"That's okay. I'm sorry I bolted from your car."

"That's alright."

We continue to stand under the protective cover of the trees. Zack has moved even closer and his breath is lightly warming my face. Neither of us makes a sound. Only the light rain's faint patter upon the branches and leaves can be heard.

"Are you guys coming or what?" Brandon yells from the direction of the house just as I feel Zack move his hand down my arm and grip my hand. With a firm hold he leads me out of the trees.

Brandon is still smiling when we find him lounging up against Andrew's front door. I pull my hand away once we near the house but immediately regret it when my warm fingertips begin to grow cold.

"You got any ice cream inside?" Brandon asks, and before I can even respond, Zack does.

"We have ice cream at home, Brandon."

Brandon laughs and pushes himself off the wall. "Yeah. All right. I know when I'm not wanted. Sorry for the scare, Kate. And hey, you should really think about trying out for the football team. I'm pretty sure I'll be feeling that tackle for the next day or two."

With that, Brandon disappears up the path. We can hear him whistling as Zack punches in the key code for the front door.

"He doesn't know, does he?"

"Doesn't know what?" Zack holds open the front door and waits for me to step inside.

But I don't move. "Brandon thinks I was just out joyriding in my Jeep and that's how it got smashed up."

"Andrew doesn't want a lot of people to know about last night."

"Brandon's a lot of people?"

"He doesn't think Brandon needs to be concerned. He gets freaked out about stuff like this."

"Why? Does 'stuff like this' happen a lot around here?"

"No." Zack reaches out and takes my hand again. But this time he only holds it long enough to pull me inside the house. Once the door is closed and locked behind us, he drops my hand and moves toward the kitchen.

"Do you want something to drink? Maybe some hot chocolate?"

NO! I want to yell. *I want to know why there are so many damn secrets around here.* But instead I say, "Yes." And it's the truth. I caught a chill out in the rain and Zack would only have to look at me — which he is — to see I'm shaking.

"Why don't you change into something dry and I'll make you some."

"What about you?"

"I'm not cold," he answers.

No. He doesn't look cold. I take in his narrowed eyes, his tense shoulders. Zack still looks angry.

Upstairs I feel like a coward leaning against my bedroom door. Lefty eyes me from his spot on my bed and then mews at his food dish.

"Can you only think about your stomach at a time like this?" I say.

When he mews again I've got my answer.

I change out of my wet clothes and even though I know Zack's downstairs I feel exposed and vulnerable as I slip on a pair of dry jeans and a white shirt. Being half-naked while he's in the house feels intimate, like we're involved or something.

And the "or something" is mostly what I'm worried about.

I leave Lefty to his meal of kitty crunchies and close my door.

When I pass Andrew's room, I duck in and grab a sweatshirt I find thrown over the back of his chair, just in case Zack wants to change his soaked shirt at least. But when Zack strips out of his wet shirt and pulls the sweatshirt on over his head, I realize I didn't completely think this one through. Seeing Zack's bare torso is a little more than I bargained for.

I hover in the family room unsure of what to do with myself until Zack places a warm mug of hot chocolate in my hands.

"Maybe I should call Andrew and see how much longer he'll be."

"I'm in no hurry, Kate."

"Great," I mutter under my breath.

Zack stretches out on the couch and instead of turning on the TV he watches me. In defeat, I slouch into the loveseat opposite him.

"Did you leave anyone behind in San Diego?"

"You mean like on the side of the road?" I'm looking up at the ceiling, anywhere but at Zack. The ceiling fans are dusted and white. So very clean. How does Andrew get up there? They're at least fifteen feet high.

"A boyfriend, Kate?"

I shrug and say, "There was this one guy, but it ended a while back."

"Let me guess, you broke his heart."

"Uh, no," I snort.

"He left you?" Zack asks with disbelief.

"And why is that so hard to believe?"

"This kid, he's in high school, right?"

"Yeah."

"Well high school guys are pretty simple. They like girls, they hang out with girls, and they stay with girls, unless there's a problem, like the girl stops liking them."

"You make them sound like machines."

"Was there a problem, Kate?"

"I don't know, ask him." I stand up and move toward the kitchen with my mug in my hands. I'm no longer interested in drinking my hot chocolate.

I don't hear Zack follow me. I just know he's there.

"Andrew called while you were upstairs," he says. "He's on his way."

"Thanks."

"He didn't find anything important but he mentioned he's going to be away again tomorrow night."

"Okay." I rinse my mug and turn to leave. "I should probably get some homework done."

"What are your plans tomorrow?" Zack asks. He's filling the doorway, and he's doing it rather well. If I want to get by I'll have to push him out to the way. And pushing involves touching and touching is bad. Or good, depending on which voice I'm listening to at the time.

"Tomorrow?" I ask.

"Yeah, tomorrow."

"Well there's school—"

"After school."

"I'm—"

"Hanging out with me." Zack grins. "Good. It's decided then."

"Now that I think about it, I'm sure I have plans."

"I'll pick you up after school." He's still smiling and for a moment his smile is contagious. And I hate him for it.

"You don't tell me," I say and then I try to push him, just slightly out of the doorway, but he's quick. Too quick. And suddenly my hands are trapped in his.

He's laughing and smiling at me with those eyes. And then he's not.

"You'll have fun." His voice is soft. My eyes feel heavy. "I promise," he adds, and the way he says those two words hypnotizes me.

"And If I don't have fun?" My voice is soft too.

"That's easy," he says. "We'll just try again the next day."

And that's when Andrew arrives. Zack drops my hands, or do I pull them away? It's difficult to know for sure.

Andrew comes in looking grouchy but when he sees me he smiles.

"Hey, Kate." No honey, or sweetie, both words my mom always used, and yet his eyes light up the same way her eyes would. "How was dinner?"

"Fine," I say at the exact same time Zack says, "Great." And then Zack grins at me.

"I've got to take off, but I'll see you tomorrow, Kate." It's not a question and the look he gives makes that rather clear.

168

"Goodnight, Zack," Andrew says with his head in the fridge. I can hear him rummaging around inside the vegetable bin.

"Goodbye," I say with a sugar sweet smile, a smile that stops Zack in his tracks. His eyes widen and then narrow upon my face.

"Not, goodbye, Kate," he says low enough for me to hear. "Goodnight. Or cheers. Or better yet, you could go with, see you later. But not goodbye."

"What was that all about?" Andrew asks after Zack closes the door. He's frying an egg on the stove, and thankfully his back is to me, otherwise he'd have more questions, like why are you blushing and using the counter to hold yourself up?

"No idea," I say. "You're the one who's friends with him. I can't help it if your friends are weird. So what happened in Tacoma?"

Andrew slides his egg onto a plate and says, "Follow me to my office."

Once he's seated behind his desk he says, "So tell me about the accident."

"My mother's accident?"

"Yes."

"What do you want to know?" Somehow I knew this conversation was coming. I just didn't expect it to be tonight.

"Do you remember anything? The person driving? Whether or not it was a man or a woman?"

"A man."

"Was there anything else?"

"I told Zack I remember his eyes." I pause. "And apparently he told you."

"He may have mentioned something. What exactly do you remember about them?"

"I don't remember much. Just that he seemed to be having a good time. Maybe he was so drunk he thought he was riding a roller coaster. Or a bumper car."

"Was there anything else? Anything at all that stood out about that day?"

"She was nervous, my mother," I explain. "I hoped that she'd relax once the meet was over. But she didn't. She kept looking around the café, almost like she was expecting someone. I asked her what was wrong but she kept telling me it was nothing."

"Café?"

"We had some time before our flight so we stopped to eat in Pioneer Square. She has this telltale sign when she's nervous. She's a fidgeter." I walk over to the photo of her on his bookcase and pick it up. "She can't keep her hands still for more than a few seconds. By the time our waitress arrived to take our order she'd sorted the sweetener packets by color and rearranged the menus. Twice."

"What do you suppose she was so nervous about?"

"I don't know. The meet was over and we had plenty of time to get to the airport." I conveniently leave out how I won the race and managed to beat a world record.

"I see."

I set the photo back down and turn around.

"Have you heard of Dr. Luke Dolus?"

Andrew takes another bite of his egg. "The name does sound familiar. Why do you ask?"

"My mother knew him. I think she may have visited with him while we were out here for the meet."

"What makes you think that?" He sets his plate aside and leans back in his chair.

I pretend to study the books on his bookcase. "I think John mentioned it to me. I'm not sure if she actually went, though." I'm hoping for some kind of reaction to the doctor's name, but either Andrew doesn't know any more than I do, or he's far better at hiding it. Not even a hint of recognition stumbles across his face.

"I'm not going to be around again tomorrow night. Will you be alright?"

"I have homework," I say. "I'll be fine."

"Zack might stop by." Andrew's eyes are on his computer monitor. He doesn't see me flinch.

"I'll make sure to lock the doors."

"Kate." He sends me a look of warning. "I don't want you here alone. Not until I figure out what's going on."

I come around his desk, mostly to see what he's up to, and notice a pen next to his keyboard. It's all black except for the silver pen cap.

"Your pen is broken," I say after I push the silver pen cap a few times and don't hear the familiar click.

Andrew glances up at the object in my hand and then he looks back at his monitor. "It's not broken, it's a camera pen."

"A camera pen?"

"Yes."

He says it so matter-of-factly, as if everyone owns one. "Where did you get it?"

"I'm not sure really. Perhaps at a convention."

"What kind of conventions are you going to where they pass out camera pens?"

He glances up at me, but I can tell he's not really paying attention.

"I mean that's kind of creepy, Andrew."

"They were security conventions. And businessmen get very bored on trips, Kate. Perhaps they figured it would—"

"Help them photograph the guy sitting next to them on the plane without his knowledge?" I finish.

Andrew smiles. "Perhaps."

"Do you need this?" I ask.

"No. I have others," he says. His monitor has captured his attention again.

"Others, huh? What, did this one come in a box of twenty-four?"

Andrew laughs. "It was the door prize."

Nineteen

Zack's Defender is waiting in the parking lot when I get out of school, and when I hesitate, he climbs out of the driver's seat, waves and then starts walking toward me.

"You got any more of those at home, Triumph?" Emily says from just behind me. "I've been seeing this guy named Travis. He's in my Calc class, nice looking but smarter than he is cute. I'd be willing to trade. You know, if you're interested."

"He's not mine," I say. But I can't take my eyes off him. He's dressed in jeans and a light green t-shirt, and when he smiles I swear the birds around me start chirping.

"You sure about that?" she asks and then propels me forward with her hand on my back.

"Hey, Kate," Zack says. He nods at Emily and then reaches for my backpack. "You ready?"

His hand is warm when he takes the strap from my shoulder. I can feel it through my light gray jacket and through my shirt. When I imagine what it would feel like on my skin heat rises to my face.

"See you later, Triumph," Emily says with a laugh, and I realize I'm still staring at Zack.

"Yeah, later," I say and follow Zack to his car.

He opens my car door for me as if this is a date. But this isn't a date. At least, I don't think it is.

"How was school?" he asks once he's in the driver's seat. "Did you learn anything interesting?"

He's smiling at me as he pulls out of the parking lot. That lift of his eyebrow is meant to tease, but it makes my palms feel damp. He smells good, like shaving cream or cologne. Really, really good shaving cream or cologne. Not the cheap kind kids spray in Target just before you walk down the aisle and then suddenly you find your tongue tastes like Old Spice or Drakkar Noir.

"School was great fun," I tell him when I realize it's my turn to talk. "I learned that it's never okay to fall asleep during a movie in Health class, even if the teacher is sleeping, and that instead of earthquake drills you have bomb drills. And that Mr. Mooney, my Calculus teacher, takes them very seriously, even when it's the third one this week." I pause and take a breath. "How about you? What did you learn today?"

"That you talk a lot when you're nervous."

I feel my face turn pink and he smiles.

"I'm not nervous," I say.

"Good. Are you hungry?"

"Not really." I'm too nervous to feel hungry.

"Then we'll eat after."

"After? After what?" I ask just as Zack pulls into the parking lot of the Mercer Island Ice Rink. "Oh, no," I say, shaking my head. "I don't think so."

"You can't tell me you've never ice skated before."

"I have. Once. When I was younger."

"So you know how fun it is."

"No. Not fun, more like torture on ice."

Zack laughs. "Come on, Kate. I'll teach you."

"I don't need instructions. I know exactly how it works. You wear these ridiculously sharp blades on the bottom of these ridiculously painful boots and then you do your best to stay on your feet so you don't fall on the ridiculously cold and hard ground."

"Yep. That about sums it up."

"And this is what you *want* to do?" I can't keep the distaste from my voice.

"This is what we're *going* to do. Now let's go."

"No, really, Zack. I don't think it's a good idea." I'm holding my seatbelt in place as he leans over and tries to unlatch it. "Let's do something else. Anything else."

"Why?" He's studying me as if he's going to find the answer to my hesitation in my expression or the downturn of my frown. "If you can give me one good reason why we shouldn't go ice skating I'll leave right now."

"I don't *want* to."

"Not good enough," he says, and climbs out of the driver's seat. He opens the latch leading to the back of the truck and when he comes around to my side he's carrying a black duffle bag.

"Come on, Kate. I promise I won't let you fall." He's holding my door open and I notice, for the first time today, it's not raining. To the side of the parking lot I can see a patch of trees hit with golden light and the combination of moss-covered trees and sunshine makes the forest appear enchanted. I expect at any moment a unicorn to break free from the trees and saunter on over to us.

Zack is patiently waiting for me to exit the car and when I finally look up at him I'm hit with one of his beautiful smiles. It's truly unfair that he's allowed to use these on me. They should at least come with a warning, a flashing light and a computerized voice that warns, "Stand back, smile coming."

"Why ice skating?" I say. I'm stalling and he knows it. He takes my hand and tugs at me to exit the car.

"It's one of my favorite things to do." He looks off at the patch of golden trees, and I realize his eyes are the same color as the forest: green, brown and gray with specks of sunshine gold. "My mom and I used to skate together all the time. I've been skating since I was old enough to walk."

Damn him. Damn him for playing the mom-card. And of course that makes me think of my mom and the one time we went ice-skating when I was five and how she fell on the ice and started laughing and I started crying and then when I tried to pull my skates off I sliced my hands.

That was the last time we went ice-skating.

"Okay," I whisper, even though I know it's a horrible idea. Even though I know exactly what will happen if what *could* happen happens. I open my mouth to try to undo what I've done and then end up saying, "Let's go ice-skating."

With another heart-stopping smile Zack grabs my hands and lifts me from the car.

"By the time we leave the rink you'll be faster than I am," he says.

But that's impossible. No one could be faster than Zack. He zips around the rink at mock speed, slicing in-between the other skaters as if they aren't there. Backwards and forwards and then when he arrives next to me he skids to a stop as I avert my eyes, anticipating a shower of ice to spray over me.

"What are you some kind of professional figure skater?"

"Hockey," Zack says. "I played on a hockey team in high school." His cheeks are pink, his eyes excited. I wonder how his lips would taste.

"Ah. Well, I can't do that," I say, pointing to the perfectly executed skid mark on the ice near his skates. "Or that," I point to the other ice-skaters, the ones who are still on their feet while I'm clutching the wall with frozen and stiff fingers.

"That's because you haven't tried." Zack pries my hands from the wall. "We'll go slow," he says and leads me out onto the ice.

All I notice is his warm hand in mine. I can feel it through my gloves, gloves he brought me. They're dark blue and masculine, and they smell like Zack: clean, healthy and male.

"You're really good at this," I say and concentrate on lifting my white figure skates off the ice like Zack told me to.

The skates I'm using belonged to his mother.

"You can't learn to skate in rental skates," he explained when he pulled them out of his duffle bag. "It's like they're setting you up for failure. They never sharpen the blades, the boots are this hard plastic that has absolutely no give and to top it off they're this ugly green color.

"I hate the color green," I say with a mock shudder. "It makes me think of trees, fresh air and newly cut grass."

"Believe me, Kate. You're better off wearing these." He slipped the skates onto my feet and laced them up, wrapping the extra-long laces around the top of the boot and then double knotting it. Just like his mom used to.

I don't know how he knew they'd be a perfect fit, worn-in exactly the way my foot would wear them. But somehow he knew. When I stood up he held my hand until I got my balance and the way he looked at me made me want to tuck his rebellious hair behind his ear and promise to never leave him.

Ever. Never.

The inside of the rink smells like greasy food and cotton candy.

What I would give for a cup of hot chocolate right now.

Zack has other plans. He grips my elbows as I skate in front of him, and when I stumble he holds me up, my back to his chest, his mouth to my ear, whispering encouragement.

"You're doing great," he says and occasionally when I hit the ice just right his hands slide around my waist. It isn't the ice and the sharp blades under my feet making me wobbly, it's Zack's body pressed against mine.

It doesn't take long for me to get my ice-legs. I increase my speed and Zack matches it, and if it weren't for the dozen or so people on the ice I would stretch my legs and kick my sauntering up a notch. Or four. But the risk is too high, and I have to admit, I like the feel of Zack too much to skate off, away from him. The way his hand slides down my back when I get a little in front of him or how when that happens his hands grip my waist and he pulls me back.

"I knew you'd be a natural," he says after our tenth or twentieth lap around the rink. "We could make this a regular thing, if you'd like," and I stumble, not sure whether or not he's talking about ice-skating or something else. Something I would definitely like, but can't have.

"Teach me how to do that slide-stop thing," I say, mostly to keep my mind on ice-skating.

"You mean this?" He drops my hand and skids to a stop.

He pulls me toward him and then moves my body, hips just so, feet like this, until I'm standing like he is. "This is how you want to stop, just turn your body mid-motion and make sure your skates lean the same direction as your body."

So I try it.

Zack catches me just before I hit the ice.

"Again," he says while laughing against my hair.

The next time I almost get it and then I catch myself just before I lose my footing.

"Lean more to your right and lift your skates so they're parallel." Zack is standing a few feet away studying my movements. He looks so serious, like my own private ice-skating coach. And cute. But he always looks cute.

I skate a small distance away and then come to a perfect slide-stop.

"I did it!" I yell and turn around, searching for Zack.

He grabs me around the waist and spins me in a circle. At first it's terrifying, my feet dangling just above the ground, my hands gripping his jacket. When he stops I'm out of breath. His smile is so close. His body. His lips. They're all just so damn close.

He lowers me back to the ground and when my skates touch the ice it appears I've lost my ice-legs. I'm still gripping his jacket. All I have to do is look up. Move my chin, tilt my head and wham. We could be kissing.

And I want to. Something in his eyes tells me he wants to too. But we don't. We hover in each other's breath, so close, but not nearly close enough.

I feel like we're still spinning, but it's everyone else on the ice rotating around us, while we remain perfectly still.

"You did it." Zack's voice is soft, almost drowned out by the classic rock blaring over the speakers. "How does it feel?"

"I. What?"

"How does it feel to get what you want so quickly?"

"I wouldn't know." I want to pull away. I want to skate to the other side of the rink just so I can escape the heavy look in his eyes.

"Yeah, me neither," he says. "But it doesn't stop me from trying."

Over the loud speaker a voice comes on to inform us that the rink will be closing in fifteen minutes.

"We should keep skating," he says, but neither one of us moves.

"Thank you for bringing me here and teaching me to skate." It's the only approved thought running through my mind at the moment.

"You're welcome."

When he smiles I smile. We're standing there smiling at each other like two stupid fools when something slams into me and knocks me sideways.

I hit the ice and lie there, too stunned to move, as a pair of black ice skates zip past my head and then skate off toward the exit. Zack's swearing and on his knees, leaning over me with a look of anger and then concern and then anger again.

"What happened?" I ask as he pulls me to my feet. My hip hurts and my shoulder, but a quick glance down my body and over my hands tells me I'm mostly okay.

No blood. No foul.

"That idiot over there ran right into us." Zack's pointing at someone near the exit and my eyes lock onto a blue helmet and hockey jersey and then move down to those familiar black skates.

"Where was he?" I ask. "He wasn't skating before. At least I didn't notice him."

"I don't know. I wasn't really paying attention." Zack is holding my hand as he leads me off the ice.

"He didn't even say sorry."

"Let's sit for a minute. I'll grab you a drink. Are you thirsty?" Zack's scanning the crowd, just as I am, barely listening as I make sense of what just happened.

"It's almost as if it was intentional. Like he was aiming—"

And then I see him. He's sitting up in the bleachers to my left, just along my line of sight. I know he wasn't there when we arrived and he definitely wasn't there a few minutes ago when I scanned the crowd for the hundredth time since we got on the ice. I always pay attention to the crowd, the bystanders who may one day play the important role of an eyewitness. So I know he wasn't here. The bald man wasn't here.

But he is now.

As I watch he stands up, wearing a long black jacket, the kind that hits you at the knees, and unlike the rest of us inside the ice rink he isn't wearing a hat — he wants me to recognize him. He holds up his black-gloved hands and blows me a kiss.

"Kate? Are you okay?" Zack leads me toward the bench where our stuff is stashed. My blue sneakers peek out at me from the open duffle bag and all I want to do is put them on and chase after the bald man, make him explain why he's following me and demand to know what's going on. But I can't. Not with Zack here, standing right over me with that look of concern. He'd never understand. Not without an explanation.

"I'm thirsty," I say. "And a little tired." I squeeze out a tiny smile to reassure Zack and he seems somewhat relieved. He must think I'm weak. One fall on the ice and I need to catch my breath.

"I'll be right back," he says and then hurries off toward the snack bar.

I don't have to look up at the bleachers to know that the bald man has moved on. He's accomplished what he came to do. I've seen him and he's seen me.

But I search the rink anyway. I take the long way to the restroom, to avoid running into Zack, and then backtrack along the rink.

He's gone. In fact, now that I'm noticing, the ice rink is pretty much empty compared to when we first arrived. Only one or two ice-skaters are still on the ice even though the music has been turned off.

I sit back down on the bench and hug my coat around me. I could have imagined him. This could be my overactive imagination creating drama when drama's taking the day off, but I don't think so. He was here, watching me, waiting for me to notice him.

The real question is, why? Why is he following me? Is he the one the letter warned me about? And if he is, then who sent the letter?

Zack is back with a bottle of water.

"It's all they had. They've locked everything up for the day."

"It's perfect," I say and drink almost half while Zack changes back into his shoes.

The sun has set by the time we leave the rink. It feels like it sets earlier here than in California. Like the trees keep the last half hour of light to themselves, allowing us a quick glimpse of yellow-orange through the occasional clearing.

Out in the parking lot the light posts flicker a warning that darkness is on its way.

"Please tell me you're hungry," Zack says leading the way across the parking lot. "I'm so hungry the dried up hotdogs at the snack bar looked good."

"They didn't smell good," I say with a laugh. But I'm not thinking of food, I'm scanning the parking lot, the cars and the shadows.

"We can grab some Italian down on Main or if you'd like Chinese…?" He stops, his eyes taking in the fear I know has whitened my face. "What is it, Kate?"

When I don't answer he follows my gaze across the parking lot to where his Defender is parked, and to where four large men in dark blue hockey jerseys are leaning against it.

"Is this yours?" The guy closest to us asks. He's no longer wearing his helmet or his black skates but I'm convinced he's the one who knocked me down on the ice. I'd recognize that rock-solid shoulder anywhere.

"It is," Zack says. "But don't feel like you have to hold it up or anything. It can stand just fine on its own."

"Well aren't you cute," the guy says, and when he laughs the rest of them laugh, like parrots imitating their owner. I'm guessing the other three aren't here to talk, they're just here to stand around looking threatening. So far it's working.

"You know I've always wanted one of these old trucks. I hear they run great."

"They do." Zack shoves me behind him as we walk and I can't help but peek around his shoulder. We're almost to the truck now and as we get nearer the three guys in the back stagger themselves so they form a wall, a wall that could easily close in on us.

"You know I'm not feeling so well," I say. "I took quite a fall out on the ice today and I'm feeling a bit queasy. I know you love talking trucks, Zack, but can we do this another time?" It's the best bored-girlfriend imitation I can pull off, considering I'm so scared my legs are shaking. And I'm not lying about the queasy part. Being surrounded by four giant-sized men in a dark, abandoned parking lot is something straight out of my nightmares.

"You heard her, boys. You wouldn't want me to end up in trouble now would you?" Zack has my arm in a firm grip. I'm not sure what he's going to do if they don't move away but when the guy in front pulls out a baseball bat from behind his back I realize I'm about to find out.

"We're going to make this as painless as possible," he says. "We just want your girlfriend here, and because I'm in such a good mood I'll let you keep the car."

"What?!" I say, followed by an even louder, "What?!" from Zack.

"She's pretty important to a friend of mine. You see, she's got something he needs and we're here to get that back."

Okay. Now I'm definitely going to be sick.

"Kate," Zack turns to me slowly, all the while keeping his eyes on the men. "I want you to go back inside the rink and stay there until I come and get you."

"No way. I'm not leaving you out here alone."

"When I say, run, I want you to run back to the rink."

"Zack—"

"Kate. Do it." He squeezes my arm so hard I have to keep from crying out, and when his eyes briefly meet mine I notice he's not terrified like I am. He's furious.

"Zack, I'm not leaving you."

"Yes. You are. When I say, run—"

"I don't have all day," the front man calls out. He taps the bat in his hand, and the movement is so unoriginal if I wasn't so scared I'd roll my eyes. Somehow it signals the men to start moving closer. Zack and I take a few steps back.

"NOW! Kate. RUN!" Zack pushes me back toward the rink seconds before he charges the guy with the baseball bat.

And I'm speechless. Out of the four men, why would he choose to attack the one with the weapon?

He's throwing punches now, and dodging the bat like this is some choreographed dance he's rehearsed.

"Kate! Go!" he yells.

But I don't run. Even though we both know I could make it. I could get inside, call the police and wait while Zack gets the crap beat out of him or possibly ends up killed.

I don't run because I won't leave him. As much as I want to save myself I don't want to leave him behind. I can't.

Perhaps I've made a mistake, at least it feels like a mistake when one of the non-talking, threatening guys grabs me from behind and forces me to watch while the other three do their best to take Zack down.

They start off taking turns. First the front man with the bat swings at Zack and then one by one the three men throw their punches until they realize they'll get much further if they all attack him at once.

I yell out for them to stop, kicking and scratching at my assailant, but when I realize it only upsets Zack I stay silent. Even though I don't want to watch, I have to. It's like watching a pack of tigers rip apart a gazelle except this gazelle is fighting back.

Strangely enough if I wasn't so freaked out by the situation I'd be impressed by Zack's fighting skills. It's almost as if he's done this before. The way he can almost read their minds, anticipate where they're going to aim next and when. But three on one isn't a fair fight and after a few direct hits to the gut he begins to slow down.

"This is stupid," I cry, doing my best to pull free. "What you're doing is crazy, beating up two kids in a parking lot. There are four of you and two of us. Does this fight feel fair to you?"

But the man holding me doesn't answer. He grips my arms even tighter and at any moment my left shoulder is going to pop right out of its socket. As if the situation isn't dire enough the man smells like fish. Not cooked fish but raw, bloody, dead fish that has been sitting around in the sun. For at least a week. It's everything I can do to keep the water I just drank from coming back up.

"What do you want from me?" I ask, because talking is easier than breathing. "Why are you doing this?"

But silence continues to be fish-man's favorite response.

Zack and the front man are still playing a dangerous game of who's got the bat, while the other two guys take turns distracting Zack with punches and kicks. They find it amusing, these two. How every time they hit him, Zack moans or grunts in pain, and I want to scream. I want to break the arms that hold me back and then break the legs of each man that dares lay a hand on Zack. This feeling racing through my body isn't exactly fear or anger. It's this strange cocktail of both with a hint of challenge thrown in.

I want to fight.

As soon as I realize this it's as if my skin is battling a fever. My face feels hot and all over my body it's as if I'm on fire.

I throw my head back and hit fish-man right in the chest. I hear him grunt but he doesn't release me, instead he wraps his thick arms around my torso and squeezes.

"Stop," I choke. "I can't breathe."

But the only one who hears me says nothing and does nothing.

I wish I could reach my cell phone. I wish I'd run inside and called the police when I had the chance. But mostly I wish I had taken up my mom's offer to teach me Karate. Her plan was to learn it herself and then teach me at home.

"It's too risky for you to learn in class," she'd said. "What if you get hurt?"

And even though her argument was sound, it didn't sound as fun.

But I never figured I'd be in this situation, gasping for air while a foul-smelling man with large hands controlled my breathing.

"I have a message for you," fish-man says, and his hold on me loosens temporarily, only to be replaced by the cold edge of a knife pressed against my skin.

"What?" I manage to choke out.

"This will happen again, unless you cooperate."

"I. I don't know." I swallow down the bile and whatever else is making its way around the pressure of the knife. "I don't know what you're talking about."

He pulls the knife closer and I feel it break my skin.

"Please," I plead.

And then something crazy happens. Zack does this round-spin-kick thing and the front man goes down without his bat.

The two guys in back scramble for it but Zack beats them to it. All he has to do is wave it in the air for them to realize the game has changed.

"This will happen again, Kate," fish-man whispers into my ear and then moves the knife from my skin. "And next time he'll make you bleed."

Twenty

By the time Zack reaches me I'm alone and fish-man has done his job. He's terrified me.

And managed to cut my throat. But neither he nor Zack will ever know this.

"Kate! Are you alright?" Zack's holding my arms, feeling my face, and staring into my eyes, searching for a way to reassure himself that I'm okay.

But I'm not, and neither is he.

"You're bleeding."

"I'm okay," he says. "Let's get out of here."

"You're not okay. Your head is bleeding, your face is bleeding." I lift his hands and sure enough they're bleeding too.

"Let's go." He drags me toward the Defender and when we're inside with the doors locked I should feel better — safer — but I don't.

He'll make you bleed. Next time he'll make you bleed.

Who the hell is *he*?

There are only a few cars left in the parking lot — a tan jeep, a broken down truck and a shiny sedan.

Zack's watching his rearview mirror and glancing back and forth as we drive through the parking lot — neither one of us feels like this is over — and thankfully he's distracted when we pass the shiny sedan. He doesn't hear my gasp or notice when my hands start to shake. His eyes skim past the man standing next to the light blue Honda Accord, smoking a cigarette. He doesn't notice the long black coat that hits the man at the knees, or how he's not wearing a hat.

But I do.

I pull my knees up to my chest and begin rocking back and forth.

"It's over, Kate." Zack wraps his arm around my shoulders and pulls me against his side. "They can't get us now."

I nod my head, a sign that I've heard him and that I'm alright, but it takes me a little longer to convince myself.

"Should we call the police?" I ask.

"I need to talk to Andrew first."

"Why? Where is he?"

"I'm not sure. I just know I should talk to him before we involve anyone else."

We pull onto the road that leads to the high school. We're only a few blocks from Andrew's house.

"He knew my name," I say. "The man holding me knew my name."

Zack's grip on my shoulders tightens but he doesn't say anything.

"And they kept hitting you!" I cover my eyes as if that will keep the scene from flooding my memory.

"It's over. I'm okay, you're okay, and that's all that matters."

But he's wrong. It's not over. And I'm definitely not okay.

"Where'd you learn to fight like that? I don't know how you did it?"

"Did what?" Zack drives past Andrew's house and pulls down the next driveway.

"You fought them off! How did you fight them off?" I turn in my seat and stare up at him in wonder. "There were four of them, Zack. What were you thinking?"

He turns off the engine once we're in his garage and his eyes stare straight ahead. I can almost see him replaying the details of the night, just like I am.

"Why'd you go after the guy with the bat? He could have killed you."

The garage light flickers off, leaving us in darkness.

"I know you have lots of questions, Kate, but I think we should get inside."

He doesn't have to tell me twice. I slide across my seat and out the door.

I don't like the darkness. Especially now. Even though I know we left the bald man back in the parking lot I feel as if he's everywhere. He could be watching me when I'm at my most vulnerable, waiting for his chance to shake me up and then disappear.

Here's the shocker, I don't really want to talk about Zack and his super ninja fighting skills or how he managed to stay calm throughout it all. Don't get me wrong. I'm totally intrigued. I just don't want him asking me any questions. And he's got to have questions, like, why those guys were after me? Or how about why danger seems to be my constant companion lately?

I should feel relieved at this point. Tonight could have gone in a completely different direction. Zack could have thrown me at their mercy, or worse, I could have ended up covered in blood. But I'm not. For the first time someone else is hurt and all I can think about is how I want to take care of him.

Zack's house is a two-story A-frame cabin that is much cleaner than it should be considering two teenage boys live here.

He moves toward the fireplace, turning on lights along the way, while I stand in the middle of the large living room soaking in the place that Zack calls home.

"This is nice. Have you always lived here?" My attempt at conversation is lame, I know, but I've got nothing else. Every other topic that springs to mind leads down a dangerous path.

"Pretty much," he says. "Except for the years we lived with my aunt and uncle, right after my parents died."

"How long was that?"

"Just until I turned eighteen, so two years."

"Oh." I wander around the living room, peering at photos of a much younger Zack or Brandon, who, whether they're playing sports or simply smiling at the person behind the camera, exude this natural confidence, like they lead a charmed life. At least that's how it appears in the photographs. But then the large family photo hanging over the fireplace catches my eye and I'm reminded that no one is safe from heartbreak.

My eyes lock-on to the happy family and I move closer. Everyone is smiling. Everyone's alive.

"You look like your mother," I say. "You have the same eyes and smile."

"Thank you." Zack's voice catches me off guard. I didn't realize he was so close. I turn and find him standing just a few feet away with his hands resting along the back of the couch.

His bleeding hands.

Instantly I feel guilty. He's bleeding because of me. Me! The girl who doesn't need anyone to fight her battles. Not when I can survive them far better than anyone else.

"Do you have any antiseptic? Or bandages? I need to clean you up," I say.

"I'm fine, Kate."

"Yeah, you keep saying that but you underestimate my need to take care of—" I stop, and Zack gets this funny look in his eyes.

"Of what? Your need to take care of me?" He's grinning now and when he comes around the side of the couch his eyes are sparkling. "Is that what you want to do? Take care of me?" He reaches up and touches the side of my face. "Do you want to make me all better?"

"What I want is a first-aid kit."

I remove his hand from my face and examine the cuts across his knuckles. "I'll get you cleaned up and then you can explain how it is you're so good at fighting." When he doesn't move I add, "I'm sure it's a great story. I really can't wait to hear it."

Zack just continues to stare down at me.

"So. Where is it?" I ask.

"Where's what?" He tugs on my hand until we're so close our knees are flush up against each other.

"The first-aid kit. I need you to get it for me, otherwise I'll be forced to search your house until I find what I need."

"I'm fine, Kate."

I reach up and brush the hair back from his forehead so I can get a better look at the gash along his eyebrow. The movement brings us even closer.

"You're not fine. You're bleeding. Please, Zack, let me get this cleaned up." I'm doing my best to sound stern but with him so close and our bodies touching the way they are there really isn't much hope. In the end I just come off as if I'm out of breath. "It's the least I can do considering you saved me from those guys."

When his eyes narrow I realize my mistake.

"What did they want with you, Kate?" He tilts my chin up when I don't answer him. "Do you know what they were talking about?"

I take a step backward but I don't go far. I'm trapped between Zack and the back of the couch.

"No. I don't."

"Why were they after you?"

"Stupid mistake, I guess. I've never seen them before in my life." And, hopefully, I'll never see them again.

Zack studies me for a minute and then walks toward the staircase. When he returns he has a large, blue first-aid kit.

"This may sting a little," I say, but Zack doesn't even flinch. He patiently waits for me to clean and bandage each wound and soon his cheek and both hands are all patched up. His left eyebrow takes me a little bit longer.

"I've never had to do this before," I say. "I hope I'm not hurting you." I dab at the cut hesitantly and then press down harder when Zack doesn't react.

"Does it hurt?"

"No."

"It looks like it hurts," I say. And it does. The skin over his left eyebrow is broken and raw, the cut underneath pink, and it continues to ooze this clear fluid even after I apply pressure to it. If I weren't so concerned about getting it cleaned up the whole process would gross me out.

"Do you hurt anywhere else?" I ask after I've applied the last bandage. "Your ribs perhaps, or —" I touch his chest with my hand and then immediately pull away when he sucks in a quick breath.

"I'm sorry. Did I hurt you?"

"No."

"Are you sure we shouldn't get you to a hospital or something? I mean if you're hurt…"

"I'm fine." And to prove it he takes my hand and rests it first against his ribs and then slowly moves it up his chest where he holds it in place when I try to pull away.

"See," he says. "All better."

I pull at my hand again and this time he lets me go. "We should call Andrew." I try to scoot around him but there's really nowhere to go. It's as if he's filling the room, his eyes watching, the warmth of his body touching me while every breath of air I inhale is laced with him.

"Kate," he says, and the sound of his voice startles me.

"Yes?"

"Were you scared tonight?"

"Um, yeah. How could I not be?"

"Were you afraid I was going to let them hurt you?"

"I was mostly worried you'd get hurt."

Zack considers this for a minute and then says, "Why didn't you go back inside? I told you to run. Why didn't you?'

"And leave you alone? No way."

"Why? I can handle myself."

"Well, I didn't realize that at the time."

"No. You didn't, did you?" Zack smiles and I feel like I'm sinking.

"Kate?"

"Yes?" I won't look up. He's probably still smiling, or worse, he's looking at me and I can't handle him looking at me especially when my knees are shaking and any minute now I just might stumble forward, right into his oh-so-kissable mouth.

"I'm waiting."

"For?"

"For you to look up for one."

So I do. And of course it's a mistake.

His eyes capture mine and don't let go. He lifts me so I'm sitting on the back of the couch, my body trapped with his arms on either side of me.

"Why don't you trust me? Why is it that every time I get close to you I feel you back away?"

When I don't answer he continues, "I know you feel this. There's no way you don't."

He leans down and we're almost touching. Our lips are almost there.

"I wasn't scared tonight," he whispers against my mouth. "All I could think about was that guy with his hands on you and what would happen if I didn't get to you in time. I've never felt that powerless before."

His hand moves up the side of my body and rests along the back of my neck.

"I won't let anyone hurt you. Do you believe me?"

I open my mouth to respond and then he's kissing me. I grab his shoulders when the pressure of his kiss nearly sends me over the back of the couch. But I'm not going anywhere. Zack's hands have moved down to my waist and he's holding me against him.

"I can't do this," I say just as my fingers slide up into his hair.

Zack deepens the kiss and I feel like I'm falling all over again. His mouth is warm. His lips soft. His hands move up my back, pulling me closer until I realize it's not enough; we'll never be close enough. But it doesn't stop him from trying.

"Kate," he whispers along the side of my mouth, while I try to catch my breath. "You have to stop pushing me away. You're making me crazy."

His lips are back, moving over mine with an intensity I can't match. I try, but with each kiss I'm weakening, my body swimming against the tide that is his hunger.

"Promise me, Kate," he whispers.

"Promise. What?" I breathe.

And then he's kissing me again, or did I kiss him? I can't seem to stop now that I've started. I don't think I can stop.

A loud buzzing cuts through my thoughts but I ignore it and then Zack's phone starts to chirp.

"I have to answer it," he says, but he doesn't. When it rings again he only pulls away long enough to say, "It could be Andrew."

He sounds as disappointed as I feel.

"Andrew?" I whisper.

Andrew.

And just like that I'm back. I push my way out of Zack's arms and this time I do fall over the back of the couch.

I hear Zack say hello but I can't look at him.

I walk over to the fire and then decide it's not safe, so I cross the room and stand near the sliding glass door that leads out to blackness. At least that's how it appears to me.

"Yeah, we're here," he says, "see you in a few," and then he tosses his phone to the couch.

"Kate?" he calls over to me.

"Yes?"

"Are you okay?" He hasn't moved. He's still standing where I left him.

"I'm fine. Is Andrew coming here or should I meet him back at home?"

Home. The word pops out of my mouth and catches me by surprise. This is the first time I've called his house, home.

"He's on his way here." Zack doesn't come any closer. He keeps his distance or perhaps it's my distance, since I'm the one who created it.

"Would you like something to drink?"

"No."

"Or something to eat?"

"I'm not hungry," I say.

"Okay." He takes a step toward me and I flinch. "Would you like to explain what you're doing way over there?"

"I'm." I look around the room and my eyes fall on the fireplace. "Hot."

"You're hot." Zack's mouth lifts up in the corner as if he's holding back a smile.

"Yes. I'm hot. Thought I'd cool down over here. Is that alright?" I ask. I mean he can't fault me for being hot now, can he.

"Would you like to step outside?" He nods toward the sliding glass door and lifts an eyebrow.

"Outside?" I know I sound like a parrot, but I can't help it. As long as he continues to look at me that way I'm going to keep repeating his questions until I have my bearings or I leave, whichever comes first.

"If you're still hot we can slip outside. That should help you cool down."

"Right. Outside." I turn around and stare out the sliding glass door but all I see is a reflection of Zack moving toward me.

I reach for the handle and pull but the door doesn't budge. When I look up Zack is directly behind me.

"It won't open," I say and hope he can't hear the panic in my voice.

"It's locked." He reaches around me and slides the lock down but he doesn't bother opening the door. Instead his hands move up my arms and I can't help it, his touch makes me shiver.

"Are you cold now, Kate?" He pulls me back against him and his arms wrap around me from behind.

I can't help but stare at the picture we make in the sliding glass door. If I didn't know better I'd say the couple staring back at us in the glass looks comfortable in each other's arms. Maybe even slightly in love.

"I can't do this, Zack," I whisper. "You don't want me."

"I don't?" There's a trace of a smile in his voice, but when I meet his eyes in the glass a shadow falls across his face. "Why don't I want you, Kate?"

"This can't happen."

"It already has."

"No." I push away from him but once again I've allowed myself to get trapped between Zack and a hard place.

"Kate. What exactly are you afraid of?"

"You mean besides the four men in the parking lot and the man who chased me down in my jeep?"

Zack's arms tighten around me. "Yes. Besides that."

"Nothing."

"I don't believe you."

"Alright then, everything!" I yell. "I'm afraid of everything." I duck out of his arms and he lets me go.

I make my way to the middle of the room. Once again I've created distance, but instead of safe it only makes me feel alone.

"This can't happen. I know you think it's fun. Like some kind of challenge but—"

"Fun?" Zack storms across the room and I stumble back a few steps. "You call this fun?" He towers over me. His eyes are dark, his expression heavy.

"No." I shake my head and keep backing up until I'm up against a wall. "I can't," I whisper.

"What happened to you?" Zack says. "Who did this to you?"

"It's not what you think."

"So tell me."

"NO!" I slink down to the floor and bury my face in my hands.

And that's how Andrew finds me when he walks through the door.

"What happened?" he asks and when I don't answer or look up he turns to Zack.

"We went ice-skating."

Ice-skating. That feels like an eternity ago.

"And?"

"And someone pushed Kate on the ice and then they waited for us out at my car and tried to get Kate to go with them but I fought them off."

"How many?"

"Four."

"And a bat," I pipe in. "Don't forget the baseball bat." I pull my hands from my face just in time to catch Zack's glance.

"Yes. And a baseball bat," he says.

"And what did they want?" Andrew asks.

"Me."

The look on Andrew's face sends a chill down my spine. "Why?" he asks.

"You know why," I whisper.

"Perhaps you should explain it to me."

"I can't. Not now." With my eyes closed I lean my head back against the wall. I can't tell Andrew what I know, not with Zack here. And if I tell Andrew everything, what will he think? Will he believe me? Will he lock me in my room or will he send me away? To be honest, I'm not sure which one would be worse.

"Kate." Andrew's voice is close now. When I open my eyes he's crouched down in front of me. "I need you to tell me what's going on."

"At home, Andrew. I'll tell you when we're home."

"Now's as good a time as any."

My eyes widen and I shoot Zack a look. "I can't talk about it with—"

"Kate. You can trust him."

I shake my head. "Not with this," I whisper.

"Andrew, there's something you should know," Zack says.

I look up and find him watching me, and suddenly my throat feels dry. He's not going to tell him about the kiss, right? Right?

"What is it?" Andrew asks.

"They knew Kate's name."

I breathe out a sigh of relief and Andrew shoots me a look.

"It's alright, Kate. They can't hurt you now." He brushes the hair off my face and then turns to Zack. "I'm just glad you were with her tonight."

"Yeah, me too," Zack says. "But maybe you should stick around for the next few days." I look up just in time to see something pass between the two. Andrew nods his head and helps me to my feet.

"We should get home. It's late, and you have school in the morning."

"Right. School." I'm avoiding Zack's eyes as I move toward the door. Just before I follow Andrew down the steps Zack stops me with a light touch on my arm.

"I'm sorry about tonight, Kate. I never should have rushed you. You've been through so much lately…" he trails off and then drops his hand.

"I'm sorry too," I say, but I'm not exactly sure about what.

"I guess I'll see you around." Zack drags his hand through his hair and I follow the movement. If I were to close my eyes I could pretend it's my hair he's touching, my face his hands seek out.

But my eyes are open. It's my heart that's closed.

"See you around, Zack," I say, and then follow my father out to his car.

Twenty-One

You'd think that after the night I've had I'd be allowed to go straight to bed.

No such luck.

The ride home is as quiet as two tight-lipped people riding in a sports car can be, but once we're home, and I turn to head up the stairs, Andrew stops me with a request to follow him into his office.

"We need to talk," he explains.

And I have to agree.

I sit down on the long, black lounge chair near the back of his office. He perches on the side of his desk, a notebook in his hands.

"I want details," he says. "Leave nothing out."

"O-kay," I say and then hide my blush from his inquisitive eyes. That's so not going to happen. "We were ice-skating. You know that part."

Andrew nods.

"And then this guy comes out of nowhere and crashes into me."

"Had you seen him around the rink before it happened?"

"No. Definitely not."

"You sound so sure."

"I am sure. I was paying attention."

Andrew gives me a look and then nods for me to continue.

"So then soon after that they start to close the rink—"

"Around five?"

"Yes. I remember it was just starting to get dark when we headed out to the parking lot."

"Okay."

"I noticed the men before Zack. There were four of them, all wearing dark blue hockey jerseys."

"Did you happen to catch any names on the jerseys or a team name?"

"No. Just numbers."

"Do you remember—?"

"14, 8, 22 and 1. The ringleader's number was 1."

"Of course it was." Andrew grabs a pen off his desk and jots something down in a notebook.

"The guy who held me smelled like dead fish," I say and Andrew looks up.

"What do you mean, he held you?"

"He had my arms behind my back while the other three were fighting Zack."

"Did he hurt you?"

"He had a knife. But Zack doesn't know that part," I add quickly.

"And?"

"He cut my throat. But I don't think he meant to. I mean, he meant to scare me but I don't think he meant to cut me."

"Why do you think that?"

"Just a gut feeling." I can't bring myself to tell Andrew everything I know. I'm sure it has to do with the fact that I have a year's worth of experience living with my mom and how I learned never to add kindling to her fire of paranoia. But then there's this other little thing worrying me. What if Andrew tried to go after Dr. Dolus and then got hurt? What if I lost him before I even got to know him?

Andrew stares at me for a minute and then nods his head. "And he smelled like fish?"

"It was more like it was coming off his skin or something. I have to tell you, I'm not so sure I could handle the smell of seafood now. It was overwhelming."

"Anything else?"

"You mean besides the fact that Zack fought them all off? He did some tricky ninja kick and knocked the ringleader right on his ass. He was still on the ground when we pulled away."

"Zack's trained in Martial Arts," Andrew explains. His head is down while he continues writing and doesn't look up when I ask where Zack learned it.

"I taught him," he says.

"You?"

"Yes." He finally looks up after a few more minutes of silence. "I tried to teach Brandon too but he wasn't interested."

"Can you teach me?"

"If you'd like."

"I'd like."

Andrew smiles. "Alright. Maybe we should start after track is over. I wouldn't want you to get hurt—" he stops and clears his throat. "I mean. I wouldn't want it to come between you and your running."

"Okay," I say.

"Was there anything else that stood out tonight, Kate?"

Yes, about a million things, but nothing I'm ready to talk about.

"He didn't bring out his tricky moves until the end," I say. "Why do you suppose he waited?"

"You mean Zack?"

"Yeah. He was fighting them off pretty well in the beginning and then they all started coming at him at once and that's when he started in on the kicks and the other cool moves."

"I guess he wanted it to be a fair fight."

"Fair?" I choke back a laugh. "What's so fair about three on one?"

Andrew closes his notebook with a snap. "Zack could have handled at least a dozen. He's trained to fight against large numbers."

"What? Why?"

"Because that's how I trained him to fight."

"Okay." I lean forward in my chair. "Then where did you learn to fight?"

"Didn't I tell you I was in the Army?"

"Yes. But I wasn't aware that the Army was big into Martial Arts training."

"They're all about the training, Kate."

"I see."

Andrew moves back behind his desk. He must think the Q&A session is over.

"And is that where you learned how to drive?"

"I learned how to drive when I was sixteen. I didn't join the Army until a couple years later."

"Nice," I say. "I see what you did there."

"What?" Andrew is looking at me as if he's as clueless as he expects me to be.

"I know when someone's avoiding a question. Believe me, I could teach lessons." When Andrew continues to stare at me as if I'm speaking another language I say, "The other night, and how you flipped the jeep around into on-coming traffic and then you shot out the tires and..." I stop and shake my head.

"What is it you're asking, exactly?"

"I'm not sure. I guess I'm asking what it is you did before my mom left you."

And just like that Andrew shuts down. I know that look. I'd recognize it anywhere. His blue eyes are wiped clean, like someone has dropped the Levolor blinds to his soul.

"Is that a goodnight I hear coming?" I mutter under my breath, and before he can answer I stand up and move toward the door. "Don't think I'm going easy on you, Andrew. Sooner or later you will answer my questions. You're just lucky I'm feeling tired tonight."

"Kate?"

"Yeah."

"I want you to stay close to the house for a while, and if Zack or I can't be with you then you're not to go anywhere on your own."

"What about school?"

"School is fine but then you need to stick around here. At least until I figure something out."

"What exactly are you figuring out?"

Andrew reaches up and rubs the back of his neck. "I made a few enemies in my last job. I'm concerned they might be trying to get to me through you."

"What kind of enemies?"

"The usual kind," he says. "People who believe they're invincible, but they aren't."

"Okay. And do these people have names?"

"It's nothing for you to worry about. I'll take care of it."

"So let me get this straight. You think the guys at the ice rink and the man who chased us down in the jeep the other night were actually after you, not me?"

"Not exactly. I believe they'll do anything in their power to get to me and if it means coming after you they'll do it."

I sit back down on the chair. "What did you do to win these people over?"

"That's a conversation for another night. Just promise me you won't go anywhere without Zack or me at your side. At least until I work this out."

He stands up as if he's about to usher me out the door, but I'm not done. Not yet.

"You're not connected, are you?"

"Connected?"

"Yeah, like, you know. Connected, connected."

"No," Andrew laughs. "Believe it or not there are other ways to make enemies."

"Yeah?"

"Yeah."

I stifle a yawn. "And one day you're going to fill me in on the details, right?"

"Yes, Kate. One day. Just not tonight. It doesn't exactly make for a very nice bedtime story."

"Alright," I say, but it comes out as a sigh. Suddenly I'm so tired I can't see straight. Or am I simply overwhelmed? How many more secrets are going to haunt my life?

"Goodnight, Kate," Andrew says and when he meets my eyes he smiles. "Don't worry, I'll figure this out."

He hovers near the doorway as I move past and then he stops me with a hand on my shoulder.

"Kate? Are you sure you're alright? I mean how are you handling all of this? Your mom dying and moving here with me."

I don't know how to answer this question. It's not like I can say, great! Or I love it here! Wish I'd come sooner! Because the truth is I do like being here. I like being with Andrew. I mostly like that it feels like an extended vacation from my mom. Since I'm not in San Diego I can pretend she's still alive. I can pretend she sent me off to summer camp even though it's fall, and I can pretend that she's back at home missing me as much as I miss her.

"Kate?" Andrew's hands are on my shoulders. I feel like this is the beginning step of a hug, but I'm not sure.

"I've been a bit distracted lately," I say. "I keep forgetting about... I mean I don't forget her, I just forget sometimes."

And then he's hugging me. His arms are around my back, his heartbeat in my ear. I don't want to cry. I do everything in my power to hold the tears back.

It's funny how the world could be ending and I don't care at all, but all someone has to do is offer up sincerity and I turn weak like some spineless girl who cries because she can't keep it together.

"I'm sorry you have to go through this," he says against my hair. His breath flutters a few stray strands near my face. "I'm glad you're here, Kate. It's important that you know that. Important to me."

Again he's left me without a quick response. It takes me a minute or two to think of what to say and in the end I come up with, "thank you."

It isn't until I'm safely enclosed in my bedroom that the events of today finally catch up with me. I flop back on my bed and cover my eyes to block out the memories, but they all come flooding back. And then I remember something. The photograph. I get up and open my backpack where I slipped the photo of Dr. Dolus and his bald companion. I got a good look at his face tonight. Good enough to ID him if I had to.

But I don't have to. One glance at the photo and I know who he is, and I also know why he's following me.

It all makes sense now. This is just part of Dr. Dolus' scheme to get to me. He must think that if he scares me enough I'll be forced to work with him. I'll beg him to fix me, turn me into a science project so that the world doesn't discover what a freak I am.

And if I continue to say no, he'll send the bald man with the long black coat to mess up my life, shake me up or worse yet, make me bleed.

Next time he'll make you bleed.

Next time.

I climb into bed, still in the clothes I've been wearing all day. I'm too cold to change. I just want to bury under my blankets and never come out.

"I can't take anymore, Lefty," I say to the little white cat at my feet and within minutes he moves closer, rubbing his whiskers against my hands. "Why can't they just leave me alone? It's not like I asked for any of this?"

Lefty rubs his nose against my cheek and when he finds wetness there he shakes my tears from his furry face.

"Bald men and baseball bats aside, I really like him," I whisper. Because after everything that has happened to me, and everything that could happen, I still want Zack. Without reservations. Without fear.

"Don't you think I deserve to be liked?" I ask the small white cat lounging near my shoulder.

Or, dare I say it, loved.

"He kissed me tonight," I whisper. "He kissed me and I liked it, Lefty. A lot. But it doesn't matter, does it? Because in the end, he's just another thing I have to give up."

Lefty blinks at me with his yellow cat eyes. I'm sure he has plenty to say, but he's the strong silent type. And when his eyes close it makes me want to close mine.

"It's your secret, Kate," my mom always told me. "It's better if you keep it from them."

While my response was always, "Better for who?"

Because how long can I pretend it doesn't matter? That I don't care if I'm alone?

How long?

If my mom were here she'd do that thing where she doesn't answer, she'd just give me that look of hers that tells me, *things will get better*. But she's not here. She'll never be here.

"You have me, Kate," she promised. "You'll always have me."

But she was wrong.

The tears are falling faster now. This is the first time I've really cried since I came to Mercer Island. I guess I did forget. I let myself forget all about her because it's easier to pretend that the one person who loved me more than anything is gone.

"How long, Mom?" I whisper. "How long can I go on like this, feeling alone?"

I lie here in the dark, petting Lefty and listening to him purr.

207

And when I finally fall asleep I still don't know the answer.

Twenty-Two

The next day I'm not surprised to find Zack waiting for me outside my school again. Andrew warned me this might happen.

"This is getting to be a habit," I say.

But all I get is a half-hearted smile.

"How was school?" he asks and I say, "Fine."

And that's where our conversation ends.

The ride to Andrew's house is quiet. Thank goodness it only takes about ten minutes. Ten awkwardly silent minutes.

"I have some homework," Zack says once we're inside Andrew's house and then he heads into the living room.

I guess this is his way of telling me there will be no repeat performance of last night.

"That's alright. So do I," I say, and then I stand there looking lost as he pulls out a stack of textbooks and plops down on the couch.

"Do you need something, Kate?" he asks and I hate him for sounding so cool. So detached.

"I have a paper due." I'm not sure he hears me, but he doesn't bother asking me to repeat it either.

Upstairs I toss my backpack toward my desk chair where it slides to the floor with a loud "thump."

"Lefty, come out, you coward. If I have to hide up here pretending to do homework then you at least have to keep me company."

"If you're looking for the little white cat, he's under the bed," a voice says from behind me.

I whip around. Leaning against my bedroom door is the bald man. His long black coat is unbuttoned and open, revealing a black shirt and black jeans. One hand is hidden inside his front pocket while his other hand rests on the butt of a gun tucked into the waistband of his jeans.

"Don't worry, Kate. I'm only here to chat. But if you feel the need to call your boyfriend upstairs I will be forced to use this."

I try not to stare at the gun, but it's difficult considering I've never seen one out in the wild before.

"What do you want?" I ask, and it comes out all shaky.

"Mostly I'm here, in your room," he sweeps his hand around my bedroom, "to show you how easy it is to get to you."

"Why?"

"It's important that you know. In case you thought otherwise."

"I know who you are," I say.

"Well that saves time."

He gestures for me to take a seat but I shake my head, no. It's easier for me to run when my feet are already on the ground.

"You've been playing a rather dangerous game, kid. Our mutual friend is growing impatient."

"You must have me confused with someone else," I say. "I don't have any friends."

The bald man smiles. "You know, you remind me of your father."

"You mean Andrew?" I can't keep the surprise from my voice.

"Do you have more than one?" he smirks. "Yes. Except when I knew him he went by the name Shortland not Shore. I guess that changed when he moved here."

"What do you mean? How do you know—"?

"Your father is rather infamous, Kate. Let me guess. Andrew hasn't told you all about his secret life? Hasn't filled in the details of how he met your mom?"

When I don't answer right away he smiles.

"Why don't you tell me what you think you know and I'll tell you if you're right," I say.

"Well done," he laughs. "Not only can the girl heal and run fast but she's got guts as well." He leans back against the doorframe. "No. I'm guessing Andrew wouldn't want to go down that path just yet. Better to come off as the nice guy before he sheds his skin."

"I'm not sure what you're implying but I'll have you know Andrew tells me everything. We don't keep secrets from each other."

"Everything, huh? So he knows all about my visit to the rink and our mutual friend?"

"Everything," I say.

"Well, that is very interesting."

"You think?"

"So then I have to assume you know all about your grandfather?"

"Of course," I say without missing a beat.

Never hesitate when lying, rule #1.

"I like you, kid." The bald man folds his arms against his chest and smiles.

"You have a strange way of showing it."

"What? You didn't enjoy the ride? Sorry it dragged out so long. I forgot how quickly your dad thinks on his feet. I'd hoped you'd stay in the driver's seat, but, you live, you learn. And I have to admit those guys at the ice rink had a little too much fun. Money can't buy you subtlety, I'm afraid."

"Have you been following me?" My eyes skim along my dresser for some kind of weapon within my reach but all I see are a few perfume bottles and a hairbrush.

"I can't help it, kid. You're fun to be around."

"Stop calling me, kid," I say under my breath.

"Believe me, *kid*," he emphasizes the last word and then takes a step closer to me. "You don't want me thinking of you any other way."

And just like that, I'm going to be sick. I know it.

"So why are you here?" I whisper. "You've made your point. You got in. Now what?"

"I'm here to deliver your last warning, Kate."

"I thought that was last night. You know, the guy with the knife and the whole 'next time he'll make you bleed' speech. It was a nice touch. Believe me. I was convinced."

When the bald man doesn't say anything I add, "So let's hear it."

And then he's on me. His hand is around my throat and he's holding me up against the wall while my hands pull at his hand. But he's stronger and bigger, so naturally he wins. No matter how hard I pull I can't get him to loosen his grip. I dig my fingernails into his skin and his knuckles but he doesn't even react.

"I. Can't. Breathe," I choke out. "Please."

"You have two days to change your mind. Two days before my patience runs out and I come after you." His eyes are in my eyes, two dark circles of nothing that completely fill my vision. I can't look away. I struggle against the wall, kicking my feet in a desperate chance that Zack will hear me, but kicking takes energy and after a few more kicks I find it's far more important to breathe.

"Do you really want lover-boy to come and rescue you right now? Have you thought that one through?" he growls against my face.

"Please," I gasp. "I can't—"

"Two days."

And then he releases me. Just like that. His large hand frees my throat and I collapse to the floor. I suck in air but it won't come fast enough.

"Don't forget to tell your father I said, hi," he says from his perch on my window seat.

"Who are you?" I choke out.

"My name's Haddock, but he'll know me as #5."

He climbs out my window and then disappears.

It takes me a moment to get to my feet. I don't have to look out the window to know he'll be gone. No footsteps in the dirt or crushed flowers on the ground. Not one thing has been disturbed other than the red, green and blue wires along the edge of my window, which have all been cut, detached from the black box in the corner.

When I realize the only way he could have dismantled the alarm is by trimming the wires from inside the house my skin goes cold.

How did he get in? I live here and know the pass code and even I've set off the alarm a time or two.

"Lefty? Lefty, come out! Please be okay!" I stick my head under my bed afraid of what I might find.

Two blinking yellow eyes stare back.

Zack knocks on my door a few minutes later.

I'm lying on my floor petting Lefty who's still under the bed. He's decided it's safer under there and I really can't blame him for not believing me when I say come out, everything's going to be okay. If I could fit I'd be under there with him.

"Kate?" Zack knocks again when I don't answer.

I nod my head, still too dazed to speak.

"Kate? Can I come in?"

"Yes," I call out. My voice sounds scratchy, like I've been crying.

"Are you alright?" Zack asks when he sees me on the floor.

"I'm perfect."

"I just wanted to say I'm sorry about last night."

And the day just keeps getting better and better.

"You've been through so much lately, I never should have, I mean, I really wish I had—"

"Zack. Please stop talking. I get it. Regrets, right? No worries. Consider last night forgotten."

"What? That's not what I meant, Kate. And you know it?"

"Do I?" My eyes are closed. I won't look at him.

"How could you think I'd regret what happened? If anything I regret that it ended so quickly, not that it happened. I'm only apologizing for my behavior after you tried to close me out again. I know you need time and I know you've been through a lot—"

"I *have* been through a lot," I interrupt. I drag my arm over my eyes to keep from looking at him when I say, "And that's why I think it's important that what happened last night never happen again."

He's quiet for a minute and then he says, "Okay. If that's what you want."

"It is."

Zack's footsteps are silent on my carpet and so it isn't until he peels my arm off my face that I even know he's kneeling next to me.

"I'm sorry, Kate."

"Yeah, you mentioned that."

I open my eyes and something in his expression nearly brings me to tears. I want to believe him. I've never seen sincerity like this before. But he's apologizing. And I don't want apologies. Not from him.

"I wish things had gone differently. I wish I'd been more patient with you. And I wish that you would believe me when I tell you that you can trust me not to hurt you."

He stares at me for a minute longer and then shakes his head, "But I guess that's too much to ask."

When he realizes I've got nothing to say he climbs to his feet.

"There is something you can do for me, Zack."

He turns in the doorway with his hand on the door handle.

"Yes?"

"Tell me what you know about my father."

"Kate—"

I sit up and wrap my arms around my knees. "You said I could trust you. Prove it."

Zack's eyes narrow and for a moment. I think he might just turn around and leave without answering me.

"They're his stories to tell. You need to understand that."

"Oh, I understand everything perfectly. I understand that my father has been lying to me, and so have you. I understand that whatever he was when he met my mom is the reason my mom left him and he probably fears that if he tells me the truth I'll want to leave him too and that's why he continues to lie to me. Does that sound about right?"

He doesn't answer. But he doesn't have to. The look in his eyes tells me I'm right.

"Okay, then." I take a deep breath and climb to my feet. "I guess we're done here. Thanks for the chat. You've been very helpful. I'm so glad I've figured out who I can trust."

And then I close the door in his face.

Twenty-Three

Two days. The bald man — or Haddock as I now know — has given me two days.

Two days to decide whether or not I want to live, because if I don't agree to Dr. Dolus' terms he's going to come after me and either kill me or ruin my life so completely I'll wish I were dead.

And the alternative?

Give my life to Dr. Dolus who will turn me into a lab rat and then once he's done using me he'll reveal me to the entire world.

Either way I'm dead. Everything I am, sacrificed for the good of Science.

"I'm going running," I announce to Zack when I come back downstairs. I've spent the last hour either pacing my bedroom, or staring off out the window feeling sorry for myself. Not to mention that stretch where I alternated between crying and screaming into my pillow.

"I don't think that's such— "

"I'm going. You can come, or try and stop me. But I'm going."

I zip up my jacket while Zack watches from the couch, and just before I move toward the front door he jumps to his feet.

"How far?"

"Does it matter?" I ask.

"I guess not."

And then we're running. I start off slow, my stride steady, until my body hits that magic place where everything comes together and creates the perfect escape. Nothing matters: Dr. Dolus, Haddock, and my father, don't matter.

For the moment I can even pretend I'm oblivious to Zack at my side. I know he's there, keeping pace with me, but neither of us says a word.

At the top of the hill, where I got lost that day in the fog, I slow down and come to a stop. Zack bends over catching his breath while I stare out over the neighborhood. Most of the houses are lit as the people inside prepare dinner or arrive home from work. Their porch lights twinkle back at me while the light rain dampens my clothes.

I can see my breath, something I rarely saw while I was living in San Diego, and it reminds me that I'm alive.

I'm human. I have feelings and a heart. I'm not some animal they can dissect. I've only had seventeen years, and yeah, they haven't all been fun, but they're mine. And the future is also mine.

Even though my first instinct is to run away, hide from Dr. Dolus and the Haddocks of the world, I won't survive on my own forever. I can't.

Out of the corner of my eye I notice Zack's bent over stretching his calve muscles. He's doing quite well considering he's running in jeans.

"I'm ready when you are, Kate," he says and then I'm kissing him.

My hands on the back of his neck, holding him close until I feel his hands move up into my hair. I can't stop. I don't want to stop. Kissing Zack sets me free. Makes me feel alive.

And that's all I want, to feel alive.

"Kate—"

Zack tries to pull back but I won't let him. I don't want to hear his words, his reasons for stopping. They mean nothing to me. All I have is this, right now. And it's all I may ever have.

He doesn't fight me for long, but it feels like forever. Soon his hands are on my body, on the back of my neck where my skin is exposed, and then burning trails of warmth down my back.

"I'm sorry," I whisper. "I'm sorry I can't give you any more than this. I'm sorry I keep pushing you away."

I don't realize I'm crying until Zack stops kissing me and instead focuses on brushing my tears away with his fingertips.

"I want this," I say in between each staggered breath. "I want this so much but there's something you don't know. Something I can't—"

"Kate." Zack pulls me against him and blocks my words with his kisses. His mouth is hard against my own and I don't even remember why I wanted to talk, why I stopped our lips from touching in the first place.

"I want this too," he says against my mouth. "Just don't close me out."

And then our bodies are touching, our tongues touching, our everything touching, until a car drives by, its lights illuminating our bonded form for everyone to see.

I should pull away but I don't want to. Zack must feel the same because when he whispers, "We should get back," his hands are still in my hair, our foreheads pressed against each other's. When we breathe our breath joins together and forms one misty cloud that hovers around us and then disappears.

It takes a few more cars driving by to get us moving and on the way back our pace is much slower. We're practically jogging. Side by side we trot next to each other, our hands occasionally linked, until we hit Andrew's driveway.

"There's something I should say before we go inside." Zack stops me by taking my hand. "There are things I know about Andrew, things even he doesn't realize I know. But he has to answer your questions, Kate. I can't. Andrew has been like a father to me. And to Brandon. We never would have made it through our parents' death without his support. You have to know I'd do anything for him."

Zack turns toward the house and I notice it's lit from inside. Andrew must be home.

"There are things he's done out of duty, things he's not proud of."

I feel myself begin to shake. I'm not sure if it's the cold or something else chilling my skin.

Zack grips my shoulders and his hands move up and down my arms, warming me, but it's temporary. The cold has moved inside where it will harden my heart if I let it.

"You have to know that he cares about you, Kate. He would do anything to keep you here. To protect you."

"Even lie?"

"If he had to, yes."

"To me?" I ask and before Zack can answer I add, "How can I trust him if he lies to me? And how can I live with a man I can't trust?"

"You can keep on pretending you don't need anything from anybody and see how far that gets you? Or you can open yourself to the possibility that someone just might care about you. Do anything to keep you safe."

"Kate," Zack whispers when I stay silent. "I promise I will never hurt you."

And when he kisses me, this time it feels different. His lips are so soft at first, they're barely a touch until I open myself up to the kiss and it becomes something so much more.

"Is it okay if I come and see you run on Saturday?" he asks right before we reach Andrew's front door.

"I'd like that." I smile at him and he smiles back and my heart does this little flutter thing that makes me feel like I've just jumped off something high and I'm hung up in the air.

And then it hits me. Saturday. The track meet.

It's two days away.

Two. Days.

During dinner I'm quiet. It's just Andrew, Zack and myself. Brandon is with Marnie tonight. I pick at the delicious dinner Andrew whipped together out of chicken, rice and steamed vegetables. Andrew and Zack appear to be enjoying it, they've nearly cleaned their plates, and while I want to eat, my stomach has other ideas. It's tied up in knots, worried about, well, everything.

Zack doesn't stay long once dinner is cleared. He makes some excuse about how he has a lot of homework and I would have believed him if he hadn't given me a look right after he said it, a look that clearly encouraged me to talk to Andrew tonight.

I walk him to the door while Andrew starts on the dishes. If he finds it odd that I'm walking Zack out he doesn't mention it.

Zack pulls me in for a quick kiss and I blush under the porch light.

"This is me giving you time, Kate," he says. "As long as you don't push me away I'm cool with keeping things uncomplicated. For now."

I'm not sure what he means, but I nod my head and then punch in the key code once the door is closed. I can't stop thinking about how Haddock got inside this house.

Or when he will again.

Andrew is placing the last of the dishes in the dishwasher when I walk into the kitchen. He looks up and smiles but I don't return it.

"What's wrong?" he asks. He stares at me with concern and I can't blame him for this reaction, things haven't exactly been normal since he took me in.

I pull up a stool and sit down while Andrew wipes his hands on a dishtowel.

"Why'd you change your name?" When I'd rehearsed this question in my mind it had come off sounding assertive and direct, but instead it sounds like a sigh, as if I'm too tired to put much behind it.

And I am tired. I'm so tired of it all, the secrets, the fear, but mostly the loneliness.

"I don't understand this question, Kate?" he leans back against the counter, his arms crossed in front of him.

"I need the truth. It's important that I know everything."

"Kate I—"

"I've told you my secrets, it's time I heard yours. Please, Andrew."

But he just continues to study me in silence.

I take a deep breath, and prepare myself for the battle that's about to begin.

"I thought I found you once," I say. "It was just after we'd moved to San Diego. I was fourteen." I lean my head against my hand, propping my elbow on the counter to help support what suddenly feels too heavy for me to hold up on my own. "I went back and forth on whether or not you were really dead. My mom swore by it but I figured I had to get this healing-thing from someone, right? I knew it wasn't my mom. So I kept my eyes open, and waited for the day you would turn up." I look off just past his shoulder to the curtain-less window behind him. "There was this man. He lived about two blocks from us. I used to ride by his house everyday on my bike." I glance at Andrew to see if he's still listening — he's so quiet — and find his intent blue eyes watching me.

"He had dark hair." I smile. "I don't know why I always thought of you with dark hair. And blue eyes, like mine, of course." I drop my eyes down to the counter. I don't want to see his sadness, my sadness, in his eyes. "So one day I got up the nerve to go up to his door. I just wanted to see him up close, you know, and have him see me. I was convinced that if he saw me, there would be some kind of reaction, a look of recognition, or something. But nothing happened. No slight gasp, or widening of the eyes. No dramatic music playing in the background or close up of our faces. Instead I stood there, forgetting my entire speech about how I knew he was my father and how I didn't want anything from him I just wanted him to know about me. And after what felt like an hour of him staring at me and me staring back at him, he finally said, 'Can I help you?' Just like that. 'Can I help you?' Like I was browsing some luggage store looking for a fourth piece to match my collection."

"What did you tell him, Kate?" Andrew's voice sounds raw, like his question scratched his throat on the way out.

"The first thing that came to mind was that I was selling newspapers." I laugh, but it comes out sounding hallow. "I convinced him I was his paper girl. He paid me twenty bucks and I took it and ran. And for the next six months I got up every morning, walked down to the newspaper stand and delivered his stupid paper."

"Oh, Kate," Andrew sighs.

"No. It was a good thing," I say. "During those six months I realized I didn't want him to be my father. I used to see him walking some girl out to the curb almost every morning. At first I thought it was his daughter but then when I'd get close I'd see she was always different. Sometimes she was blond and tall or dark and tall or, well, she was always tall." I shrug and stare down at the matching tiles along the countertop, my finger tracing the line of grout around each tile. "I think I always knew he wasn't you. I just couldn't believe you'd be dead."

"Listen," I say after a minute or two more of silence, "I know you're hiding something from me, and I know there's a reason my mom kept you from me. She protected me my entire life." I shake my head and stare up at the ceiling, forcing back the tears that are desperately trying to slip free. "Every single second of every day she worried about me," I continue. "But I came out here with you because I hoped you would eventually tell me the truth. And," I pause and take a breath, "I wanted to get to know you. But if you don't tell me soon, I'm going to suspect the worst." I brush my hair out from behind my ear and it hangs down, blocking my face, when I whisper, "And I don't know if I can continue to live with someone I don't trust."

When I finish the room is so silent I'm afraid to breathe. My chest is tight from holding back my tears and the other things I want to say, but can't, like, why weren't you there for me? And, please don't make me have to leave.

"What would you like to know, Kate?" Andrew's words come slow. "Ask me anything," he whispers.

I look up and find whatever I'm holding back he has right there in his eyes.

"Let's start with why my mom left?" I say.

Andrew leans his head back against the cupboard and closes his eyes. "We should probably start earlier than that."

His face is tense, almost cold, like he's second-guessing what he's about to tell me.

"I enlisted when I was eighteen. There weren't a lot of options for a kid with no funds. College was out of the question, and the Army promised me a bed and three meals a day. That was more than anyone else could offer."

"Didn't you have parents? Or family?"

Andrew shrugs. "My father died when I was sixteen and I never even knew my mother. I had two options come graduation day, live on the streets or enlist."

"But I thought you went to MIT? You told me—"

He holds up a hand to stop me and then slips both of them inside his jeans pockets. "I did, Kate. Once the Army discovered my special talents went beyond standing in formation and drinking to fall asleep, they moved me on to Special Ops. That's when things got a bit interesting."

"What do you mean, interesting?"

Andrew reaches a hand up and drags it through his hair. "I never designed security systems, Kate. The Army, they trained me to be a spy."

"A spy?" I shake my head in disbelief. "You're a spy?"

"A spy, an acorn, a mole," Andrew pauses, "a contract assassin. To me it was just a job."

"Like a James Bond kind of spy?"

Andrew smiles. "It's not that glamorous, trust me."

"But. You. They." Apparently I can't form a complete sentence. I squint back at Andrew like I'm trying to see him clearly. He doesn't look like spy, no twirly mustache or Inspector Gadget trench coat. "I don't understand."

"Obviously the life of a spy requires a certain amount of discretion. Nobody was supposed to find out. Not even your mother. And living in Washington helped," he gestures outside at the light rain hitting the window, "no one makes eye contact when the sky is falling."

I take a breath, my mouth poised with another question, and then I get it. I know why she left.

"She was never supposed to find out, Kate."

"But she did."

"Yes. She did."

"And so she took off." It's not a question but Andrew nods anyway.

"Somebody leaked her some false information and by the time I got home she was gone. She left me a note, told me she never wanted to see me again and to leave her alone. At the time I wasn't exactly happy to oblige, but I did it anyway. There aren't too many happily married spies. I knew the risks."

"What was this false information? And who told her?"

When Andrew turns back to me his eyes are haunted, like I've drudged up a ghost he thought he'd outmaneuvered years ago. "She believed I killed her father," he says. "And that I used her to get to him, but it's not true. I was hired to take him out but after I met your mother I turned the assignment down and someone else went in to finish the job."

"I don't know how she found out. I came home and found she had photos of me in her father's house the same day he was killed."

"What?"

"I went in thinking my hate for her father would get me through it, but it wasn't enough to pull the trigger."

"Why didn't you try to explain?"

"Because I couldn't prove it. And until I could she wouldn't see me, hell, she wouldn't even allow me near enough to explain."

My head feels so heavy right now I can't make sense of anything. I can see my mother, pregnant and scared, running, just like she always has, thinking she'll never be safe, that her baby will never be safe.

"So she didn't know about me before you... she never."

"She must have found out soon after."

"Oh." I stare up at Andrew until I realize he's interpreting my silence as blame.

"I was assigned to take out her father," he explains. "He was a very bad man, Kate. He'd hurt a lot of people to get where he was."

"And what was that?"

"He was a diamond dealer. He had a chain of stores throughout Europe but he never came upon his diamonds legally. Or ethically."

"Did she know? Did my mom know what he was?"

"No." Andrew shakes his head and in his eyes I see his sorrow. "She adored him. Your grandfather could do no wrong."

He rubs the back of his neck and I can tell this story isn't easy on him. But I don't want him to stop.

"I didn't use her to get to him," his eyes plead for me to understand. "I was following her, yes, but only to learn as much as I could about her family. She used to love this one tree in Hyde Park. She'd go there to read every day at lunch."

His eyes stare off out the kitchen window and I can almost see her, my mom, with her sun hat and her large sunglasses, sitting under a tree with her legs crossed.

"When I finally got up the nerve to go talk to her, she said, 'I was wondering when you were going to come over.'"

He smiles and my heart tightens.

"'You weren't very subtle, you know,' she continued. 'I saw your intentions the moment you walked into the park.'"

"She shook my hand and then slipped it inside the book she'd been reading — marking her place — while she waited for me to respond. But I had nothing. Your mother," he stops and shakes his head, "she only had to look at me with those enormous green eyes of hers."

He turns away without finishing his thought and I realize I'm holding my breath. "I didn't do it, Kate. I never would have hurt your mother like that. I loved her very much." He's gripping the edge of the counter, his knuckles white from the pressure of his hold.

"And she knew that," he says, his voice louder than it has been all night. "I thought she knew me."

"I don't think she did," I say. "I think she was scared. And whenever my mom was frightened about something she ran." Just like me.

"But *I* believe you," I say. "I believe you didn't kill him." And once I've said the words out loud I realize they're true. I do believe him. At this point, why would he lie?

"I'm actually having a difficult time getting over the spy part," I add and he smiles. It's not a big smile but it's something.

"So am I to assume you got your information from Zack?"

"No. Zack wouldn't tell me anything."

Andrew shakes his head. "I don't understand," he says. "How did you know I changed my name? That's classified information."

"Well, see, that's kinda why I needed to talk to you about all of this. That and I've been driving myself crazy trying to figure out why my mom left you. You seem nice enough to me."

And there it is, a real-life smile.

"So then, where exactly did you get your information?" he asks.

"I know you think whoever is pulling all these stunts is after you, but I don't exactly believe that."

"Why? What happened, Kate?" I wish I could remove the worry from his expression but I'm pretty sure my next words will only bring it back.

"I had a visitor today. A man named Haddock."

I wait to see if Andrew reacts to the name but he only looks confused.

"Should I know that name?"

"I'm not sure. He said you'd know him better as #5."

The lines around Andrew's mouth thin out and his eyes grow dark. For a second I'm almost afraid of him.

"Are you sure about that?" he says slowly.

"Yes. I'm sure."

Andrew grips my shoulders and I can feel his tension pulsing through his fingertips. "And where did this conversation take place?"

My eyes widen when he shakes me.

"Kate! Where did you see him?"

"Upstairs. In my bedroom."

Andrew goes still. It's as though his breathing has stopped. His fingertips dig into my skin, but I don't dare complain. I'm so frightened by the look in his eyes I don't dare blink.

"Here? Are you telling me he was here? Today?" he asks softly. Each word clearly enunciated so I don't miss the question.

"Yes," I whisper. "He was in my room when I got home from school."

Andrew grabs my hand and drags me toward the garage.

"What? We're leaving?" I try to pull back from him but my legs are too shaky and instead I stumble along behind him. "Wait! I can't leave Lefty."

Andrew curses under his breath and then pulls me toward the stairs.

"Stay close to me," he whispers. "When I say run, you run."

"Where?" I whisper back, but he doesn't answer. He's practically carrying me up the stairs. After he's checked my bedroom thoroughly he motions for me to grab the sleeping cat on my bed and throw him into his cat carrier. When Lefty lets out a howl of protest I nearly hit the ceiling.

Once I have Lefty zipped up and inside the cat carrier I find Andrew examining the cut wires along the edge of my window.

"Looks like he cut them from inside," I say and when Andrew looks up I wish I'd stayed silent. It appears he's already come to this conclusion and he's not too pleased.

"That son of a bitch was in my house," he says once we're inside his car. He reaches across my seat and slips a shiny, silver gun out of the glove box.

"What is that— why do you need a gun?" my voice is quivering. I can hear it so Andrew must hear it.

"Did he hurt you, Kate? Touch you in anyway?"

"He only came to chat," I whisper.

Andrew slams on his brakes, nearly missing a stop sign.

"Andrew? What is happening exactly?"

"We're not staying here tonight." And that's all the explanation I get until we arrive in Downtown Seattle.

I follow him up to our room at the Hilton, all the while avoiding the curious glances thrown our way. I mean, I get it; an older man, a young girl, and neither of us have any bags. I'm sure the staff sees this kind of thing all the time.

But gross. He's my father!

If Andrew notices he doesn't react. The last thing he wants to do is draw any attention to us right now.

Once we're in our room I watch him check the locks, the windows and the phones and then when he's finally satisfied he pulls up a chair and faces me.

"Tell me everything. From the moment you arrived here in Seattle with your mother to every detail leading up to today."

And it takes a while. We order room service around 2AM, chocolate ice cream for me, and a pitcher of coffee for Andrew.

It's close to five in the morning before his questions finally ease up.

"Get some sleep, Kate," he says, and he doesn't have to ask twice. Once my eyes close, I'm there. When I wake in the afternoon Andrew's still in his clothes from the night before and I can tell by his hunched position in the chair that he hasn't slept at all.

He hears me stir and turns to me with tired eyes. It's everything I can do to keep from throwing my arms around him and telling him I'm sorry. Sorry that my mom didn't believe him. Sorry that she left. I'm sorry he never got the chance to explain his side of the story, but mostly I'm sorry she died believing the worst.

"I'm sorry," I say and his eyes do that thing my eyes probably do when I don't understand.

"Why, Kate?" his voice is clear and deep as if he's been talking on the phone for hours and now that I think of it, I know he has. A few hours ago I heard him, and when I opened my eyes he slipped into the other room.

"Kate?" he asks again when I don't answer.

"I never meant to cause so much trouble."

"This isn't your fault." He sits down next to me on the bed and takes my hand. "This will never be your fault."

"I'm the one they want," I say.

"Yeah, well, they'll have to find a new hobby."

I smile up at Andrew, and even though it's a half-hearted smile, he smiles back.

"Are you hungry? I sent down an order for some breakfast a few minutes ago. Why don't you go take a shower and I'll listen out for it."

"Okay."

"I called the school and told them you were sick. And then I called your coach and let him know you won't be competing tomorrow."

"Okay." I manage to keep the disappointment from showing on my face, but I can't keep it from tugging at my heart. I was looking forward to Saturday, but we decided, Andrew and I, late last night that it was better if I laid low until Haddock was found.

"And he will be found, Kate. You can take my word on that," Andrew assured me repeatedly. "He's been running long enough. This time he's not going to get away."

It appears our dear Haddock, or #5 as he's referred as around Andrew's old agency, is on some list of the world's most dangerous criminals.

Lucky me.

With the help of a few old contacts through the agency, Andrew has a team out looking for him right now.

I'm on my way into the bathroom when Andrew calls out, "Zack and Brandon will be here in about an hour. They're going to stay with you while I run across town and meet with one of my contacts."

"Alright," I say, "but I'm going to need some new clothes if you expect me to entertain men in my hotel room."

"Yesterday's clothes will have to do," Andrew says and from the look on his face he doesn't find my comment amusing.

But I do. I chuckle under my breath, amazed that I can find humor in all of this. I should feel terrified. I should be hiding under the bed with Lefty, who the moment we slipped him into his cat carrier went into survival mode where he doesn't eat or drink until he's returned to his original location. But instead I'm laughing as if today is just another carefree day in Kate Triumphland. And my stomach is even thinking about breakfast.

"We should be able to go back home tomorrow," Andrew calls out to me.

There it is again, that word. Home. How quickly Andrew's house has become my home.

"The new alarms should be installed and up and running by then," he says.

"Great," I mutter under my breath. "Just when I was getting used to the old key codes."

I close the door and catch a glimpse of myself in the full-sized mirror.

The girl staring back at me looks different. Same long auburn hair, same dark blue eyes, but there's something in her eyes that I've never seen before. If I were to pinpoint it I would say she looks comfortable.

Safe.

Two words I'd never use to describe myself.

Something must have changed between yesterday and today to turn my eyes this comfortable shade of blue. Was it me or was it Andrew? Last night he stopped being my father, the stranger, and became my protector. Which is funny because I never thought I needed anyone to protect me.

Something must have changed in the last few weeks because, normally, I take care of myself.

But I never feel safe. Never.

I take the world's longest shower and then wrap myself in the hotel's terrycloth robe while I take my time blow-drying my hair. As long as I'm in the bathroom I don't have to listen to Andrew's plans or strategies on how he's going to bring Haddock down, lock him away and then swallow the key.

It's not that I feel bad for Haddock, quite the opposite. I just don't want Andrew involved.

Which is what he wants to be.

I know he used to do this kind of stuff for a living and from what I can tell is pretty good at it, but I have one family member left. One whole person in the world who cares if I eat a good breakfast, floss my teeth and go to school. I don't care how evil Haddock is, if he takes that person away I'm left with nothing.

But then on the flip side, if Andrew does lock Haddock away does that mean I don't have to worry about Dr. Dolus anymore?

When I mentioned his name Andrew vaguely remembered some doctor my mom was going to for fertility treatments. But Andrew wasn't around much during that time, and therefore never went with her to any of her visits.

"She wanted a baby more than anything," he explained to me last night. "And she blamed herself for not getting pregnant."

"It probably would have helped if I'd been around more…you know, to keep trying—" he stopped and cleared his throat and the blush that spread across his cheeks made me want to laugh.

And I had to love him for that.

Zack and Brandon show up as I'm finishing a large plate of hash browns. Brandon spies Andrew's half-eaten sandwich and after gaining permission swallows the entire thing in one bite. Soon after, Andrew leaves. He hovers in the doorway with his eyes trained on me and when I give him a hug he holds me a bit longer than normal.

"Nobody comes in until I'm back, do you understand?"

When the three of us nod he appears satisfied and then closes the door.

"What kind of channels do you get here?" Brandon asks and for the next few hours we lose him to sports, while Zack steals twenty bucks off me in a "friendly game of Blackjack."

"I never took you for a cheater," I say as he's shuffling up the cards.

"I'm not cheating, Kate. Counting cards is a skill, it's not cheating."

"You don't!" I exclaim and he laughs.

"I don't," he says, but the smile on his face makes it difficult to believe him.

During our game Zack decides to play twenty questions, which feels more like a hundred and twenty, but I play along.

He asks me things like, what is my favorite flavor of ice cream, and, who was my favorite cartoon character when I was young? All safe questions, as far as I can tell.

After about an hour of this Brandon joins in. I can feel him watching us from the couch. He pays attention to the way Zack and I laugh or talk over each other. When he catches my eye he smiles.

It only turns serious when I start laughing so hard I'm almost crying and then I realize I haven't laughed this hard since before my mom died and because I'm feeling so relaxed at the time I say this out loud.

It's moments like this that come out of the blue and make you stop laughing altogether. Zack and Brandon immediately notice the switch in my mood but they don't say anything. Brandon goes back to the TV while Zack deals up another round of cards.

"I hate that thinking of my mom brings me down," I say. "Because she was never down, even when I drove her to the edge of her sanity, she was rarely in a bad mood."

"She would want you to be happy, Kate," Zack says. "Eventually you'll stop feeling guilty for feeling happy."

"I don't believe that." And to lighten my response I add, "I'm pretty good at feeling guilty. It's one of my many skills."

"You mean like losing at Blackjack?" Zack throws down his cards and sure enough, I've lost again.

Andrew returns around ten. He comes in looking exhausted but satisfied and I feel a tiny burst of hope.

"It's over, honey," he whispers against my hair and with his arms around me, I've never felt so safe.

"My contact found him a few blocks from here. He's been staying in the city. They transported him down to Burien where they'll hold him until our guys can pick him up tomorrow afternoon." Andrew smiles at me looking tired, but happy. "And you know what that means, right?"

"Haddock's gonna wish he brought his own soap?" Brandon throws out.

"No," Andrew laughs. "Kate gets to race tomorrow."

"Woohoo!" Brandon yells and Andrew's smile widens.

"I plan on paying a visit to our friend, Haddock, tomorrow but not until the afternoon. So we can all come and watch you race, Kate. You still up for it?"

"Sure." I look around the room at their three smiling faces. I want to feel relieved, like this solves everything and all my problems have disappeared. But I'm still me. Even with Haddock behind bars and Dr. Dolus minus his scare tactic, I'm still a freak.

"So it's really over?" I ask Andrew again later. Zack and Brandon have gone on home and Andrew is making notes in his notebook while he rubs the back of his neck in concentration. "You're positive you caught the right guy?"

"It's him, alright. They found a photograph of you and your mom in his pocket and a box of explosives in the back of his car. I guess he had some plans for me tomorrow."

"Wait! What?" I can feel the blood rushing from my head to the tips of my toes. "What do you mean, plans?"

"I shouldn't have mentioned it. Kate, I'm sorry. You see, Haddock and I go way back."

"What does that mean?"

"Well, let's just say he wouldn't exactly cry at my funeral. But we have him now," Andrew adds when he notices the look on my face. "You don't have to worry."

"No. I guess not," I say. "So where's the photo?"

"Right now it's with evidence but I got a good look at it." He taps his pen against his notebook, his eyes narrowed in thought. "When you were here for the track meet did you and your mom stop and eat lunch at a café in Pioneer Square?"

My stomach drops.

"Yes. I told you. We grabbed some lunch right before our flight back."

"And your mom had already visited with Dr. Dolus by that time?"

No. No, this can't be happening.

"Yes," I whisper. "She met with him that morning. Just before my first race."

The room is so silent I can hear the TV from next door.

"He killed her," I say. "He followed us back and killed her."

"We don't know that for sure, but it's starting to look that way, Kate." Andrew is watching me uneasily as if he's afraid I'm going to collapse and when I sink down to the floor he wraps his arms around me. "He may not have meant to, I believe it was his way of testing out your ability."

"A test? Well that makes it all better, Andrew. He killed my mom as a test for me!" I try to pull out of Andrew's arms but his hold is too strong.

"I'm so sorry, Kate," he whispers over and over again. "I'm so sorry."

"Whether he meant to or not, he killed her." The tears run down my face and the pain from holding back a sob is choking my throat. "You know him. You tell me, did he get some kind of sick satisfaction from killing her? Because he looked like he was enjoying it."

"Kate—"

"He smiled at me, Andrew! That sick son of a bitch smiled at me! He knew the car was going to hit us and he smiled!"

Andrew is rocking me back and forth the way my mom used to. His hands rub my back, soothing the sobs that are breaking me. When I breathe in it sounds like I'm gasping and when I breathe out it comes with a cry of rage.

Every few minutes I pound my fists against his back and he lets me. I know he's tired and, man, so am I, but my mind won't rest.

"He killed her. Killed her!" I cry over and over again until the words slur into something that resembles "killer."

Just before the room gets light again Andrew promises me he'll make Haddock pay. He'll make him suffer. And it feels good, this thought. It comforts me when I drift off to sleep. But in the dreams that follow I'm the one torturing him, making him bleed. He begs for mercy, mercy from me, and when he looks up, I'm the one reflected in his eyes.

Twenty-Four

San Diego

The cool waves rush over Jonah's feet. For hours now he's been sitting behind Kate's house. Or to sum it up more accurately: days, hours, and many contemplative minutes.

Where is she?

He'd ventured up to her house a couple of times. Even wandered the perimeter, staring through windows, but no one is living there. He is sure of it.

"I'm trying, Nanna," he whispers into the light breeze. "I'll wait forever if I have to."

But maybe Sara was right. She must not have missed him much. Or perhaps she'd been forewarned.

Jonah rests his head back in the sand, covers his eyes and tries not to think about how much he hates Sara. But it just seems impossible.

It had been exactly twenty-four hours from the time he and Nanna had arrived in San Diego that Jonah had gone searching for Sara — otherwise known as the woman who showed up to his eighth birthday party and slapped him across the face for calling her "mom."

The neighborhood was quiet when Jonah stepped from the taxi.

"You sure you want me to leave you here, son?" the driver asked.

Jonah wondered that himself. But instead he said, "I'll be fine," and turned to face Sara's house.

The taxi pulled away. No reason for it to be soiled by the derelict neighborhood any longer. With its boarded-up houses and overgrown lawns, Jonah was surprised someone he knew would choose to live in this part of town. But then again, he'd never really known his mother.

Sara's house stood out mostly because it looked lived-in rather than abandoned. Jonah could hear yelling when he approached the front door, but it wasn't clear whether it was coming from inside Sara's house or from the house next door. Before he could knock, the door flew open. Jonah leapt back in surprise.

"You're trespassing! We don't want anything you're selling, so take off, kid." The man was large in height and girth, and the smell of alcohol spewed from his mouth.

"Is Sara here? I need to talk to her."

The man stared blankly at him, his eyes bloodshot. "Sara! Sara, get out here!" he slurred.

Jonah held his ground when the man swayed toward him and stumbled onto the front step.

"What is it Tom? You know I'm watching my soaps. What could possibly —" Sara took a step out onto the porch and stopped.

Jonah hadn't seen her since his eighth birthday. She still had that long, black braid that whipped against her back like a horsetail, but her face was now weathered from the sun.

"What do you want?" Her gray eyes squinted at Jonah, even though the day was cloudy. "What are you doing *here*?"

"Do you need me to make him leave, Sara? 'Cause I don't really like him." Tom stumbled into Sara and she pushed him away.

"What are you going to do about it, huh? You can barely hold yourself up."

Tom grunted in response.

"I just need to ask you a question, Sara, and then I'll be on my way." Jonah didn't take his eyes off the woman he'd always believed to be his mother.

She stared back and something in Jonah's eyes must have convinced her to let him stay. "Tom. Leave us alone, would ya?"

"Who is this kid, Sara? How do I know I can trust him?" Tom was leaning against the doorframe now, his head swinging slightly with each word he spoke.

"He's—" Sara didn't continue.

"I'm Jonah. I know Sara from the hospital."

Tom perked up slightly. "Tell them to take her back! The money was real good when you were working there, huh, Sara?"

"Tom. A minute please?"

Tom gurgled something Jonah couldn't make out and tripped back into the house. Within seconds Jonah heard a crash from the next room.

"Well, what is it you wanted to ask? Is it Nanna? Did she finally run out of money and now she's looking for a hand-out?"

Jonah's eyes went flat. "No, Sara. She's dead." It was only a slight lie and he had his Nanna's permission so it made the lie a little less painful.

"Oh." Sara's hands twitched slightly at her sides but her face didn't react. "Well? What do you want then?"

"Her name."

Sara's face went white. "I-I don't know what —"

"I know you know who she is. Just give me her name and you'll never have to see me again."

Her face tightened when she smiled as if it wasn't used to the expression. "You think it's that easy? I spent four years of my life locked up in a loony bin for taking you! And by the time I got out, I wasn't so sure I didn't belong there."

"I have no intention of ratting you out. I just want her name."

Sara snorted. "Why should I believe you? How do I know you won't go straight to the cops and spill the whole story?"

Jonah slipped an envelope out of his back pocket and handed it to her. "Because of this, and the fact that if I told, not only would they come after you, but Nanna's name would be disgraced as well. And *that* I can't have."

Sara took the envelope and opened it slowly. When she looked inside her eyes widened.

"Keep it, Sara. I want you to have it. Just give me her name."

Sara's shifty eyes moved around the yard, but not once did they meet Jonah's. "If I tell you, you'll leave me alone?"

Jonah nodded.

"And I can keep this money?"

"Yes."

"You won't want anything else from me?"

Like what? Jonah wanted to scream. A mother? But instead he asked, "Why'd you do it, Sara?"

Sara snorted again and something inside Jonah turned cold. "Believe me, kid, you weren't worth it. Thought it would help me at the time. You were an easy take. Your mother believed you were dead. Stillborn. So I took you and tried to pawn you off as my own, but the guy I was trying to trap didn't want you neither." Sara's face piqued with curiosity. "She must have told you. Yeah, no other reason you'd be here. The old cow must have told you then. I swore she never would, what with her growing all attached and all."

"Yes. She told me."

Sara's smile nearly made Jonah sick. "You must hate her for it. Sweet old Nanna. Not so perfect anymore, huh?"

"No, Sara," Jonah hissed. "I don't hate *her*."

Sara shifted her feet as if she'd lost interest in the conversation, or perhaps she simply couldn't handle the look of revulsion in Jonah's eyes a moment longer.

"Well, it's been a while but it'll come to me. You staying around here?"

"I'll wait, Sara. As long as it takes, I'll wait." And he would have. But luckily for him, she remembered rather quickly when she realized he wasn't going to leave.

"Olivia. Her name was Olivia. Not the smartest cookie but you can't have it all, you know."

"Goodbye, Sara." Jonah was walking back toward the street when she called out to him.

"You want to know the strangest thing about it, kid?"

Jonah paused but he didn't turn around.

"They never reported me — the hospital, the mother — neither of them filed a claim."

"Then why'd you serve time?" Jonah couldn't help but be intrigued.

"The dead baby. They thought you were dead and I wasn't about to tell them otherwise. So, they locked me away for that." Sara tapped her forehead lightly and said, "You gotta be sick in the head to steal a dead baby. But the jail time is less so I went along with it. Acted it up too. Told them I threw you in the ocean. Fish food." She laughed and Jonah's stomach lurched. "They searched the beach for a couple days but the mother, she never wanted to make a big deal of it. You know, get in the papers and stuff." Sara had moved closer and when Jonah turned around she was almost in front of him. "Must not have missed you much, huh, Jonah?"

Those parting words had kept him company on his long walk back to town.

Jonah thought about the countless beatings he'd welcomed from Ricky's hands. Sara's words hurt more than the lot of them.

"Did she remember, Jonah?" Nanna was sitting up in bed when he'd walked into the hotel room.

"Yes."

"The whole name? Can't do much with just a first name."

Jonah had walked to the window and stared out at the view of the ocean. In that moment he could feel his world changing. With each wave that touched the sand, the life Jonah had always believed to be true was washing away.

"Jonah?" His Nanna's voice was anxious and Jonah turned and offered her his best impersonation of a smile.

"Yes, Nanna. She remembered everything."

Three weeks later his Nanna died. She closed her eyes, went to sleep and by morning she was gone.

"We found her," Nanna had whispered over and over again. "We found her Jonah, now go make it right."

Twenty-Five

Seattle

"Up and at 'em," Andrew says and I open my eyes. "We're going to be late if we don't get moving."

"Late?" I squeak out. "Late for what?"

"The track meet." He sits down on the edge of my bed and I realize he's already showered and dressed.

"Do you ever sleep?" I ask.

"Are you up for this today, Kate? You don't have to run. I know you haven't had a lot of rest and with everything that's happened..."

"I want to." I always want to.

"Alright." Andrew smiles and stands up. "If you're sure."

In the shower I let the water run down my body. It's so hot it feels like tiny pinpricks of fire. The warm steam slips into each corner of the bathroom and spills out under the door, but it doesn't touch the cold inside of me.

My mom is dead. Murdered. And it's all my fault.

"Try not to think about it," Andrew says. "We don't know for sure."

He watches me pick at my breakfast while he talks on the phone, and once when his back is turned I see his face reflected in the mirror. He may not want me to think about it, but he sure is. I've never seen him look so intense. If I didn't know this man, he would terrify me.

On the way to the meet we swing by the house so I can grab my running clothes. Upstairs I release Lefty into the wild that is my room while Andrew talks to the three pirate-looking men working on the alarm system.

"They'll be finished by noon," he explains once we're back in his car. "They managed to get the system set up much faster than they expected."

"And you trust these guys?" I ask. "I mean, I'm sure they're great guys and all and they probably buy their moms flowers on mother's day but if I saw them on a perfectly lit street, swimming with cops, I'd still run in the opposite direction."

Andrew smiles. "I trust them, Kate. They're also retired from the agency. They do this on the side now."

"How convenient."

Andrew doesn't say anything more but I do feel his occasional glance as he's driving. I can only imagine he's waiting for me to break under the stress of it all. Between my mom dying, finding out I have a father, finding out I have a father who's a spy and that other little matter of the man who wants to place parts of me in a Petri dish, not to mention his psycho henchman, I really shouldn't be expected to be out performing normal right now.

A dark cave with soft pillows would be my first choice.

We pull into the parking lot of the high school and that cold, lost feeling I woke up with burns off like the fog that rolls in most mornings. I can't help but feel a stirring of excitement when I see the other athletes heading toward the track.

"You really love it, don't you?" Andrew is studying me. A hint of a smile plays upon his lips.

"I can't explain it, it's like this rush of adrenaline, and even though I know it's risky and it used to stress my mom out like nothing else, I can't stop." I shrug my shoulders, embarrassed that I've said so much, and that absolutely none of it makes sense to anyone but me. "When I'm out there, I'm in control."

"I think I know what you mean. Whenever I was on an assignment I was always aware of the risks and yet it didn't matter. What mattered was taking the target down. I knew if I kept my senses clean I could get through anything."

Up until this point Andrew has been staring out the front windshield, watching the parking lot fill up around us, but when I ask, "What was it like, being a spy?" he turns to me, his expression dark.

"Dangerous."

"Too dangerous for Zack?"

His eyes widen upon my face and then he says, "Yes. Zack needs to continue his interests in engineering or architecture. Something more suited to—"

"A life of ordinary?" I ask. "Something safe and boring?"

"Something practical," Andrew says.

"And what about me?"

"What about you, Kate?"

"Do you think I'd make a good spy?"

It's meant to be a joke, an attempt to lighten the dark mood I've been living in for the last twenty-four hours or possibly seventeen years, but Andrew doesn't take it that way. He stares at me for a minute as if he's deep in thought and then his entire body goes still.

"What? What is it?" I don't like the look in his eyes. It frightens me. But it passes so quickly that I wonder if I was mistaken. He shrugs it off and then nods at something behind me.

"You should go. I think one of your teammates is looking for you."

And sure enough, when I turn around there's Emily. She and a few girls from my team have just arrived and they're waiting for me on the edge of the parking lot.

"Good luck, Kate." Andrew gestures for me to go on ahead. "I'll see you after the race."

"Is that your dad?" Emily asks when I join them on the sidewalk. "Crepes, Triumph! Don't let my mom catch sight of him. She'll have her tentacles around his flashy sports car before you can say, evil step-mother."

"Crepes? Don't you mean cripes?"

"Maybe if I were like a thousand years old."

245

"Okay." I make a face at Heather who smiles at the ground.

"Are you ready for this?" Emily asks and then begins kneading the back of my shoulders as if I'm a prizefighter and I'm about to go into the ring.

"It's just a race, Emily."

"Oh, give me a break with this, 'it's just a race' crap." She looks back and forth between Heather and me and then says, "do you know I've had to endure about five separate 'Kate Triumph is a God' conversations with this girl," she nods at Heather and then continues, "it's like racing you again is on her bucket list or something."

"We're racing each other today?" I ask, and Heather just nods.

Her cheeks are red with embarrassment and her eyes downcast.

"How many races?"

"Just one."

Emily throws her arm around Heather as if in apology. "And you better bring you're a-game, Triumph. Heather here has been practicing."

For a split second Heather looks up and our eyes meet.

"I'm just excited to race with you. When we competed at Husky I got bumped up as an alternate. But like Emily said, I've been practicing."

From across the field I hear a whistle blow and then Coach Abrahms is yelling at us.

"Can someone please explain why half my team is still standing in the parking lot? Triumph? Have you even warmed up yet?"

"I'm coming coach," I yell back and then start jogging toward him.

"Don't forget, Kate! After the meet we're headed to the mall."

When I don't respond Emily yells," You said you'd come Triumph! I'm holding you to it!"

Once I reach the track I go through my warm-up instinctively. I can feel the coach's excitement. I've seen it before. He watches each move I make, jotting down notes on his clipboard.

"Do you feel ready?" he asks.

It's always the same question.

"Of course," I say, which is always my answer.

I sit back on the grass and watch Heather do her sprints. Back and forth, back and forth, and then she jogs in place. Her face is radiant. Her eyes lit with adrenaline. She finishes her warm-up and stretches her arms above her head. When she catches me watching her she waves and had I not seen her earlier I wouldn't recognize this girl in front of me. She's confident and lit from inside, like a whole new girl.

"Hey, Kate." Brandon trots up to me with Zack right behind him.

"Has anyone ever told you that you look great in running shorts?" Zack whispers in my ear when Brandon turns to talk with the coach.

I feel my face heat up but I can't hold back a smile.

"There was that one guy," I say. "You know, back behind the bleachers. But I think he felt he had to since he was kissing me at the time."

Zack's smile disappears and his eyes narrow. "What guy?"

When Brandon hears me laughing he walks over to us.

"What'd I miss?"

But I can't stop laughing. It feels so good to laugh, even if it sounds slightly out of tune, and when I continue Zack joins in.

"You're up, Triumph," Coach Abrahms yells.

"Give 'em hell, Kate," Brandon thumps me on the back and when I spring forward he says, "That's what you get for tackling me the other night."

And of course that gets people talking, "Kate tackled Brandon. At night, he said!" I hear them twittering like chickens, but I ignore them because Zack is smiling at me and I like his smile. It makes me feel lucky, like out of all the people he could choose to smile at, he chose me.

"Good luck, Kate," he whispers, and it's everything I can do to keep from throwing myself in his arms and kissing him in front of everyone. From the look in his eyes it appears he's thinking the same thing.

I walk with Heather to the line. She takes her place three runners down from me and just before the warning whistle blows she mouths, *good luck*, and I mouth it back.

When the starter pistol fires I start running.

I pass the other girls easily; I don't even have to try. I slow up near the bend just like my mom always told me to.

"You don't want to slip coming around the corner, Kate. Remove the risk."

I'm so used to hearing her voice in my head while running it shouldn't affect me, but it does.

Why can't you be here with me? Why did I have to compete at Husky? Why did you have to die? The whys chase me around the track. They fill my head with white noise, blocking out everything else. Out of the corner of my eye I notice Heather is coming up from behind and suddenly all I can hear is her voice inside my head.

"I'm kinda a freak around here."

"They all make fun of me because I love running so much."

I'm not sure if I'm just distracted or simply tired, but suddenly she's right next to me, running as if it's everything to her.

"I don't care if I win, I just like to run."

Up ahead is the finish line. A few more strides and we're there.

Heather is panting, pushing her body beyond its limits. I haven't even broken a sweat. *You can do it, Heather. Keep going.*

And it's like she hears me. Her feet kick up dust and she sprints past me just as we reach the line.

Heather lights up when she realizes she's won. She looks back at me, her face a picture of disbelief, and then she's jumping up and down as the rest of my team converges on her.

The crowd is cheering. My teammates are cheering. Somewhere my mom is cheering, smiling from the sidelines. Just like Andrew. When I catch his eye, he winks, and that's really all I need today to feel free.

Heather's parents materialize from the crowd and they couldn't be more excited if they tried. They're all smiles as they hug her. Their enthusiasm is contagious.

I'm about to walk away when Heather turns and runs over to where I'm standing.

"We did it, Kate!" She pulls me in for a hug and squeezes me so tight I feel the hug even after she's let go. "That was amazing!"

"It was," I say. I have to admit it felt pretty damn good.

Heather hugs me again and then runs back to her friends and family.

"That was a great race, honey."

"Thanks, Andrew." I turn around and there he is, leaning up against the fence.

"I need to take off right after your next race so I wanted to make sure I got a chance to say congrats on your win."

"Who says I'm going to win?" I say and Andrew grins.

"What? You're feeling overly generous today?"

"Not exactly."

He winks at me again and says, "You're getting soft, Kate."

"Me?" Who'd a thought?

"So, what are your plans for the rest of the day?"

"World domination, perhaps?" I'm feeling that good.

Andrew laughs. "Can you keep it to a twenty-mile radius? Until Haddock is locked up I'd like you to stay close."

Haddock. His name creates cracks in my good mood leaving me shaky.

"Some girls on my team want me to go to the mall."

"Which mall?" Andrew asks. If he's surprised to hear I have friends he keeps it from me.

"Belleview, I think? Is that far?"

"It's within your boundaries." He winks at me. "But just to be safe, why don't you have Zack take you?"

"Please tell me you're paying Zack well for all this babysitting."

"It's not babysitting, Kate. And from what I can tell he's happy to oblige." Andrew waggles his eyebrows and that's where the conversation ends.

"Drive safe, Andrew," I say with a backward wave. I'm so not going down this road with him.

His laughter follows me across the field.

"So let me get this straight, we're going to the mall?" Brandon is tossing a football in the air in the backseat of Zack's Defender. I'm not sure where he got the ball, and I'm pretty sure he doesn't play football, but one of the things I've learned is that Brandon is always in motion whether he's sitting, eating or talking.

"No. You and Zack are going to the movies while I do the girl-thing at the mall with Emily and her friends."

"You should totally ask for a sports car?" Brandon says in typical random-Brandon fashion. "That is if Andrew decides he trusts you to drive on your own again."

"He trusts me." I turn around to glare at him and Zack shakes his head from the driver's seat.

"Don't bother, Kate. He's just jealous you have a car."

"I have a car," Brandon pouts from the backseat.

"Yes, but until you pay me back for all of your parking tickets this baby is mine alone."

"Good job on your second race, by the way," Brandon says in an attempt to change the subject. "Coach was pretty impressed with your time."

"Yeah, he mentioned that," I say. "He seemed a bit put out by the first race though."

"Well, you can't win them all," Zack throws in.

"So they say."

We pull into the parking lot of the Bellevue Square Mall and Zack drives up to the front entrance.

"Where are you meeting them?"

"In the food court."

"Okay." He points to a suspended, glass walking bridge. "You have to cross that bridge to get to Lincoln Square, where the movie theater is. We're headed there now to catch the matinee and then we'll be at our Aunt Patrice's house until I hear from you. Will that give you enough time?"

"I should think so." I turn and stare at the mall behind me. "I can't even think of what I'll do in there for over two hours, let alone more."

"You're welcome to come to the show with us," Zack says and his smile is more than enough to help change my mind.

"Yeah, you can ditch your friends altogether and come with us to our aunt and uncle's too." Brandon winks at me and says, "They're dying to meet you."

Oh boy.

"I promised Emily. That is, she says I promised, but I don't remember."

"Emily has that effect on people," Brandon says from the backseat.

"That's alright. Maybe next time." Zack squeezes my hand and when I look up he winks. "Have fun, Kate. I'll call you when we're done, if I don't see you beforehand. And remember, the mall doesn't get very good reception so you may have to step outside to get a signal." He tugs on my hand when I turn to leave. "Just don't go out by yourself. Promise me."

"She promises, Zack," Brandon pipes in. "Can't you tell by her face?" And then he starts laughing.

"I won't go anywhere on my own," I say. "Unless he's cute and smells good. Oh! And he has candy. I can't resist candy."

"This isn't a fun game for me, Kate." Zack's still holding my hand and when he pulls me toward him for a second I think he's going to kiss me, right there in front of Brandon, but instead he gets right up in my face and the look in his eyes tells me this is his way of getting me back for teasing him. "Play nice or I'll join in on the game." He must find my deer-caught-in-headlights look amusing because he chuckles just before he releases my hand.

Truth be told I wouldn't have minded a goodbye kiss, I'm just not sure I'm up for an audience quite yet. Or the commitment that follows.

I wander the mall until I find a directory and discover the food court is directly above me. I'm in no hurry to catch up with Emily and the other girls from my team so I do a little window-shopping. I can't remember the last time I went to the mall. Two stores down from the escalator I notice a beautiful display in a jewelry store window and recognize the pieces immediately. They're my mom's designs, her latest collection actually. I can't help it; I have to get closer, as if touching them will bring me nearer to her.

Once I'm inside the store the noise from the mall disappears. It's like I've slipped into a soundproof room. I lean up against the glass of the display case, bewitched by the sparkling jewelry. How many nights did I stay up with her while she designed and redesigned these pieces?

Too many to count.

"Such beautiful pieces, aren't they?" the small dark-haired woman behind the counter says softly. "It's her newest collection."

I glance up and smile. "Yes, they are."

"I absolutely loved her work. Her pieces are so difficult to keep in stock with our frequent customers. Especially now."

My eyes widen in surprise and the sales girl takes her opening.

"Yes. It's awful. Just awful. She was so young and talented. I've never met her but the owner has, and he says she was truly beautiful — inside and out. I never got the chance to meet her. She was killed in a car accident about a month ago."

I can feel the room shrinking. Listening to a perfect stranger describe my mom and the loss of her life as some kind of sales pitch is the last thing I need right now.

The door chimes as additional customers enter the store. The young salesgirl excuses herself quickly with a promise to return. She hurries over to a young couple grinning by the diamond ring display case. There's only one other employee in the store — a young man — who is changing a watch battery under a small bright light. An elderly man taps his fingers impatiently as he waits for the sales boy to finish.

I glance back down at my mom's collection. Each piece arouses such a strong memory that my eyes move over the collection like an addict.

"Turn around and greet me, Kate." I feel something cold and hard press between my shoulder blades. "And if you make it look like you're not happy to see me, the sales girl is dead." He emphasizes the last few words by jabbing what could only be a gun against my skin. I try to pull away but he's trapped me up against the case.

"Now, now, Kate," he whispers in my ear. "Don't make me hurt the poor salesgirl. She doesn't appear much older than you."

I look up and catch the young girl's eye. "What are you doing here?" I whisper through a forced smile. "How did you get away?"

"Guns are magic, Kid. They can do all kinds of neat tricks."

"What do you mean? What happened?" My stomach drops and my skin feels slick against the glass counter.

"We're going for a walk now. Do you think you can handle that without anyone getting into trouble?"

No. No, I don't. But I nod anyway.

"Good. Now tell the nosy girl 'thanks' and don't forget to smile."

I do as I'm told and then we're moving toward the exit.

His arm wraps around me as we leave the store, and I'm pretty sure that thing digging into my side from underneath his jacket is his gun.

We start walking down the mall and I stare at each shopper, pleading to them with my eyes. *I need help! Please! Someone help me!* But to them I'm just another teenage girl in a mall. The noise around me is spirited and lighthearted and the twinkling sounds of everyday conversation are the background to my nightmare.

I flinch when Haddock leans close. "So many kids here tonight. If you decide you don't like my company it would be like shooting ducks in a row."

My stomach continues to roll and my head feels dizzy.

"Where's Andrew? Did you hurt him? I swear I'll kill you if you hurt him!"

"Wow! Kate. Them's fighting words!" He jabs the gun into my side again and says, "Pretty sure you're in no position to issue threats. Keep moving." He drags me down

254

a hallway where a red sign reads, To Lincoln Square, with an arrow pointing in the opposite direction we're headed.

Lincoln Square. The glass bridge.

If I can just make it across the bridge I can find Zack.

Problem is I have to escape Haddock first.

"Where are you taking me?" I'm dragging my feet and pulling as hard as I can, but Haddock's grip on my arm is too strong. He jerks me forward and I almost lose my footing.

"It's not important," he says.

"Just like my mom wasn't important?"

He glances down at me as a sadistic smile inches across his face. "Figured that out, did you?"

"You're sick," I hiss.

"I've been called worse."

We turn a corner and I notice at the end of the hall is an emergency exit. I don't know where it leads but I do know the further away I get from the crowd the less likely I'll be able to escape.

I give my arm one last tug and he pulls me so hard I fly into the wall. He lifts me back on my feet and then slams my shoulders back against the wall. I feel the cold steel of his gun pressed against my rib cage. "I can make this real easy on myself, kid. I can hurt you so bad you'll pass out, and lucky for me the doc will never know."

Lucky. Haddock doesn't get to feel lucky. I take a short breath, the only kind I can squeeze in because of the way he's holding me.

"Go ahead and shoot me then," I say. I don't know where this is coming from, but at this point in time bravery is the only thing I've got left. "If you shoot me, someone will hear you. And I'll scream so loud at least a dozen people will come running. You can't take them all out, can you? In fact, screaming sounds like a really good idea right now." I open my mouth to scream and he immediately covers it with one of his large hands.

"I don't know what you think you're doing, kid, but making the guy with the gun mad is never the best idea."

He's probably right. But I've never been good at listening to reason, so I bite him. Hard. His skin against my teeth feels rough and tastes salty, and I try not to think about where his hands have been or when he last washed them. It's far more important that I get away.

Haddock pulls at his hand but I won't let go, so he shoves his knee into my stomach and I gasp as the air leaves my body and falls to the ground with the rest of me. He grips my hair and drags me back up the wall until I'm standing just inches from his face.

"Listen, kid," he spits. "I'm going to get you out to my car one way or another. I'd prefer it if you were walking, but carrying your limp body out is starting to look like the better plan."

"Kate?"

NO! My heart stops. Not now!

I ease my head slowly to the right and find Heather standing at the end of the hallway.

"Are you okay? We've been looking for you." She takes a few steps closer and then stops when I shake my head, no. "Zack called Emily's phone, he said he couldn't get a hold of you and that your dad needed to talk to you immediately." Her eyes drift between Haddock and me. "He said it was extremely important that you call him."

Haddock is glaring at me and I don't have to look at him to know what he wants me to do. Or what he will do, if I don't do it.

"I'm fine, Heather. Why don't you go and tell everyone I'll be there in a minute."

But it's pretty obvious I'm not fine. I'm barely standing on my own with a man twice my size holding me up against the wall by the hair on my head.

And Heather's no dummy. She shakes her head and says, "Why don't you come with me, now, Kate. I think Zack will feel much better once he's seen you," and when I don't move she adds, "in fact why don't I call him right now and let him know where you are?"

Haddock moves so fast I don't see it coming. One minute he's in my face and the next Heather's falling to the ground while the sound of a gunshot echoes down the hallway and out into the mall.

I hear screaming and it takes me a minute to realize it's me. I'm trying to run to her, both my legs and arms are moving, but Haddock is holding me back.

"Help!" I scream, and it's loud, so loud it's startling, and then my head explodes.

Twenty-Six

When I open my eyes I'm against a wall in what looks like a storage room. To my right and to my left are stock shelves piled high, each one labeled. My eyes scan down the first row, reading off words like, *summer collection* and *backlogged*. My head is pounding so hard I can't think to figure out what I could be doing in this place. Until I see him. Haddock is standing next to the back door, peeking out into the night.

Just like that I'm back. The jewelry store. The gun. And Heather.

Heather!

"Why are you doing this?" I whisper. "Why do you keep hurting people?" The pain in my head is beginning to ease up but I still feel foggy.

Haddock doesn't even glance at me. "Don't take it personal, Kid. You're just a paycheck." From his pocket he pulls out a small rectangular device. "I've got a few things to take care of before we hit the road. Just sit tight and do that healing thing you do. That should keep you busy for a few minutes, right?"

I feel a faint rumble tickle the wall behind me and I look up in time to catch another of Haddock's menacing smiles.

"That should do it. Just a little diversion to steer the troops in a different direction." He slips the black box back into his pocket.

"What do you mean, troops? What did you do?"

Haddock grabs me off the floor and drags me toward the back door. "Let's go. We've got one chance to slip through the cracks."

"What was that? What did you do?" I ask again.

"I blew up a car." He says it so matter-of-factly, like this is something he does every hour.

"Why?"

"To distract them from our escape. Come on now, Kate. Keep up. You're smarter than this."

"No," I whisper, softly at first. Then I say it again, louder. "No. I'm not going with you." I push against him with all my might and slam him against the door. This is my opportunity.

He'll never catch me. Just turn around and run!

"Say no again, Kate." Before I even take a step he's on me, his hands on my shoulders, pulling me back against him. "It's my least favorite word but when you say it, it turns me on."

My hands ball up in fists and I start pummeling him, hitting his arms, his chest, everything within reach. "Why? Why? Why did you do it? You bastard! You had no right to kill her!"

Haddock fights off my attack with a tolerant amusement, but his mood soon changes when my fist connects with his right eye.

"That's enough, Kate. Enough!" He grips both my wrists in one of his unyielding hands.

"Let her go!" Brandon's voice echoes through the stockroom and Haddock's head whips around.

Almost ten feet away, holding a metal shelving rod in the air like a knight wielding his weapon of war, stands Brandon.

"NO! Brandon," I cry out, but it's too late.

Haddock aims his gun and squeezes the trigger. It looks like something invisible grabs Brandon's shoulder and yanks him back. His knees buckle and he collapses to the floor.

"Damn these distractions! Now move!"

But I can't move even if I wanted to. I'm frozen.

Brandon. Heather. My mom. How many more people have to get hurt because of me?

I whip around and punch Haddock right in the mouth. "What is wrong with you? Stop shooting people!"

Haddock wipes the blood from the corner of his mouth all the while staring at me as if I've gone insane.

I take a step forward, then another, until I'm standing over Brandon's body. His eyes are wide. He's breathing, but barely, and his skin is pale.

"Pay your last respects quickly, Kate. I'm losing patience here."

I stiffen. "He's only seventeen!" I yell. "You can't tell me this doesn't affect you!"

I remove the black hoodie I'm wearing and wrap it tightly around Brandon's bleeding shoulder.

"I've had years to get over stuff," Haddock says from behind me. "Ask your dad. He'll tell you. It gets easier over time."

"Don't touch me!" I shriek, when he grabs my arm. Twisting and pulling I wrestle with my captor, desperate for escape. Haddock continues to drag me toward the back door, but then suddenly he goes still. In one swift movement he grips my throat with one hand and pushes me against the wall. In his other hand he aims his gun once again.

The stockroom door has barely made a sound but Haddock apparently hears everything. I close my eyes just as he says, "Oh, look, Kate. It's your boyfriend."

My eyes flew open just as Zack's head disappears behind a stack of boxes.

Haddock follows Zack's movements with his weapon and his eyes.

"Zack, please just go! Please!" I plead. "Go get help! Brandon's been shot!"

But Zack isn't leaving. He's moving further into the room on all fours. Every few seconds his head appears and Haddock shoots at him like he's playing a carnival game. I flail my arms at Haddock each time he raises his gun, but he shrugs me off effortlessly and reloads his weapon.

Zack is now within a couple feet of Brandon — not close enough to touch him but close enough to see the stillness of his body. When Zack's face loses its color, Haddock snorts.

"Brandon doesn't need help. He needs a casket."

Zack dives toward Brandon and Haddock raises his gun. I scream when I hear the gunshot just as Haddock springs back. He spins to his right, his gun cocked and loaded, and I notice there's a tear in his jacket along his left shoulder.

"I should have killed you years ago." Andrew's voice is like a blow to my knees. My legs threaten to buckle right out from under me.

He points his gun at Haddock, who switches his target. Their weapons level on one another like cowboys in a showdown.

Haddock laughs and his smile only makes him look more evil. "Hello, Daddy. Did you miss me? Or should I call you Shore? I hear that's what you're going by these day."

He yanks me by my hair again and my scalp burns like he's ripped out a chunk. "I really wish we had more time to catch up. It's been ages, right? But I really need to hit the road. You see, I've got plans for your daughter."

Andrew's hand doesn't move or shake. The barrel of his gun remains centered on Haddock's chest. "I suggest you let her go."

Haddock presses his gun up against my temple and I suck in a breath. The cold steel begins to lightly massage my skin. "I'm afraid that's not going to happen. Now put the gun down."

I stare straight ahead at Andrew. His face is expressionless, his eyes hard. I'm pleading with him to do, what, I'm not sure, something, anything, that will keep him safe and me safe, and kill Haddock.

"I know this kid is magic and all but I'm pretty sure if I blow her brains out she won't recover too well."

And he's right. I don't know how my ability works exactly. I've never believed I'm immortal. If Haddock pulls the trigger I should die. I mean, even I can't recover from that. Can I?

My eyes are on Andrew. I can tell he's debating the same thing.

"Well, Daddy," Haddock says when the standoff continues. "We're waiting. I'll only ask one last time. Put the gun down."

This time Andrew doesn't hesitate. I watch him place the gun upon the ground, my hopes falling with it. When he kicks it toward us, I close my eyes.

We're all going to die.

My life is now in the hands of a man who gives no thought to taking it; first my mom, then Heather, Brandon and soon Andrew and Zack, until my world is void of everyone who matters and I'm left to fend for myself. Alone.

I look up and find Zack watching me. He has blood on his hands but really it should be on mine. If everyone dies, they die because of me. No one else.

"I'm sorry," I mouth. For a moment he looks stricken and then his face takes on that same hard look that Andrew's has.

Haddock rubs my burning scalp with his long fingers and gently moves his hand down my face. "Now comes the good part, Kate. You get to watch me clear the room, one annoying hero at a time." His fingers slide up and down my cheek, and I stiffen at his caress. Waving his gun back and forth between Andrew and Zack, Haddock smiles. "Hmm, who should I kill first? Daddy or Boyfriend? You pick, Kate."

"I hate you," I hiss. "I will make sure you pay for this."

Haddock just laughs.

"They grow up so fast, eh, Andrew? One minute you're rocking them to sleep, oh, wait. You missed that part." He rubs his mouth along the side of my face, his breath warm against my skin. "Good thing she got your wife's looks, although it's a shame she didn't get her sexy green eyes." He pulls me even closer and his arm wraps around my waist rubbing circles along my abdomen. "A man can lose himself in those eyes," he drawls.

It's like Haddock is poking Andrew with a long stick, goading him to try something, make a move, or fight back. But Andrew doesn't react. He continues to watch Haddock with a look of indifference, his body as still as a statue.

"So, Kate. You decide. Daddy or Boyfriend? Daddy or Boyfriend?" Over and over he whispers the words like he's making a decision on what to eat for dinner. The room grows quiet except for the deafening rhythm of my pounding heart. Inside I'm screaming so loud it's impossible to think. My eyes move with the gun in Haddock's hand, willing him with my mind to aim at the floor instead of at the men who are most important in my life. Zack has slowly climbed to his feet, his hands raised, his eyes wide, while Andrew's expression has taken on a look of boredom. It's his eyes that tell a different story. They don't blink nor do they stray from Haddocks face.

I'm debating whether or not I have the strength to knock the gun from Haddock's hand when he makes his next move.

"Boyfriend?" He swings the gun on Zack and fires off a shot near his head. When Zack dives to the ground, Haddock laughs. "Nah, I'd rather start with Daddy." And then his gun is aimed at Andrew's heart.

I've never wondered if I were faster than a speeding bullet — until now. His grip on me has grown slack, his attention diverted, and I easily break free. It isn't entirely a conscious decision; my body seemed to know what I was going to do before my mind did. With an effortless burst of adrenaline I throw myself into the path of pain before Haddock can even release the trigger.

The bullet slices through my right shoulder and then fire engulfs my back. Withering in agony, I hit the floor.

"Kate!" Zack's cry is drowned out when Haddock roars in rage. He swings the gun around the room wildly, he doesn't seem to know what to do first: run to my side or throw himself at Andrew.

Andrew doesn't give him another second to think. He dives for the ground and in one swift motion rises up on one knee and steadies his arm. A bullet pierces Haddock's chest. Andrew storms forward, barreling toward Haddock like a train. When he's within a foot of him, he slams the side of his gun against Haddock's face and shoves him to the ground.

Andrew is holding Haddock down by his throat while his other hand aims his gun right between his eyes.

"Kate, are you alright?" he calls out to me and my only response is a slight moan. "Kate?"

I close my eyes and concentrate on each tiny breath that fills my lungs until the miraculous gift of numbness begins to trickle into my shoulder.

"Kate?"

When my eyes open I find Zack hovering over me. He's naked from the waist up and when I look down I see his shirt balled up and pressed against my shoulder.

"Kate! Are you okay?"

I manage to nod my head, but the pain is too much for me to speak.

"You're going to be fine. The police should be here any minute. Just lie back and keep breathing."

"Zack..." My voice is scratchy and faint and Zack only knows what I've said from the movement of my lips.

"Yes?"

"I need to get up."

He shakes his head. "No. You need to stay right here. The police are on their way. Any minute now, Kate. They'll be here any minute."

I know he's only trying to keep me calm but his words are having the opposite effect. I push against his body with a surprising strength. "I'm getting up, Zack. You can either help me or get out of my way."

"There's some clothes on the shelf behind you, Kate. Hurry and change," Andrew yells over his shoulder.

"Are you both insane?" Zack cries. He's still bullying me back to the ground, but my strength is improving and I fight steadily to my feet.

"She's been shot," Zack exclaims, as if it isn't already obvious. "She needs to lay still. She's losing too much blood."

But I'm already moving behind a shelf with a pair of jeans and a t-shirt in my hand.

"Hurry, Kate!" Andrew doesn't take his eyes off Haddock.

"What's going on, Andrew?" Zack yells.

His answer is a balled up sweatshirt to the back of his head.

"Wipe up the floor, Zack. Now!" Andrew's voice is urgent with more than a hint of desperation, which turns to impatience when Zack doesn't move quickly enough. "Kate's blood!" he yells. "Get rid of it!"

"What? Wipe what?" Zack's face pales when he notices the puddle of blood collected on the floor, where I was lying.

"Do it, Zack! NOW!"

"I've got it, Zack," I say and he looks up, dazed, from his position on the floor. I'm standing over him. My borrowed clothes are loose fitting but clean — the sales tags missing. I tug the borrowed backpack containing my bloody clothes tight over my shoulder, my injured shoulder, and turn away from the questions in Zack's eyes.

"Brandon? Is he...?" I don't finish. Truthfully, I don't want to know. Especially if the news is as bad as I imagine.

"He's alive. His breathing is strong but he's lost a lot of blood." Zack's eyes move over all sixty-nine inches of my upright position and it's like I can read his mind.

Just like you.

"And Heather?"

"She's fine. She's probably already at the hospital."

Which is where we should be.

I look away from his expressive face. This is the part I hate most. It starts with surprise, then relief, which always leads to fear.

But Zack — I never wanted to see it on Zack.

He lifts his hands and then lowers them as if he's afraid to touch me. He then moves over to check on Brandon.

"Kate? Are you...alright?" Andrew's words are few but I clearly understand their meaning.

Are you healed?

I take a deep breath to calm my nerves. I can feel eyes upon me; Zack's eyes, Andrew's eyes, even Haddock, who's still slouched against the wall, has lifted his head and is watching me with an intensity I can feel from across the room. The only eyes turned away are Brandon's. His breathing is shallow and his skin is now grey, but he's alive.

I bend down and start cleaning my blood from the floor, but Zack stops me. He takes the garment from my hands and wipes the floor clean, unaware that he's removing the last remaining evidence of my injury.

When he finishes, I place the cloth deep inside my backpack and pull the zipper tight over the bulging garment. I won't look at Zack, not again. But I can feel him watching me.

The silence of the room stretches on far too long but it's only a matter of minutes before the room erupts in chaos. Local police officers and two separate SWAT teams burst through the door. They move like shadows along the perimeter of the room.

Andrew has already stashed his gun and when the police approach him, he willingly surrenders his hostage. They drag Haddock off in handcuffs. Just before he's out of sight he smiles back at me. His message is clear, *this ain't over yet.*

Up to this point I've been battling off a war of feelings. When Andrew wraps his arms around me the dam that has held my tears back threatens to break.

"How did you find me?" I whisper.

"Oh, Kate." Andrew is holding me so tight I can barely breathe, but I'm not complaining. His grip on me is pushing the fear away.

"When I arrived at Burien, the two guards who were assigned to him were dead and Haddock was gone. I called your phone and when I couldn't reach you I called Zack's." Andrew pulls back so he can see my face and that's when the tears start. They race down my cheeks and pool in the folds of my shirt when Andrew isn't quick enough to catch them. He crushes me against him, holding me closer than he ever has before.

"I love you, honey. I don't know what I'd do—"

He doesn't have to finish his thought, and thankfully he doesn't, because neither of us wants to go there.

Zack is hovering over Brandon as they whisk him away on a stretcher. I can see him over Andrew's shoulder. Just before he leaves the storage room he looks back and our eyes meet.

"We'll see you at the hospital," he says.

And then he's gone.

Twenty-Seven

Seattle

"Kate Triumph to see Dr. Dolus."

The young blonde behind the desk glances up briefly and I smile.

"Yes, he's been expecting you. I'll let him know you've arrived."

I take a seat in the doctor's waiting area. The white walls are littered with expensive artwork and his furniture is all plush. Everything appears costly. And clean.

"Dr. Dolus will see you now, Miss Triumph." The young blonde leads me down a long hallway and stops in front of a large metal door. "Miss Triumph is here, Doctor."

"Thank you, Janet."

The soft muted voice behind the door is familiar, and I step forcefully through the doorway.

"Kate! It's so nice to see you again." Dr. Dolus takes a step forward eyeing my bright red skirt and ivory blouse. Offering me his hand, he says, "How nice it will be to have someone so pretty working alongside of me." When I ignore his handshake his eyes take on a wounded look and then he drops his hand back to his side. "Did you have any trouble finding us?"

"No."

"Good. I'd hate to hear you were inconvenienced. Seattle can be quite complicated when you don't know your way around."

I don't respond, instead I squint back at him while my eyes grow accustomed to the brightness of the room. Everything in here is blindingly white and spotlessly clean. I have a sudden impulse to take the bottle of 'Hazard Red' nail polish from my backpack and splatter it about his office.

"So here's how it will go, my dear," he begins quickly once he's taken a seat behind his desk. "You'll need to move here to the facility, for only a short time, of course—"

"No."

The doctor's eyes widen at my blatant interruption and then he scowls at me.

"I didn't come here to work for you. I came to offer you a deal."

"A deal?" Dr. Dolus leans back in his chair and folds his hands neatly in his lap. "I'm not sure I follow."

"Well, let me spell it out for you then. H-A-D-D-O-C-K. I'm sure you know by now your henchman was arrested after attacking me at the mall last night." When Dr. Dolus' expression doesn't change, I continue. "But what you don't know is before he was dragged off in handcuffs with a bullet in his chest we had a nice little talk." I take a step forward and the doctor's eyes narrow slightly. "He told me all about your plans, Dr. Dolus."

"I have no idea what you're talking about. I don't even know this Haddock person you're referring to."

"You mean him?" I reach into my backpack and pull out a photo of the doctor and Haddock getting into a long black limousine. "I'm sorry I can't believe you. You see, I have proof. A tape recording to be exact. Haddock gets rather chatty when he thinks he's going to die." I pause for dramatic effect and to let my words sink in. But the doctor is either too cold to react or too polished to show emotion.

"Haddock seems to be under the impression that you hired him to kill my mother."

Dr. Dolus leans forward and I can almost taste the sweet smell of his aftershave, which doesn't mix well with the acidic feeling in my stomach. I allow my revulsion for him to show distinctly when I look deep into his eyes. "I have copies and I made arrangements so if something should happen to me, or anyone close to me, those copies will be sent to some very interested parties. I'm sure they'd find Haddock's tale rather intriguing considering you've made so many friends around here." The doctor's arrogant expression begins to falter and I continue. "In exchange for my silence, I ask two things from you. One, leave me alone and leave my family alone and never contact me in the future. And two," I lean across his desk, "I want you to tell Haddock to make a full confession that he was after my father and not me. I want to stay out of this story and all stories in the future. Do you understand? I'm not to be involved. Ever."

I stand back and wait. I've said my peace, now it's time to sec how he will react.

"Done."

My hands ball into fists. "And all this time I believed it was an accident."

I clench my jaw in an attempt to hold back all the things I want to say but shouldn't. But it doesn't work.

"You are a selfish bastard and one day this will come back to haunt you." I turn and head for the door before I can slip and say anything more.

"Kate." His breathing is heavy and his eyes wild. "She wasn't supposed to die. I never meant for her to die!"

"What do you mean by that, Dr. Dolus?"

"He was only supposed to scare you!"

"Rolling our car along the highway was only supposed to be a scare?"

"Dammit!" Dr. Dolus jumps from his chair and comes around his desk. "He's sick! He gets such a thrill from the hunt. He never knows when to—" he stops and his eyes darken. "He wasn't supposed to kill her."

I smile but it doesn't quite reach my eyes. "Thank you for that."

Leaving the door wide open, I walk back down the hallway. I can hear him yelling for his secretary. His voice filled with rage. I step into the elevator and when the doors are just about to close the women behind the desk looks up.

It's as if she's frozen, her hand reaching for the phone while Dr. Dolus screams at her through the intercom on her desk.

My fists are still clenched and there's a blazing fire of retribution raging through my body. It's as if I'm daring her to try and stop me. The doors close just as she opens her mouth to call out. But it's too late. With a soft ding of the elevator, I'm plummeted down into the lobby of the big glass building.

I walk out the revolving doors in the lobby and when I'm safely outside I reach up and remove the small video camera pen from the front pocket of my blouse.

It worked! The bluff has paid off.

I smile into the lens of the camera pen just before I hold it in the air to signal to Andrew, who's waiting out in front, that today was a success. My smiling face will make a good ending to the doctor's confession, the first step in the downfall of Dr. Luke Dolus.

As I stand on the top of the steps I unzip my backpack and pull out the bright pink orchid I purchased just before my appointment. From behind a cloud the sun peeks through, warming my shoulders and illuminating the beautiful flower. I swear it glows in the daylight.

I lift the flower gently to my lips and whisper, "For you, Mom. May you rest and I sleep."

And then I drop it at my feet.

I hurry forward to Andrew's car, while the big glass building retreats from behind me. I don't turn to look back. I don't have to. I know the orchid will be forever dancing on the steps of Dr. Dolus' grave.

I climb into the passenger seat and smile at Andrew.

"You did great, Kate," he says and the look in his eyes confirms it.

I'm stronger than I think.

Twenty-Eight

There's a strange peace that arrives when the dust settles. Although, I'm not entirely convinced it isn't just the wind shifting in a new direction. Even though the dust is only resting at my feet I can sense its potential. Any minute now the wind could start up again.

The water on Lake Washington is still, the air dry, and the sound of footsteps on the dock somewhat comforting if not repetitious. Is this the fifth or sixth time Andrew is coming to check on me? Each visit out to the dock has a new reason; a sweatshirt (in case it gets cold), bug spray (they swarm us this time of year), and my favorite, just checking to make sure you're alive (after five hours sitting on the dock, alone).

Andrew is as restless as I am but not for the same reasons. While he's worried that I've retreated back into my world of solitary confinement, I, on the other hand, know Brandon is arriving home from the hospital today. Twice Andrew has visited him in the hospital and twice he's asked me if I'd like to go as well, but I'm not ready to see Brandon just yet.

From what I hear Heather is doing well, although no one has seen her yet. Emily has called me repeatedly expressing her annoyance over the situation.

"She's out of the hospital," she informed me yesterday, "but then her parents whisked her away to some family get-together down in Oregon."

I don't mention how Heather called once to check in on me, and how when I asked how she was feeling she rushed off the phone. I never got the chance to thank her for saving me that day. Because, truth be told, if she hadn't gotten shot no one would have known where to find me.

"They wouldn't release her from the hospital if she wasn't strong enough," I explained to Emily, but that didn't seem to ease her displeasure. I get the feeling she's just upset she missed the entire thing.

"Something finally happens around here," she muttered for perhaps the third time, "and I'm on the opposite side of the mall."

I'm not sure what she expected me to say to that. "Maybe next time you can stop the speeding bullet," seems wrong so I don't say anything, and eventually she lets me go.

The day has been warm — an Indian summer — but now that the sun is going down, the evening chill is settling in. I wrap my arms around my legs not for warmth but protection. I need the comforting touch, even if it is my own.

"Hey, Kate." Zack's voice is low and unexpected.

I flinch but I don't turn around.

"Have you been out here all day?"

"Not really." Technically speaking there was that one hour between waking up and walking outside.

"I wanted to stop by and make sure you were okay."

"Yep. Just fine." I glance back at him and then wish I hadn't. Zack is leaning against the railing. In his dark jeans and orange sweater, he's easier to ignore with my eyes on the water.

"You sure?"

I take a deep breath and hug my knees closer. "What do you want, Zack?"

"Brandon came home today. He wants to see you."

"Maybe I'll stop in tomorrow."

"I'm sure he'd like that."

The silence stretches on for so long that I finally turn to see if he's left. Nope. Still there.

"I'm not leaving, Kate."

"I see that."

"I came to talk to you, and if you want to stay out here all night that's fine by me."

"I don't really have anything to say."

"Oh, really? Well, I do. I thought you agreed not to push me away anymore?"

I jump to my feet and face him. "What more do you want from me, Zack? I gave you an out, just take it!"

"An out? Is that what you call not speaking to me, and ignoring my phone calls, avoiding me and Brandon who's been in the hospital for the last two days?" Zack moves toward me and before I can back away he has hold of my arms. "Is it that easy for you, Kate? Just turn your back and walk away?" His hands are slowly moving up my arms until they slide underneath my hair at the base of my neck. "Because truthfully you never really had me convinced. I was willing to give you time if that's what you needed. But not forever."

I'm losing my concentration. Each time his warm fingers brush against my skin I inch closer to him. We're so close now I'm a mere nod away from his lips.

"Unless you don't really like me. I'll leave you alone if it's like that."

Zack's breath is warm against my mouth. When he leans his forehead against mine I close my eyes.

"Do you like me, Kate?"

"No," I whisper. "I don't like you."

Zack's low chuckle makes my heart flutter. When I raise my chin his kiss stops it altogether.

"Well if that's true, I must not like you either," he whispers against my mouth and then playfully bites my bottom lip. "This should be interesting. I've never had a girlfriend that didn't like me before."

"Girlfriend?" *Girlfriend!* I try to pull away but Zack resists.

"Do you prefer significant other?" He's laughing at me now while I untangled myself from his hold.

"I can't, Zack. I can't —"

"What? What can't you do? You can't let yourself get too close to someone who already knows your secrets?"

274

My eyes widen and I instinctively try to pull away. I don't want to talk about it. I just want to end it.

"I'm a little beyond the mystery by now, wouldn't you say? I've already witnessed it first-hand. And yeah, it's pretty crazy. So crazy for the last few days I've been convinced it was just a reaction to shock. But it wasn't, was it? You really did get shot. And you really did heal right before my eyes." When I don't respond, Zack continues. "We can talk about this, right? I want to talk about this."

"I guess," I say, while my body language says anything but.

"You have to know how cool I think this is. I mean, I grew up reading comic books. It's like you're a super hero or something."

"Super hero?" The look I give him is incredulous.

"Yeah. We should get you a cape and a tight outfit or something. Don't you think?" He tugs at my hand, his smile melting some of the fear around my heart.

"Sorry, you lost me at comic books."

"Seriously, Kate, what are you afraid of?"

"You're kidding me, right?"

When Zack sees the troubled look in my eyes he leans forward and kisses me. "Tell me what you feared would have happened," he whispers.

"I didn't think you'd want to—" I stop there and shake my head. "I didn't think you'd want me."

"Ah, I see," Zack cups my face and kisses me softly. "And now what do you think?"

"That you like kissing me," I say.

"Yes. And what else?"

"That you want me to wear some kind of catwoman outfit."

Zack laughs against my lips when he tries to kiss me again. "I like *you*, Kate," he says. "Don't you see that you're amazing?"

"No. Not amazing." I pull away and take a step back.

"You're unbelievable! Do you know how lucky you are—?"

"No! Not unbelievable. Not lucky!" I'm steadily increasing the space between us. My heart pounding so hard I can hear it inside my head. "I'm none of those things, Zack. I'm, I'm…"

"You're?" Zack reaches out and grabs me right before I take that last step off the back of the dock and then he pulls me back into his arms.

"I'm, I'm…" When I can't bring myself to say all the hateful words I use to describe myself in my mind, I sigh. I don't really believe them anyway. "I'm—"

"Unique." He silences me with a kiss. "Remarkable." He moves up and kisses my left eye. "Gorgeous." Then my right eye. "Frustrating." Back to my mouth. His hands move to my waist and the kiss deepens. "Too distracting," he murmurs against my lips and then gently pulls away. "Kate," he sighs, "there's nothing *wrong* with you. Bizarre maybe," he says and then chuckles when I glare back at him, "but not wrong."

"Weird."

"Not weird."

"Gruesome."

Zack laughs. "Definitely not gruesome."

I tilt my face up so I can see his eyes. "Distracting?"

"Yes. Very."

I like that one. "In a good way of course."

"Of course." And to confirm it Zack pulls me in for another kiss. When he moves away, I'm too distracted to notice he's leading me back toward the house. "Brandon wants to see you. He's inside talking with Andrew."

My eyes go wild. "I don't know what to say to him, Zack! I don't…"

"He doesn't know, Kate. He didn't see anything."

But Zack did, I tell myself. And he's still here.

Twenty-Nine

San Diego

Jonah almost doesn't recognize the house from this angle. He's used to approaching it from the beach. Even from the street it looks empty. He tells himself it's still empty and turns back to his rental car just as "Scrubs" pulls into the driveway.

Jonah watches as the man walks up the front porch and unlocks the door. He envies his quick footsteps and knows when it comes time for his feet to travel that path they won't move as swiftly. Even with his Nanna's letter burning a hole in his back pocket, and her dying wish haunting his restless sleep, Jonah can't convince his feet to take the steps.

He's read the letter so many times that he could probably recite it.

Olivia,

You don't know me, and chances are you never will. But I've been dreaming of contacting you for as long as I've known, which sadly has been far too long.

I'm sorry. I'm so sorry. If I said it every minute of every day I was alive, it would never be enough. So I've sent him to you. My Jonah. He never should have been mine. He never should have ended up in my arms. He should have fallen asleep with you that first night and stayed there until he was old enough to hold your hand as you awaited death. Not me. He was a gift, one I never deserved but now I'm giving him back. And hoping you will in return forgive a dying old woman for her selfishness.

For years I've held the pieces of your broken heart in my hands and now I must return them to you, once and for all.

I'm sorry, Olivia. All I can say is, I'm sorry.

Please tell Jonah I love him. He knows the story. He knows everything. And as proof of his goodness he stayed with me anyway. He held my hand like he has since the night he came into my world and didn't let go.

Now that he's back in your life, please make sure you do the same.

One last time, I'm sorry.

Anna Selby

"It's time, Nanna," he says and takes a step. It's just one step but it perpetuates a motion that leads Jonah across the street. Two steps and then three until the last fifteen steps to the driveway are slowly eaten up by his heavy shoes. He takes the front steps two at a time. His confidence increasing and his curiosity like a strong wind behind his back.

With one deep breath Jonah lifts his hand and lightly taps the back of his knuckles to the solid wood door. In the time it has taken him to cross the street he's worked out a plan. The letter. If he can't say the words he'll just hand her the letter.

Scrubs opens the door.

"Yes, can I help you?"

Jonah clears his throat and says, "Sir. My name is Jonah Selby. I'm looking for Olivia Triumph. And Kate. I was told they live here."

Scrubs doesn't answer right away, His eyes study Jonah as if he's seen a ghost and then he apologizes.

"I'm sorry. I don't mean to stare but, you look so much like someone I know." He swallows and then clears his throat. "You have her coloring."

Jonah smiles and asks again, "Do you know where I can find Olivia or Kate Triumph. It's very important that I find them."

"And why is that, son?" Scrubs asks.

"I'd prefer it if I could speak with them personally, sir."

"Well I'm afraid that's not possible." Scrubs rubs the back of his neck and says, "Kate is with her father out in Washington State."

"Father?" Jonah takes a staggering step back. "I didn't know. I'm sorry. I thought."

"Are you alright, son?"

"And Olivia?"

Scrubs narrows his eyes but doesn't answer.

"Sir, it's very important that I give her this letter in person." Jonah holds up the letter as if to show proof of its importance. "I promised my nanna—"

"Can I read the letter?" Scrubs asks and then holds out his hand. "Please, son. I've afraid I can't tell you more until I better understand the purpose of your visit."

•   •   •

Mercer Island

"Kate! Watch out!"

Ducking quickly, I avoid the soccer ball that whizzes by my head.

"Sorry!" Brandon races past with three guys from his soccer team close behind. Even though his left arm is in a sling it doesn't appear to be slowing him down.

He maneuvers the ball smoothly down the lawn as if he wasn't just laid up in a hospital bed a mere week ago. The bullet damaged some muscles when it exited his shoulder, but the prognosis is strong. And so is Brandon's spirit.

I move along the side yard. If only I could find the birthday boy.

Andrew has been MIA for the last hour, and I have a sneaking suspicion he's out on the back porch. No one has ventured back there yet so it only makes sense that he would seek out the quietest spot in the yard.

"Happy Birthday, Andrew," I sing when I scoot up next to him and kiss his cheek.

He smiles. "You've already told me at least a dozen times, Kate. I'm not old enough to forget that fast."

I stare out over Lake Washington. "Maybe I'm just making up for all the birthdays I never said it. Anyway, you're avoiding your own party and it's almost time to bring out the cake."

"Double chocolate with chocolate frosting, right? I'm ready when you are!"

I laugh and look up into my father's smiling blue eyes. A weakness for chocolate is just one more thing we share. "I'm bringing the cake out in a couple of minutes," I explain and move off the back porch. "But you'll get nothing if you're still back here staring longingly at the fish."

"I'm right behind you, Kate!"

He slips his arm around my shoulders and we dodge the playful soccer game on the side lawn. Zack is coming out of the house as we round the corner and when he spies Andrew he says, "Did you see those fish jumping out there? That patch by the dock is completely alive!"

I punch him lightly in the shoulder. "Don't you dare encourage him, Zack. We'll lose him for the rest of the day if he goes out there."

Zack reaches over and playfully tugs on my ponytail. "Sorry." With a smile that makes my knees buckle, he jumps in front of Brandon and manages to steal the soccer ball right out from under him. I turn and watch him race down the lawn, wondering how I ever believed I'd be able to resist that?

"The cake, Kate? Didn't you say it was time for cake?" Andrew's voice is insistent in my ear. I turn and smile innocently up at him.

"Did I say we were having cake, now? No...I meant after we'd eaten and possibly played a few party games and..."

"Party games? No way, Kate. I don't play party games. And if you think I'm going to wait for that cake

now, after you tricked me into coming with you..."
Andrew's voice trails off as he marches toward the house. I
watch him, smiling.

"Come with me," Zack whispers in my ear. His
hand slides down my arm and then grips my hand, tugging
me toward the side door.

He leads me through the kitchen and toward the
front hall, where it's quiet and people-free. I look up and
notice Lefty loitering at the top of the staircase, sniffing the
air suspiciously. Earlier he made it down to the kitchen but
when Brandon tried to put a bow on top of his head he
hissed and disappeared back upstairs.

"I just wanted to tell you how amazing you are,"
Zack says, walking me backward until I'm pressed up
against the front door.

"Amazing, huh?" I say. "It's only eleven o'clock in
the morning and already I'm amazing?"

"Mmm," he nuzzles against my neck. "You smell
like chocolate."

"That's the cake." I sigh and then my eyes flutter
closed. I move my mouth a little to the left and he takes the
hint. Zack's kisses make me forget everything else: my
father, who's moving around in the kitchen, the birthday
party going on outside, and every single person who could
walk into this room and find us making out in the front hall.

You make me happy, Zack.

I'm so close to saying the words they tickle my
tongue.

When the doorbell rings we jump apart, and my
nose collides with his chin.

"Son of a—" Zack swings around as if he's
expecting someone to jump out and attack him and I can't
help it, I start laughing.

"Someone's at the door," I say through fits of
laughter, and eventually he smiles.

I'm still chuckling when I open the door, but it comes to a stop when I find John and a young man on the doorstep.

"Hey, John." My smile wavers when I notice the look on his face. "What's going on? What are you—" I stop and my eyes lock on the young man at his side. He's about my age, tall and slender with auburn hair.

"How are you, Kate?" John asks and from the tone of his voice I can tell this question isn't just a formality. The look in his eyes asks more than that.

"What's going on?" I say, but my words are directed at the young man. He's watching me with the same level of intensity. His eyes are a familiar shade of green.

John clears his throat and says, "This is—"

"Jonah," the young man finishes. "Jonah Selby."

"Kate? Who is it?" I hear Andrew come up behind me but I don't turn around.

"Jonah," I say, and then repeat it once again.

Jonah.

Andrew walks up and stands next to me. "What is this, John?" he asks, but he is also staring at the young man.

"Jonah," I say again, and the young man smiles.

Acknowledgements

Without the support of friends and family a writer's existence would be very lonely. I'm lucky that even when I'm alone, writing, I still feel them near. Thank you Lynne and Mike Novenstein for the support and the babysitting. =) Thanks to Michael Weaver for the reading and the editing and all the book-talk. Thanks to Judi, Lori and Barbi for listening to ALL THE STUFF (good or bad) and, you know, still loving me through it. Thanks to Kaitlin, Morgan, Chandler, Sawyer, Taylor, Freddy, Brett, Emeli, London and Haven. I truly started writing for you. Thanks to Michelle Tolman for encouraging my relentless imagination and still wanting to be my friend. Thanks to Rachel Rothman-Cohen for talking about all the friends we share (who actually don't exist in real life) and for being just as excited as I am about books.

To my greatest fan (that's you mom) I owe you immeasurably. Thank you for always believing even after I'd stopped. And thanks for always loving my writing. (Or at least pretending to)

Thanks to Keelin O'Reilly for the amazing cover. I told you my vision and you made it come true.

Thanks to Tracy Banghart. Thanks is such a small word. I owe you so many more. Without you, well, you know where I'd be. =)

You owe me another Pinkberry date, Emily Liebert. And I owe you far more than a thanks on my acknowledgement page. But I'm pretty sure you're simply happy I'm writing one. =) Thanks for the phone calls and the check-ins. And for always making me feel there was someone on my side.

My poor children have inherited my imagination, but luckily that means they will never feel bored. I love you bunches and lunches.

And then there's Jay. See that? I saved the best for last. Thanks for getting chills when the words were right and telling me, "yeah, no," when the words were not. Thanks for all the late night brainstorming, for listening to pages of my imaginary friends when you could have done something, ANYTHING, else. Thanks for holding my hand and believing.

Made in the USA
Charleston, SC
11 August 2015